The Right Rose for Mano

The Right Rose for Mano

Joseph F Harden Jr.

Order this book online at www.trafford.com
or email orders@trafford.com

Most Trafford titles are also available at major online book retailers.

Printed in the United States of America.

ISBN: 978-1-4669-0042-4 (sc)
ISBN: 978-1-4669-0043-1 (e)

Trafford rev. 10/05/2011

 www.trafford.com

North America & International
toll-free: 1 888 232 4444 (USA & Canada)
phone: 250 383 6864 ♦ fax: 812 355 4082

PREFACE

The Right Rose for Mono

He was only fifteen and had tried to keep his family functioning after his mothers passing. No time to attend school now he planted the garden and hunted for meat for their table. All of the time seeing anything of value disappearing from the farm. Everything going to support the drinking habit his father and two older brothers had acquired.

They'd leave for town in the morning after eating what ever there was for breakfast and not be back until suppertime. He would lie in his bed in the evening and hear them argue about the problems the country was having at that time. When all he wanted was some help so they keep the farm as it had been.

After cooking a meal of the rabbits he had hunted and what was left from the root cellar there was nothing left. He would have to hunt if he going to be able to cook another meal.

In the morning he went down to find the only animal they had left, the old horse that he could have used to pack in a deer, gone. That was almost the last straw and the last straw was when he looked where he always left his rifle, and it too was gone.

By Joseph F Harden Jr.
The Right Rose for Mano

CHAPTER 1

Opening the door he set his rifle against the wall then took the three rabbits he'd already skinned and cleaned to the table. There was no salt pork to render and fry with the pieces of rabbit the way he thought was best. The lard bucket was near empty but by heating it on the stove there was enough to do the frying.

There were no more potatoes or turnips in the root cellar, just a few woody parsnips and rutabagas. "They would have to do", he said to himself, "though they're not really to my liking."

Then he had to cut firewood before he could cook, the wood box having nothing but a few small sticks left in it. Now cut up the rabbits and put the pieces in the frying pan. The water put on to boil the vegetables in, on the stove. There was no salt and no flour to make gravy or biscuits.

Since his mother died nothing had been getting done around the farm, only if he did it himself. He couldn't go to school, but he really didn't care, they argued and even got in fights in the schoolyard. All over what was happening in the country now.

His father or his brothers one eight the other ten years older then him, hadn't done a lick of work on the farm since his mother passing. The farm deteriorating, the fields choked with weeds and almost every thing of any value now gone. Yet every evening his father and brothers seemed to be able to conjure up a bottle or two of whisky, and then they too argued the pros and cons of the countries problem.

Finishing the cooking he set the frying pan and pot on the back of the stove, where the food would stay warm. He was chopping wood when he saw them walking in from the road. Laying the axe down he picked up the bucket and headed out to the pasture to water the one horse that was left. That done he came back to the house, picked up an arm full of firewood and going inside he dumped it into the wood box.

They were all eating and had their tin cups full of something besides coffee, which there hadn't been any of, for a month.

Talking his plate to the stove he found there was only one piece of rabbit left and the boiled vegetables hadn't been touched. Though he didn't care much for them he took some, remembering how his mother always said, they were good for him. He ate, then put his dish in the dishpan and went to his room, leaving them to argue the pluses and negatives about what was happening. From his bed he could hear the murmur of their voices and was glad they were never really all that loud, like so many others when they got drunk and did their arguing.

Waking in the morning he heard some one talking in the kitchen and after listening for a minute he knew it was his brothers. He didn't get up knowing there was nothing to fix for breakfast anyway. If they were hungry they could eat the parsnips and rutabagas. Then he realized if he wanted anything for breakfast that's what he'd have to have also. He waited until the house was quiet before he rose and dressed.

In the kitchen he stoked up the stove and put on a large pot of water. Clean the dishes off the table, then the kitchen. After the water was heated he washed the dishes, then bathed and washed his soiled clothes. Hanging out his clothes he looked toward the pasture knowing the horse would need at least one bucket of water this morning. There was no horse and he knew right away where it had gone. Now he wondered what else would go, not realizing right then that it would only be just a few minutes until he found out.

With no horse now to pack in a deer Louis knew he'd have to concentrate on small game, rabbits, squirrels or maybe grouse. In the kitchen he looked by the door where he left his rifle and it wasn't there, he started looking around for it, puzzled for a for only few seconds before he realized it was gone too.

Going to his room he got out the little pistol he had hidden. The only thing left that his mother had given him. It had been hers, a small thirty-one caliber but with it he could knock over a rabbit. Then sitting down on his bed he thought about how things had been going for only a few minutes and realized it was no use. The one who had held his family together was gone.

Hearing his father in the kitchen he went down knowing he had to talk to him. His father turned hearing him coming behind him. "The horse is gone Pa," he said," and so is my rifle, how can I get something for us to eat?" His father looking at him with blank rheumy blood shot eyes seemed to think for a second. Then told him, "it will be alright son". "No it won't Pa" Louis answered, "thing's have gone to far." His father face saddened, and he looked down at the floor and then walked slowly out of the house.

Sitting on the edge of his bed he wanted to cry but for some reason he couldn't. Rolling his blanket in a piece of canvas he tied it with a rope so he could carry it on his shoulder.

His pistol he could carry inside his rifles leather possible pouch, out of sight. The pistol bag held everything he needed for the pistol including its powder flask. No place for his rifles powder horn but he'd take it and maybe sell it for a little cash. His boots and still damp clothes he'd carry tied outside his bedroll for now. He only looked back once as he walked down the road heading toward St. Louis.

Mrs. Kerr the neighbor seeing him as he walked past her house came out to ask him, where he was going. "I don't really know," he answered, "I just can't stay here any longer." "You wait just a minute Louis", she said, and went into the house. When she came out she had a cotton flour sack that she handed him, and a large still warm biscuit with butter. "You take care Louis," she said, as she turned and walked back into the house dabbing at her eyes. Louis walked down the road eating the biscuit and wanted to kick at the rocks along the edge of the road but he was bare footed. Now the tears came streaming down his cheeks and he wiped his eyes on his sleeve. There was no way he could reach his bandanna with everything he was carrying. Finishing the biscuit he walked on unable to stop the flow of tears, yet.

Walking on through the heat of the day the tears had subsided but the turmoil within him continued. Now he had to come to the realization that running from the problem was the right thing to do. The only other answer would have been to stay and end up fighting what he'd held so dear before.

The sun was well past its zenith and sinking in the west when he sought a place to rest for the night, knowing he'd never be able to reach St. Louis this day.

Coming to a small stream he crossed the road turned and walked up stream until he found a small hidden glen, and there lay down his meager belongings. Here he'd spend the rest of the day and sleep the night. He gathered wood and built a small fire. Then wondered why because he'd brought no pot to heat water in. Then too realized he had nothing to brew anyway. He ate the fried chicken and the biscuits Mrs. Kerr given him, savoring every bite. He chewed slowly as he watched the flames dance and smoke rise. There was corn bread too but that he'd save for another meal.

Washing in the stream he drank from it then rolled out his blanket and lay down. Again as he relaxed he sought the justification he needed for his running away. Then he realized there was no other way, how he could have ever turned three grown men from the trail they were following. It was their responsibility and theirs alone. From now on he would seek his solace in the memory of his mother. He fell asleep watching the stars wink on and sound of the stream running its course.

I was full light when he awoke though the sun wasn't up yet. He rolled his boots and now dried clothes inside his bedroll making it into a bundle to carry. A drink from the stream and he was on his way, eating the corn bread Mrs. Kerr had given him.

The sun fully up after he had walked for only a while. Then the wagon stopping and the man asking if he could use a ride, "I be obliged sir," Louis answered and putting his gear under the seat he climbed up along side the driver. The man studied his rider a moment then asked him, "where you headed son?" "St. Louis right now", Louis told him. "Kind of looks like your packed to go a bit farther," the man said. "That's true", Louis said, "but I haven't figured where yet." "You go west as fast and as far as you can young Hand, this countries going to be a damn mess in a short time." "You know me?" Louis asked. "I don't know you personally." "That's because you don't frequent the same establishments I do son, but I know your Pa and brothers." "You can just call me Hap, and I won't say I saw you." "Thanks", Louis answered. "I guess old John Barley Corn effects others beside those who imbibe", Hap said." "Something like that I guess," Louis answered, looking down. He remained quiet and Hap took him all the way to the warehouses on the river. "This is where I pick up my load," Hap said, and Louis grabbing his gear stepped to the ground. "Thanks Hap", Louis said. Hap flipped him a five dollar gold piece. "You don't have to do that," Louis told him. "I know", Hap answered, "but you remind me of somebody I knew some time ago". "Thanks again," Louis said. "Remember what I said, young Hand, you get as far west as you can." "I'll do that", Louis answered and thanked him once more.

Walking along the beach he looked at the boats, stern-wheelers, side-wheelers and a couple of flat barges. He had plenty of time to find a place to sleep before dark, so he watched the activity there. Mostly the loading and the unloading of the wagons that where hauling to and away from the boats there.

He heard the man holler, "hey kid", and looked up to the second deck of the stern-wheeler that he was walking past. "Yeah you," the man in the soiled apron said, "you looking for a job?" Walking down closer to the boat, Louis asked, "doing what?" "Mess man" the man said. "What's that?" Louis questioned. "Washing dishes," he heard the man say. "That's a job I've done for a while now", Louis answered, and the man motioned him to come up. Louis went aboard, then on up to where the man stood. "They call me Cooky," the portly cook said, "the job don't pay much but you'll sleep dry and eat good."

"Where's the boat going?" Louis asked, "I was thinking about going west". "You don't want to do that from here kid, that's going up the Missouri and right into the arms of a bunch of red sticks." "Go south with us and we'll get ya to New Orleans." "I guess,"

Louis answered. "Bring your gear I'll show you where you can stow it, you'll bunk above me."

His things up on a top bunk the cook took him to meet the captain. "He's been the only kid that's come by captain," the cook said. "Then he might have to do double duty Cooky." "I'm Hiram George son, but call me Captain just like everyone else and we'll get along, and your name is?" "Louis Hand sir," Louis said, "glad to meet you." "Ok Cooky you can put him to work, but first get him some clothes and shoes." "Done Captain," the Cook answered.

"Come on kid," the cook said, and taking off his apron he headed ashore, Louis following. "I've some money," Louis said. "Learn kid," the cook told him, "when the captain says something you do it, it's an order and if he wants your money he'll take it out of your pay at the end of the trip."

Two white shirts and pants, a pair of shoes plus socks and they headed back aboard. A clean apron for the cook and one for Louis, and he was put to work on a stack of dirty pots and dishes. He didn't finish before dark, ate the sandwich the cook made for him and went to bed. At first light Cooky was shaking him awake and after a quick breakfast he was back at it again. He was determined to catch up, and thankful that there was plenty of hot water. By noon he was done but there would now be the noon meal to clean up after. There was no way he was going to let the work get behind again.

Two days later the boat headed South with six passengers aboard but still only one mess man, him. "You'll have to do double duty Louis," Cooky said. "You'll have to wait on the tables for the passengers plus Captains table too." "The engineer, fireman and roustabouts will serve them selves." "I don't know how to wait tables Cooky," Louis said. "Just be pleasant and always serve from the left side, you'll be all right." Cooky had the tables set up before the meal. Though uncomfortable Louis did the best he could with the passengers. Then the Pilot taking his meals in the wheelhouse the Captain taking most of his they're also and that did make serving their meals easier. With the kitchen and scullery work caught up Louis found time to bathe and wash his soiled clothes, enjoying the hot water that was always there.

Passing near one shoreline or the other Louis could see the boat was moving fast, very fast he thought. "We're sure moving fast," he told Cooky. "Got to," the cook told him, "gotta move faster then the river, so they can steer. Be a lot slower when we go back, you'll see if you go back with us." "I'm probably going to miss that," Louis answered.

Evenings and the boat was nosed into the bank of the river, usually at a beach where some wood hawk would be selling cordwood to the steamboats, that where always in need of fuel.

Cooky would go ashore and buy what he needed fresh from local farmers, meat of all kinds, fresh milk, eggs plus all kinds of fruit and vegetables. They really ate well aboard the boat and Louis could eat his fill even having a piece or two of pie in the evening.

The boat stayed tied to some tree or stump during the night, then at first light slipped away from the shore and continued on its run down river.

Louis was really enjoying the trip even though he had to put in long hours the work wasn't all that hard. The roustabouts were the ones who had to work hard, when they were hustling cordwood aboard the boat from the beach. Once under way though they had it comparatively easy only having to keep a supply of wood close to the boiler where the fireman had ready access to it.

He had lost track of time, one day running into the next much like the muddy river moved. A great surge of muddy water roiling from one side to the other sucking at the shores and changing the rivers banks, and bottom constantly.

Evenings were the only time when he could have a few minutes to spare and look at what was happening around him. Then the boat would stop for the night, the Pilot no longer able to read the river after dark.

When taking the meals and coffee to the wheelhouse Louis always saw the pilot at the wheel. Talking with Cooky one evening he learned the pilot was the one who knew the water. "He's the one who knows his river and how to read her, she may not breathe Louis," he told him, "but she is alive. That pilot has to know her and every little sign she gives him. Here every eddy, back current and swirling whirl pool means something and shows him where to steer for the deepest water, and that needed channel." "It doe's seem alive sometimes," Louis said, "you can feel how the water moves the boat even side ways sometimes".

Just two more days and in the afternoon they docked in New Orleans. "Well serve supper to any of those who wants to eat aboard," Cooky told Louis. He served the passengers and the Captain, Pilot and Engineer who sat at the table this time to eat supper. This was the most sit down meals Louis had been called on to serve at any one time. He got through the whole meal fine though and as the passengers left each gave him some money. Going into the galley he had to show Cooky. "I guess I earned it," he said happily. "You surely did," the cook told him," you didn't spill nothing hot in any ones of their lap, that counts for something."

"Stay on board the night," the Captain told Louis, "I'll settle up in the morning." "Right now I've got a lot to do on shore." "That's fine", Louis answered, "I'll be here in the morning."

After everything was done Cooky and Louis sat out on the top deck and watched the activity on shore. The unloading of their boat continued by lantern light after dark and Louis said, "I wonder why the rush." "The captains anxious," Cooky said, "he wants to get loaded then get back up river." "He doesn't want to get caught down here in the south if there's trouble." "You think there's going to be trouble Cooky?" Louis asked. "Ain't no way around it," the cook told him.

He sat quiet thinking and not really understanding only knowing that he had to continue to look for his way west.

Packing his things in the morning he had left the things out that Cooky had bought. "Pack those too," Cooky told him," they're yours, I sure can't wear them." "Besides, if you get a mess berth going where you want to go you can use them."

Cooky made breakfast for anyone coming in all of them hungry most from their working cargo. When the Captain came he gave Louis his pay envelope and told him he had a wagon going to the ocean docks to pick up cargo. "You can ride with the driver; it's a bit of a walk. He'll show you where the ships post the list of the crewmen they're looking for, you can read can't you Louis?" "Yes Sir I can," Louis answered." Get your gear then and I'll take you to the driver," the Captain said. Louis said his good byes to the cook and thanking him for all he'd done, then followed the Captain.

"If your ever back on the river Louis look me up," the Captain told him. "Thanks for everything Captain." "You earned it son," the Captain answered, "you did a good job."

His things in the wagon Louis got up in the seat and sat down next to a very large black man. As they moved off he turned to wave but the captain was already going back aboard with two men.

Turning to the black teamster Louis put out his hand and said, "Louis Hand". The man looked for a second, then moving the reins, to his other hand, smiling he took Louis's hand and said, "I'm Tow". Just Tow?" Louis asked. "Yes, just Tow," he answered. It was a ways but he could have walked it, if he'd known the way. Tow took him right to the board where some ships had posted wanted lists for crewmen. Mess men, one said, see purser at the small boat dock and that was the one that said, destination California. "You know where the small boat dock is Tow?" he asked. Tow told him to get up that it wasn't to far.

CHAPTER II

A small boat with two men sitting on the thwarts and a man pacing the dock in uniform. "Are you looking for a mess man?" Louis hollered and the man motioned him to come down. Picking up his things he offered his hand and said thanks to Tow. The black man smiling said, "Your welcome young man and Louis wondered why Tow sat so long watching him and he waved before turning to talk to the man in uniform.

"You need a mess man sir?" he asked the man. "You experienced?" he was asked. "I just came down river on a sternwheeler from St. Louis," Louis told him, "both passenger and the captain's table." "Load your gear; well be leaving as soon as the captain returns." "I'm the ships purser," he said, "I'll sign you on as soon as we get onboard". Getting into the boat Louis sat down on one of the crates then said, "I'm Louis Hand sir".

Some minutes later he saw the man striding down toward them. Not a big man but a man who walked with a straight back and his head held high, walking with conviction lake a man who knew exactly where he was going.

"Mr. Neil," he said as he approached the boat. "Two-sea man already to the ship with the long boat," the Purser said, "this is Louis Hand a mess man he fills out the crew Captain." "A full complement sir." "Good, cast off," the captain said, as he stepped into the boat and sat down at the tiller. "Be glad when we get to sea this country is about to come apart at the seams," the captain said.

The purser untied the boat and pushed it away as he stepped aboard. The men on the thwarts started rowing as soon as they were clear of the dock.

"How old are you son?" the captain asked. "I'm fifteen" Louis answered. "Runaway?" "Yes sir," Louis answered. "And of course you haven't been to sea before," the captain added, "that could be a problem."

As they talked Louis tried to figure what the captain was thinking as he asked these questions. His face not unpleasant was passive. No change of expression that Louis could possible read. But the mans eyes were soft, brown colored and right now Louis could see no animosity there what so ever.

"You're carrying a power horn?" "Yes sir," Louis answered, "but I don't have a rifle." "Loose it?" the captain asked. "Some thing like that," Louis answered, "John Barley corn got it." There was no change in his expression but the captain nodded and said, "I understand." "From your dress I'd take you for a farm boy not a mess man," the captain went on. "I've done both," Louis answered, "and I do have other clothes rolled up in my bed roll."

They were close to the ship now and Louis was looking up at a giant of a ship, larger then anything he had ever been on.

"Up oars", the captain said," then, boat your oars," and he brought the boat right up along side the ship. Right to where two rope blocks were hanging, and a rope ladder with wooden rungs.

"You can leave what you want in the boat Louis," the Captain said, "they'll bring everything aboard." He then took to the ladder and climbed up to the deck of the ship. Louis watched how the captain climbed and knew he'd have to climb that ladder the same way.

The purser came to the ladder as the seaman was hooking up the blocks. "Go ahead Louis," the Purser said, "but watch it, take your time and check each step." With both his leather possible bags and his power horn hanging on his shoulders Louis climbed to the deck.

The captain was waiting on the deck as the purser came aboard and told him," show the young man what he has to do." "Then assign him to the Captains mess, that way I can keep an eye on him." The boat brought aboard, Louis retrieved his bedroll and the purser led him to the mess men's focsle. Being he was the last mess man aboard of course there was only a top bunk left. His things up on the bunk and the purser led him to the galley to meet the cooks. Then to the scullery where he met one of the other mess men and then to the dinning area where he'd work. After assigning the hours he would be required to work to serve both the officer going on watch and the officer going off watch. You'll be required to work a lot of hours, but you will have hours off between watches. Seeing the some what concerned look on Louis, the purser said, "don't worry you'll be awaken by the seaman on watch. Report to the cook he'll help you with the meals you'll serve and I'll be around to give you a hand until you get used to the routine."

"Now go change into the clothes you wore aboard the sternwheeler and come back here to the saloon. If you have any valuables you want locked away bring them."

Dressed Louis took the pay envelope from the riverboat and his rifle possible bag with his mother's pistol in it and headed back to the saloon. The captain sat talking with the purser and Louis stood by the table until the captain nodded, and asked, "What have you got Louis?" "The things for the purser to put away for me Sir," Louis answered. The captain checking the envelope counted the money and wrote the amount on the out side. "Nest egg Louis?" he asked. "My pay envelope from the steamboat sir," Louis answered.

The captain slid the envelope over to his purser to read. Then asked Louis what mess duties he had on that vessel. "The captain, pilot, four passengers, dishwasher and scullery Sir," Louis answered. Smiling the captain turned to the purser saying, "I think he earned it".

He picked up the possible bag then and took out the pistol. "That was my mothers captain," Louis said. "Glad your checking this for safe keeping," the Captain said sliding the bag to the purser he stood up. "Every thing stowed aboard Mr. Neil"? "Done Captain," the purser answered. "Ten minutes and we'll pull the hook Mr. Neil," the Captain said, as he walked out.

Louis met the first class passengers mess man Thomas Drake who told Louis that he'd answered to Tom when he was on duty, but that Quack was his nickname that he didn't mind answering to when he wasn't. He wasn't much taller then Louis, but he was quite a bit older. Said he'd been going to sea for a time, mostly as a mess man. Tried cooking he told Louis but first class passenger mess is where the money was. "Thanks", Louis said, "I'll remember that, but that this was his first trip on a big ship and only his second on any boat. "Aye you'll love it," Tom told him, "and this ship is about as good as you can get, plus she's fast.

They could hear the commands being hollered on deck, the rattling of rope blocks and the snapping of sails as they caught the wind. The slight change in the movement of the deck told them they were now under way. "I'll have an easy time of it for a few days," Tom told Louis, "it'll take the land lubbers a few days to get their sea legs, happens every time". Falling into the rhythm of a ship at sea was difficult but with the watch waking Louis so he could get to his duties on time, and the purser and Thomas making sure he was getting things right, he was doing fine in just a few days.

The hours he was required to put in serving at each meal were fairly long. Having to be there to serve the officer going on watch and then wait to serve the officer coming off watch. The morning and mid day meal were the easiest with the Capitan the three officers, the Purser and a Cadet, the only ones he had to serve. But the evening meals were different the Captain always inviting a few of the first class passengers to his table.

The Cadet was a few years older then Louis, a half a head taller but not heavier. He acted rather snooty and aloof when it came to the crew, and Louis thought he spent most of his time on the bridge or following one of the Officers around the deck. "Be careful of that one," Thomas told Louis one day, "he's some kind of a relative of the ships owner." "He's been no problem so far," Louis said. "Just watch it," Thomas warned.

Most of time Louis had to spare he spent around the kitchen and mess talking with Thomas and the cooks. During these times he learned that Thomas owned a farm near New Bedford, had a wife and seven children.

His farm was next to his wife's father's farm, he told Louis and how with his father in-law and both families the farm thrived. "We save the money I make going to sea," Thomas told Louis, "and soon I'll be able to retire to the farm as a gentleman farmer." "Then I can watch my seven children grow up." "You have seven children?" Louis asked. "Maybe eight before I get home form this voyage," Thomas answered smiling, "and you listen to me Louis, big families are good, their strong, and they can help each other."

"You get your self a piece of land Louis and a good woman and you wont be sorry believe me." "Someday," Louis answered, "I'm a little young yet." He did think about his future, usually when he was alone and it did concern him, he knew nothing about the land called California or the people there. But he knew fretting about it would do no good, when the time came he'd face it, he'd have to and he'd have to learn.

Right now it was pleasant the weather warm, the sails full as they moved through the gentle swell. He stood learning over the rail looking and listening to the noise as the ship moved through the water. He didn't hear the Captain walk up behind him until he asked, "you all right Louis?" Turning around, Louis answered, "Yes Sir, I was just watching and listing to the water." "I thought you might be ill." "Not yet Sir," Louis answered. "She doe's sing when she moving this fast doesn't she," the Captain said," as he listened. "You could say that," Louis answered. "As you were," the Captain said, as he walked away looking up at the sails above. Right then Louis knew the Captain had changed his thought from a rather trivial item back to his most important and his primary responsibility, the ship.

Even careful as he could be with his white shirt and pants he always got them stained during his work. Not easily washed with only the water from the sea to wash in, when worn again they felt gritty against his skin. His clothes though clean and white did look wrinkled compared to his friends. He asked Thomas what his secret was. "I can't help you with the way the salt stays in your clothes," Thomas told him, "not until we get into some rainsqualls." "The wrinkles are easy when your clothes are almost dry turn then inside out, lay them flat under your mattress and let them finish drying there. Seemed all right to Louis and doing it with his next washing, did really improve the way his clothes looked.

They must have looked better to the cadet also because he brought a bag of his soiled clothes to be wash and his dress boots to be polished. Louis didn't say anything to any one and went ahead washed the Cadets clothes and polished the boots. The day he finished he brought them to the evening mess setting the clean laundry on an extra chair away from the captains table. The polished boots standing in front. As he stood up he saw the Captain looking toward him with out expression or question.

The Captain as usual coming to mess early always ate slow, seeming to enjoy his meal and the leisure moments. This the only time that Louis knew he relaxed. He wondered sometime when the man rested, always seeing him some place on the deck be it day or night. Mostly near the helm or in the chart room yet many times walking the deck. He checked the ship daily from stem to stern and always more then one time.

When the Cadet came to the table he pointed to the chair and asked," your boots and laundry Cadet?" The Cadet sat impassive. And the Captain asked, "are you taking on extra duties, Louis? Because, if you are make sure they don't take away from your regular duties." "And you Cadet make sure Louis is compensated for his labor, that's not his regular duties." The Cadet didn't answer and the captain continued with his meal.

Louis continued doing the cadets laundry for weeks but when the ship reached the Southern Latitudes and with the inclement weather he had a problem with drying his own things let alone all of the Cadets. The Cadet had left his clothes in the mess men's focsle and Louis took it back to the Cadets focsle and hung it on the door. Not sure of what the consequences might be. He wouldn't find out for a couple of days until coming to do some of his work in the pantry he found the Cadet sitting at the captain table. Can I get you something Cadet, "Louis asked. The officers did sometimes come in for coffee and maybe something sweet". "Coffee and what ever there might be," the cadet told him.

Louis brought him a piece of pie made with dried apples, a fork on the dish and a cup of coffee. Turning to leave he heard the utensil hit the deck. Turning back Louis picket it up and went to the pantry for a clean fork. Placing the fork on the table Louis watched as the Cadet slid the fork off the table letting it drop to the floor. Twice more he brought clean forks, when the forth fork hit the floor he just picked it up and set it back on the table. "It's dirty," the Cadet said. "Get me a clean fork, that's an order". Louis just stood as the Cadet push the fork over the edge and said, "Pick it up".

The Cadet stood up now and seething with anger struck Louis in the face with an open hand, the stinging blow turned his head to the side. Louis reacted quickly, turning his right fist catching the Cadet full on the mouth. Knocked onto his rear the Cadet sat sputtering and bleeding down the front of his uniform.

Louis heard the Captain voice asking, "what's going on here?" The Cadet answered," he struck me Captain, I want to press charges." "You struck him the Captain said", looking straight at Louis." "I did sir," Louis answered.

"Hold it Captain I saw the whole thing," and Louis turned to see the second mate standing near by. "Well number Two," the Captain said, fill me in I've got to get to the bottom of this." The mate was telling the Captain

13

what he saw and Louis then realized there were two others who witnessed what took place, the first cook and Thomas. When number Two finished the Cadet was on his feet bleeding down on the front of his uniform and on to the deck at his feet.

Reaching out the Captain took Louis by the chin and turned his head so he could look at the left side of his face. Swollen now and purplish red in color. Turning to the Cadet he asked, "what do you have to say for your self Mr." "He refused to obey an order," the Cadet said, "he should be brought up on charges." "First you have no right to give orders on this ship, you're a cadet and no more, understand. Secondly you bated my mess man and then struck him," the Captain told him." This is my uncles ship," the cadet answered, "and he's going to hear about this." "On this ship Cadet you have no rank, you give no orders I'm the Master when at sea and your right your uncle will hear about what's happened here, because it will be entered into the ships log. Now go to your foscle, clean your self up and take care of your uniform. Your restricted to your quarters until you hear different, dismissed," the Captain told him.

After looking down at the blood on the deck the Captain turned to Louis and asked him, to get a mop and clean that up, will you Louis?

The Captain was talking to number two as Louis worked and he couldn't help hearing what was being said. "I don't know why I let them talk me into taking that insolent pup to sea. I see more of my mess man in the chart room then him. That's where he should be if he's ever going to learn but he always has some excuse. Hows he ever going to captain a ship of his own." "You think that will ever happen?" the Mate asked. "Not if his uncle cares anything about the ship he Masters," the Captain answered, "but you just never know, nepotism has been known to cause some to turn a blind eye toward reality."

They had just finished their supper when the Captain said he wanted to see both the second Mate and Louis in the chart room in thirty minutes. Louis wouldn't have time to finish cleaning and knew he'd have to come back later. Right now his biggest concern though was what it was the Captain could possibly want. Reporting to the chart room he found both the captain and the Mate there by the chart table. Turning toward him the captain said, "Just a few questions Louis then you can get back to your duties".

Some weeks ago you did some work for Cadet Webber out side your regular duties." "Mostly laundry sir", Louis answered, "and since then every week until this week when I could no longer continue." "With the weather the way it is there's no place other then the mess men's focsle where I could dry that much laundry. I couldn't expect the other mess men to put up with that much of an inconvenience." "What compensation have you received from the Cadet so far, Louis?" "Nothing Sir", Louis answered." "Your excused Louis," the Captain said, "you can go back to your duties."

The Captain turning to his second Mate asking, "you got any ideas George?" "I'm afraid you've got a bit of a dilemma Captain," the Mate answered. "Your not much help." "No Sir", the Mate told him, "but maybe, just maybe that bloody mouth did some good."

"Go get him will you George, I've got to find some kind of a solution to this if it's at all possible." The Cadet came to the chart room his lips cracked and swollen but the bleeding stanched from his lip and nose. "Mr. Webber, I have some questions I need an answered. You were told that any work you had done by the officer's mess man would have to be paid for by you. Have you compensated him?" the Captain asked?" "No," the Cadet answered, "I spent my allowance before we left port." "It's no Sir Cadet when you answer me, you understand. So now just how did intend compensating Louis as I ordered you to, how did you intend on taking care of that responsibility?" the Captain asked.

The Cadet just stood looking ahead. And the Captain posed another question, "did you have any intention of paying him?" The Cadet continued standing. "Then you had no intention," the Captain said, "all right what do you have of value with you on board".

"Number two I'll take care of the helm, you and the Bo-sun go through his cabin and bring back anything of value you find." The Captain left the Cadet standing as he worked his chart while waiting for the Mate to return. Thirty minutes later the Mate and the Bo-sun came to the chart room with just two items, an officers dress sword, and a loaded forty-four caliber pistol. Hefting the pistol for just a moment the Captain handing it to the Bo-sun, and told him to take it out on deck and remove the caps. Then picking up the sword examined it, saying, "nice Sheffield." "It belonged to my grandfather," the Cadet announced rather pointedly".

The Bo-sun back with the pistol handed it back to the Captain. "When you came aboard you were told all firearms were to be surrendered to the purser Cadet, why did you retain the weapon and keep it in your cabin?" "It was under his mattress Captain," the Mate said.

"All right Cadet which of these weapons would like to surrender to satisfy your debt?" the Captain asked. "Not the colonels saber, I could never give that up Sir," the Cadet said. "Sit down Cadet," the Captain said," and write a note saying you relinquish owner ship in the pistol, put down the serial number and sign it." Satisfied with the note he gave both the Cadet and the Bo-sun their leave. Turning to the Mate asked, "what are you thinking?" "Any ties below the Mason Dixon line Captain?" "Large holdings in Mississippi," the Captain said, "and they have a tendency of treating those they feel below them no better then slaves, but lets just keep this to ourselves George but I'd appreciate it if you'd keep your eyes peeled."

CHAPTER III

The weather progressively worsened as they moved south. Thomas had told Louis to hang his clothes out in the rain and that was a plus. His clothes felt so much softer now with the gritty salt washed out of them by the rain.

Having to do no more laundry other then his own it was better. The Cadet was coming to the table for his meals and Louis could feel the hostility, and disrespect. But the Cadet never tried to exercise any authority over him, like he did before. Things seemed to be better between the Cadet and the Captain even through Louis felt sure there was a feeling of distrust between them.

The Mate and the seaman on watch had a pretty rough go of it now. Having to tend the wheel out in the weather. Louis when he could would bring a pot of coffee up for them. It was miserable just being out in weather for a few minutes and the wheel watch had to endure the wet and cold for their four-hour watch. Bringing coffee to the chart room gave Louis a chance to look at the chart. The Captain telling him the line on the chart was where he thought they were. But when we get a clear sky I'll find out where we really are. "Its not like being on land," Louis said, "there's nothing but water, nothing you can see to go by," "There is though," the Captain said, "it's the stars and the sun, once you learn to use the instruments its easy and you know right where you are".

The weather continued cold and wet and progressively getting colder. Thomas told him to come out on deck one evening and see the lights. Out on the deck he pointed up and Louis saw the blue green light around the sails and rigging above them. Beautiful in away but scary too, not knowing why or what it was. "It's called St. Elmo's fire," Thomas told him, "it happens sometimes when there's storms." "It was alright" Louis said, "but personally I'd feel better with out it."

Days of wind, rain, snow and rough seas a couple of days of fog and then flat seas. Then more seas and wind, a clear cold day and the Captain putting a dot on the chart said, "that's right where we are now, see Louis my other mark I wasn't that far off now was I?"

The watch had shaken him awake and he stood on the deck dressing. The movement of the ship told him there had been a change. The pitch and roll of the ship was different now and not until after he was through serving that morning did Louis know that the ship had changed direction. The sun now more on his right shoulder as he faced the bow then on his back as it was before.

The weather still cold though as he took coffee to the chart room and there confirmed that they had changed direction. Now they were moving more toward the top of the chart, and North. Bringing coffee to the chart room then taking a cup out to the helmsman, and he came back in soaked and cold. "You should wear oilskins going out in that," the Captain told him." "I don't see how they do it Sir," Louis said. "He stays pretty dry the way he's dressed," the Captain answered, "and it could be a lot worse, it's not freezing right now. It will soon be warmer through, even hot enough during some mid days that you'll wish for some of this cool."

Even during this weather Louis saw the men work aloft. A long way above the deck and when the ship rolled they were out over the water. One slip and he knew it could mean the end of the man. There was little chance that the ship could be brought about in time to save him.

Other then at meal time he seldom saw Cadet Webber and wondered why or what was happening. Though he would have liked to know he felt it prudent not to inquire. I don't think it's any of my business any way, he told himself.

Days went by as the sea fell behind them and the weather got warmer. Valparaiso Chile and they anchored off shore. The Captain and the Purser going ashore in the long boat. The Purser using the long boat hauled fresh provision and water to replenish the ships store. None of the crew where allowed to go ashore and they sailed out of the harbor as soon as the Captain came back aboard. Thomas told Louis that if the skipper had allowed shore leave, that it might take him a week to round up all the crew again.

With the fresh provisions the passengers and crews spirits buoyed considerably. The foul weather over for now, the excellent fair for their meals and water that tasted its age, behind them now.

On North and the weather warmed considerably. "We'll be crossing the Equator soon," Thomas told Louis. The crew started holystoning the deck working with their pants rolled up they sloshed the deck with buckets of sea—water that cooled their feet. The Captain walked the deck checking it with his pants rolled up and bare foot too. The men making sure the Captain got his feet cooled when ever he walked by.

"Better cover up," he told the men, "and that there would be no going with out their upper body covered." "I know it's going to be uncomfortable but I don't want anyone down with blistered hides or a fever from exposure to the sun."

Any man now ordered a loft to work the sails eagerly scrambled up the ratlands to get aloft and into the more favorable breezes that were up there.

Again crossing the equator the captain allowed little celebration but did allow the crew each a ration of rum. Louis tasting his told Thomas he thought it tasted vile. "Put it in your coffee with sugar," Thomas told him. After tasting it that way he told Thomas, "it wasn't all that bad, but if he never had it again he wouldn't miss it."

The Captain and the mates even in the hot weather drank the coffee Louis brought to the chart room so he continued with out being asked. Glad to do it, it gave him the opportunity to take another look at the chart that intrigued him. He asked Captain Bolt questions, which the Captain always answered, never denying him. When Louis had seen the change in the color and clarity of the water he asked about it. "Remember when I told you about the currents that cause a ship to move off its course. What you're asking about, that's the visible evidence of the currents. We left the Southern Artic water and entered a current coming from the South. Before we reach San Francisco we'll enter another current coming down from the North. The ocean currents are a constance challenge for us always moving and always changing, pushing us one way or the other. That's one of the reasons I spend so much time here Louis," he told him. Louis knew the winds changed too but he'd have to think about that for a while before broaching the subject.

More days through the blue water and warm weather before the ship turned into the bay at Monterey. A group of ships at anchor and they'd have to also, while the Captain and the Purser went ashore in a small boat. While the watch held the ship ready to get back under sail just as soon as the Captain was back on board. Louis standing at the rail with Thomas watching and Thomas told him that they'd arrange for the cargo here that they'd haul back. "We'll need a lot of hides and tallow to fill the ship," Thomas told him.

"Those other ships?" Louis asked, "what are they there for?" "Crewless derelicts now," Thomas answered, "abandoned by their crews, they left them to go hunt for gold." "That's just a few, wait until we get to San Francisco you'll see a lot more there." "What a waste," Louis said.

The Captain and Purser barely on deck and the ship was underway again, heading North along the coast of California. Sailing through the night they were at the entrance into the bay at full light and the flowing tide. With the fast flow of the water and the inshore wind, they moved rapidly through the throat of the bay, a wall of white fog following on their heels.

Anchoring off shore they'd take the passengers ashore in the long boat staying at anchor until they made the arrangements for offloading.

Coming on deck the first thing that Louis saw was the derelict ships farther up toward the north of the bay. Minutes later the shroud of fog enveloping their ship and the derelicts were hidden. In just a minute every thing around them had disappeared, even the tops of their own masts were shrouded in the mist.

It was after lunch and Louis had finished his cleaning then he again had time to come back up on deck. North across the bay and now he could see there in the rising mist the forest of leafless trees, or what? It wasn't until he borrowed the Captains telescope to look at what he first thought were trees, but in reality were the masts and spars of many ships. All at anchor in that bay, and all derelicts.

When he went back into the chart room the Captain seeing the look on his face asked, if he all right? "You look almost ill Louis," he said. "There's a graveyard of ships out there Captain," Louis said, "I don't think I like this place." "That is sad isn't," the Captain answered. "The lure of finding a fortune in gold is so much greater then a mans commitment to a ship. But men have done worse things I guess seeking fame or fortune."

"You were planning to get off here Louis?" the Captain said. "It was what I had intended," Louis answered. "Take a hour or so and go ashore Louis, take a look at the what's here, you might want to change your mind. I don't think your going like what you see. If you don't like it stay on board and go back to Monterey with us, I think you'll find it more to your liking. But don't you go ashore here alone," the Captain told him.

With the passengers having already left the ship Thomas having little work to do, said that he'd go ashore with Louis, and have a look around. Shortly after noon when they went out on deck they found the fog gone and they were greeted by a bright sunny day.

The crew was already off loading heavy boxes of mining machinery onto a riverboat. "The easy pickings are about through, I guess," Thomas said, "I think they're going to sweat for the gold they get now, digging down deep underground."

Just before they got aboard the small boat to go ashore they learned from one of the deck hands that the country was at war. That the South had fired on Fort Sumter not long after they'd left New Orleans. "I heard it from one the men on the riverboat," he told them. "I wonder how the news beat us here," Thomas said, "we just got here." "I wondered about that too," the deck hand told him, "and they told me that they have pony riders bringing letters, and news to Sacramento from Independence in under two weeks now." Thomas and Louis talked about what they heard on they're way ashore. How they had left before the trouble started but the news had reached California while they still at sea. Thomas told Louis that he was concerned about the trip home, that they would have sail by the southern states, that were a part of the Confederacy to get back to their homeport. "I'm sure the Captain will figure out something though," he said to Louis, "I don't think he's going to let anyone take his ship, the crew or his cargo,"

Once on the shore Thomas led the way having been there before. He pointed out things as they walked, the bars and gambling halls, the shills and prostitute's, all hawking their wares in the middle of the day. Passing one door with two young ladies standing in it, Thomas asked, "do you know what those two ladies are Louis?" "I think so," Louis answered smiling. "I didn't know, your pretty young Louis," Thomas told him. "I do have two older brother you know Thomas," Louis answered. The seedy looking characters walking the streets and on every corner, and Louis said, "I've seen enough Thomas lets go back."

They stood on the shore waving but it was some time before they were able to get the attention of someone on board, all of the unloading being done on the other side of the ship now. Finally the small boat came to the beach. The sailor on board saying, "well that didn't take long." "I saw all I wanted to see," Louis told him. "Must have been the Barbary," the sailor said laughing, "you can sure get yourself a gut full of about anything you want there and in a short time."

The talk on board the ship now was about the war and the way the Pony Express had brought the news so quickly to California. Louis listened as he served all the officers at noon, there being able to take their lunch together with the ship at anchor. They too talked about how the news had reached California and the Pony Express was a wonder that they talked about, but it was the war that they discussed at length. It was the Captain that he heard say, "that it was a sad day for their country. They'll be family against family, and that he couldn't imagine what it would be like to see one of your own relatives, maybe even your own brother over your rifle sights." It was the second time this day that something would cause Louis think about his brothers and what they were doing now. He continued listening as he waited for the meal to be finished and the conversation to come to an end so he could clean off the table.

Cadet Webber sat for a few minutes after the others had left, and as Louis waited he wondered why the Cadet had never entered into the conversation or expressed an opinion. The Cadet left, and the Captain coming back asked Louis if he had decided yet about going back to Monterey. "I'd like to go to Monterey Sir," Louis told him. "Good," the Captain said, "I think you'll find it better place Louis, and I'm going to introduce you to a man who can help you there. But you know you can still go back with us." "Thank you Sir," Louis answered, "but now more then ever I know there's no place for me back there."

Louis was just finishing with cleaning after breakfast when the Purser came with his replacement. After he introduced the man, Anthony Rose to Louis, he told him, "I could use your help for the next couple of days. I'm going to really busy for the next few days. I've got the new passengers to get settled in, and be ready to unload the rest of the cargo at Monterey. Then get things ready to load the cargo there and provision for the trip home. If you would show Anthony serving supper this evening and breakfast in the morning when we reach Monterey, it would be a great help for me."

"Are we leaving this afternoon?" Louis asked. "On the evening tide," the Purser answered. The Captains anxious and I think nervous about what we could run into on the trip home. We're faster and can out run about everything on the sea but we have no armament for are own protect, so it's a different run for home this time."

The new mess man, Anthony was a bit older then Louis closer to Thomas's age. He told Louis that he'd been up in the gold country but had gotten there a little late for the easy pickings. "I did pick up some color though," he told Louis, "but not enough to retire on, or go home first class. That's why I figured I'd save some and take this job, then I'd still have enough for a start again when I get home."

"Some of those fellas going home first class are going home fat, and others are alright but there's one fella in second class that's about like me. But there's a lot more who are still back there trying and some working in the mines. That's a lot of hard rough work breaking ore out hard rock, with little satisfaction unless you like make some one else rich."

There wasn't a whole lot to learn to be a good mess man as long as you were willing to work, and Anthony was. "It's a lot easier then shoveling gravel into sluice all day," he told Louis.

Thomas was busy at the dinner hour and getting the first class passengers settled in after. Louis and Anthony were busy too cleaning up and going over other duty's Anthony would have, as the anchor was pulled. They knew the ship was under way and heading out to sea just by the movement of the deck under them.

By now Louis knew a little about this clipper ship and how fast she was at sea, but that she was not the easiest vessel to maneuver. He wanted to watch as the Captain worked the Kestrel out through the narrow neck of the bay. They had to leave on the out going tide but tack into the prevailing inshore winds, making it difficult in the narrow rocky passage. The watch would change at eight and the Mate was already at the table but Louis knew the Captain wouldn't be. He wouldn't leave the helm until the ship was clear of the dangerous passage, well out into the open sea and the watch was ready to change.

Louis told Anthony that he would take the Captains supper to the chart room and come back after to help him clean up. The ship was in the tidal flow and he remembered how the steamboat had to maintain steerage by going faster then the flow of the river. But the steamboat had the steam—powered paddle wheel to rely on. Here the men had to harness the wind by changing the position of the sails and the rudder, and all at the Captains commands. The sails would snap, the ship would shudder for a second then the ship healing over would change direction and charge forward on a different tack, each time angling out toward the open ocean.

Once close two the open ocean and the Captain continued watching but turned the helm over to the watch, letting the Mate call out the orders. Eating a bite now and then but he continued watching, the near shore, the water and the sails. Louis was watching as the ship was again changing direction and again when the Captain walked up beside him. "It's something to see isn't it Louis?" he said. "It really is Sir," Louis answered. "This is what many of us go to sea for, the Captain said, "much of what we do is routine, but this is when you're challenged, and what makes it all worth while."

"Thank you for my supper but I could have eaten later, Louis." "Then I wouldn't have been here to watch," Louis answered. "That's true," the Captain said, smiling, "I hope you enjoyed it as much as I did. I'm afraid that it will one day in the not to distance future be a thing of the past though, they'll have steam powered ships and all the romance about going to sea will be gone Louis." And Louis wondered about men like the Captain.

After taking the dishes down to the galley, Louis checked on Anthony. With only the Mate going off watch to serve he knew he'd be all right, and with a fresh pot of coffee he headed for the chart room. They were now heading south, and he found it difficult walking with the pot in his hand. He had to hold on with his other hand as the ship listed to port, rising up on one of the large round topped waves that were coming at them from the west, and the open ocean. As the wave passed under her she would roll to the starboard almost to her rail. The Captain was smiling as he came into the chart room. "The water doesn't look all that rough," Louis said. "They're ground swells," the Captain told him, "there here all the time and remembered by most who have had to sail through them. She wouldn't roll like this normally though, but we have very little cargo left on board."

"I don't think Thomas is going to have to many for breakfast," Louis said as he put the coffee on a small table away from the chart table." "You might have to take care of the officers mess at the change of the watch by your self too, Louis," the Captain said," the man that's replacing you might have a problem also."

Shaken awake by the seaman going on watch Louis got up and dressed, and saw that Anthony was having a problem. He was up and trying to dress but was having trouble. "Go up on deck and get some fresh air," Louis told him. "I'll take care things, if you feel better later I'll see you then." Louis was cleaning off the table when he came in looking a little peaked but said, that he'd be fine in a little while. Louis gave him some crackers and told him to eat them. "I've been told they'll help," he said. "I hope," Anthony answered.

Again the watch was changing when the ship was being brought in to the anchorage at Monterey. The Captain, Louis knew he would remain by the helm until they were anchored. This time he asked him if he wanted his breakfast there. "That would be fine," he answered, "I shouldn't have a problem eating and watching at the same time. We're just going to anchor, it's not going to be near as dramatic as last evening."

The ship at anchor and the Captain told Louis to get his things together that he'd be back in an hour. Packing only took him a few minutes and he went to help Anthony clean up after the morning meal. His things at rail he and Anthony waited for the Captain to return. Coming aboard the Captain told Louis to meet him in the saloon, that he had something for him and that he wanted a cup of coffee. Anthony left to get the coffee and the Captain handed Louis a piece of paper.

"Sit down Louis, he said, and slid a piece of paper across the table," that's the name of man you want to see when you get ashore. He said he could use a man that could count, write and spoke English. I told him you could do that, but your going have to learn Spanish Louis if your going to stay here. Pablo speaks English, so you'll be able to talk with him and there are some others."

The Purser came in carrying an arm full of things and Louis recognized his possibles bags and his money pouch. Two canvas bags that he didn't though, a small one and one to large to fit in either of his bags. The small one he gave to Louis and told him it was the money he'd earned on the voyage and Louis put it into his large possibles bag. Handing the other bag to Louis the Captain told him, "don't open this one until you're on shore Louis."

"Aren't you going to count your money Louis?" the Purser asked. Smiling Louis asked him if he thought he should. "It's of course up to you Louis, but I am happy you trust me, thank you," the Purser said.

They walked together out on to the deck and watched as the lighter was being pulled out from the shore with the first load of hides. The crew had brought up from the cargo hole half a dozen boxes that looked like small caskets. The hides were brought aboard the boxes lowered on to the lighter, and it was time for Louis to say goodbye to his friends. He shook their hands then before started down the ladder he turned around, taking one last look at those on the deck. He saw the Cadet standing at the other rail watching.

Turning back he tossed his bedroll to one of the sailors on the deck of the lighter and climbed down. The lighter moving toward the beach as the other lighter loaded with hides and tallow moved out from the shore. Louis looking back waved one more time to his friends standing at the ships rail.

On the beach he watched as men carried the off loaded cargo across the beach, up the bank, across the road and put it on the loading platform in front of a warehouse. Other men were bringing hides and skins of tallow down to the lighter.

Not knowing how to speak Spanish he simply said the name, Pablo Luna, and one of the men pointed to a man standing up on the loading platform. Going up on to the platform, he said, "I'm from the ship." "Ah yes," Pablo said, "your the young man Captain Bolt said he would send." "Give me a minute senor, I'll be through here in a bit then we can talk."

Louis put his things on the platform next to the door then helped the men carrying the boxes inside. They were done when Pablo came back and said, "gracias senor for your help, now come with me I've got work for you on the other side." They walked through the warehouse to another large door opening.

Introducing him to his son Pepe, Pablo said, "he can show you what needs to be done and where you can stay." Pepe was making a simple stroke mark tally for the good hides that men were bringing in. Then told Louis what to look for when a hide should be rejected. "You're not going to find many bad ones," he told him, "just one now and then, put them aside and we'll figure if there worth anything later. When you've finished counting one mans good and bad hides, mark down the number and sign the paper. He can then take it to my father and collect his money. In another couple of days we should have the ship loaded plus a few hides to store." They checked hides until mid day when everyone stopped their work. "Time for us stop for siesta," Pepe said, he closed the door and told Louis to bring his things that he show him where he could put them. A little office with a small room next to it with a bunk, where he said Louis could leave his things.

"Now lets go get something to eat," Pepe said, "there's a cantina around the corner." They sat at a small table and Pepe told Louis that he came along at the right time. "Somebody's got to stay in the warehouse at night now, it's not just a hide house anymore, there's other things we have to store there now. Years ago it would have been all right but not anymore, I'm afraid we have some people we can't trust here now."

"I don't know how much I can do," Louis said, "but I'll be there." "Just so they know someone is there," Pepe told him, "should be enough. Now what will you have senor, beer or wine?" "I'm afraid neither," Louis answered, "water will do fine."

Pepe ordered for both of them, telling Louis, "I think you'll like what I've ordered." As they were waiting Louis asked Pepe why his father would hire him instead of one of the local men? "Few of the men here can read or write," Pepe told him, "girls are sent to Convents, but young men learn to work. Most of the Dons though they have large ranchos that they control can neither read or write." "But you Pepe," Louis said, "you read and write don't you?" "My mother taught my father when they were first married, then insisted that her children learn when we came along. When she couldn't do it any longer, my sister taught us."

"Aren't there some Americans here your father could have hired?" Louis asked. "I'm afraid there's more bad then good here Louis," Pepe said, "and if your Captain wouldn't have told my father that you were honest and trustworthy, he wouldn't have given you a job."

"Doesn't your father stop to eat" Louis asked. "He's gone home," Pepe told him, "he'll eat there, take a siesta and come back later." "The warehouse," Louis said, "we left it unlocked." The workers are there, they'll eat then take their siesta there in the shade, and nothing will be bothered while they're there. They're poor men Louis but honest." "I know I've been asking a lot of questions," Louis said, "but everything is so different here, can you excuse me?" "If you don't ask your not going learn, so you had better ask, and if it's me you ask I will help you if I can," Pepe answered.

Their food there and Louis was eating slowly, when Pepe asked him, if it was alright?" "It's fine," he answered, spicy and warmer then I'm used to, but I like it."

Walking back to the warehouse Louis asked about the men that were resting in the shade there, knowing they would be the ones he'd be working with. Pepe told him, you dress like them, except for your shoes." "There the clothes I've been wearing as a mess man and I don't have a lot of others," Louis answered. "Their not going to judge you by the clothes you wear," Pepe told him, "it will be by the way you treat them." "Get yourself a pair of sandals, a serape, a sombrero and learn Spanish and you could pass for one of the peons," Pepe laughed. "The clothes will be easy to come by," Louis said, "but learning Spanish will take me a while, but I'll do it." "I believe you will'" Pepe told him, "now its time for us to rest for a while, Papa will be back later and want to take a few more hides in."

He unrolled his bedroll, took out his clothes and put them on one of the shelves that were there. Hung up his power horn and possibles bag then open the canvas bag the Captain had given him. Inside he found the pistol a few caliber forty-four balls for it, caps, and the paper Cadet Weber signed relinquishing ownership of it. He had to smile as he thought about it and put it on the shelf. His caliber thirty-six pistol he loaded, and then put by the bed where it would be handy.

The window he found barred when he pulled back the curtains and knew that had to be there to keep some one out, not in. Laying out his bedroll on the mattress stuffed with cornhusks he lay down and drifted off to sleep. Waking to the sound of voices he went out to find Pablo talking with one of the other men. They were speaking Spanish, not able to understand he stood and waited until they were through, and Pablo turned toward him. "You ready to start counting hides?" he asked. "Your board, paper and pencil are right here Louis," Pablo said, "you know what to do, I'll be out on in the back."

There were fewer hides for him to check in the afternoon then in the morning, only three men bringing hides in. The men working inside were taking the hides from the other side of the warehouse. That side almost empty now and he knew they must have already taken thousand of hides out to the ship already.

He watched what they were doing and helped them carry the hides from near where he had been checking them to the other side. Checking to see if anyone had hides to check in every time he came near the door.

The other men were talking in Spanish and he heard two words that he did understand, peon and americano. But they were laughing so he figured it should be all right, they were just having a little fun. He had these clothes and he'd just as well wear them so they'd get used to it.

Pablo came in said something and the men quit working, and left. Pablo going to the large sliding door closed it behind them, and put the iron lock pin in place. The small door by the office he showed Louis how it could be chain locked from the outside or barred on the inside. The rear door was double barred and the rear sliding door pinned to the floor with an iron pin.

"We usually only store hides here," Pablo told Louis, "but now we need to leave other things here. Some of them very valuable," and Louis saw his eyes move to the coffin like boxes." "There's silk from China, cotton cloth, seeds, tools, iron, brass, and all kinds of hardware. So you see I need someone to keep a eye on things here, Louis." "I'll be here." Louis said. "I need to take a quick dip in the bay but, I'll do it before dark."

"There's a barrel of water next to the inside wall by the door if you get thirsty," Pablo told him.

It was still light when he took his soap a towel and going out the back door went down to the beach. He could watch the door from where as he bathed and washed his clothes. The Kestrel riding on a calm sea there only a few hundred yards away. With his clean white cotton clothes on he wrung out his wet things, and walked back up to the warehouse. In a bucket of water from the water barrel he wrenched the salt water out of the clothes he'd washed, and hung them up to dry.

His pistol stuffed in his belt under his blouse he put his possibles bag over shoulder chained and locked the door and walked to the cantina. He couldn't order in Spanish but the man who came to the table could speak enough English to help him. No cerveza or vino but he got his chocolate all right. The food was good and reasonable but different of course then what he was used to.

Walking back the sun already down for a while but the sky was still light as he hurried and heard the first guitar music. They must really care about their evenings he thought, why else would the play music and sing.

Back inside he barred the door and going into the room he undressed and went bed, though he wasn't really tired he soon fell asleep listening to the music that seemed to be coming from all around him.

He didn't know how long he'd slept but he didn't hear any music now. This was different sound, that had awaken him and he heard it again and thought it might be mice or rats. The noise persisted and he realized that it was a little too loud to be small animals and seemed to be coming from the rear of the warehouse. He slipped on his pants and stuck his pistol in his belt. Out into the warehouse, he walked gingerly on the rough splintery wood floor in his bare feet. It was dark in the warehouse and he found it difficult feeling his way as he tried to remember where things were. He remembered where the half barrel of pick and axe handles were against the wall, then only inches away from it when he saw them in the darkness and closed his hand on an axe handle. Close to the big sliding door now he saw in the pale night light that came in from out side a piece of something between the door and the wall. Then the pale hand and arm that reminded of a snake as he realized it was trying to find the pin that held the door closed. He brought the axe handle down as hard as he could on it. There was a cry of pain from outside, then the report of a large pistol and splinters of wood stung him but the lead ball missed. Pulling his own pistol he fired a shot at the movement he saw outside through the gap between the wall and the door. A scream of pain, some cussing, then the sound of more then one person running away across the wooden loading platform outside. Then nothing, and the night got awfully quiet.

He made his way slowly back to the office and sat down. He didn't know how long he sat, but there was the morning light coming through the curtained window. He heard voices out side the rear door, and going to it, "he asked who it was?" "It's Pablo Louis," he heard a voice he knew answer, and removing the bars he opened the door.

"Are you all-right?" Pablo asked as he walked in, taking Louis by the shoulders and holding him, looked at the red marks on his face where the wood splinters had stung him.

Taking a deep breath, Pablo asked again if he was all right? "People came to my house and told me that they heard a shot early this morning," he said, "I was scared for you, Louis."

"Someone was trying to break in through the big door in the back," Louis said as they walked together toward the door. Pieces of heavy wood in between the wall and the door and a long piece they had probable tried to pry with. The pieces removed Louis lifted the pin out and slid the door back. The hole through the door easily seen now as was the trail of blood across the deck of the wooden loading dock.

Pablo visible shaken now as he looked at the hole in the door, said, "I'm sorry Louis you could have been hurt." "I'm fine" Louis answered, "but there's some one around with a hole in him."

Some of the workers were there now and Pablo seeing the Captains skiff coming in went down to the beach to meet him. The other workers were standing in a small group talking and looking him and Louis wondered why. Until he looked down and saw he still had the axe handle in his hand and his pistol stuck in his belt. Going in he put the axe handle back in the barrel and going into the bedroom put the pistol away. Then put on his blouse and went back out side.

Pablo and the Captain were both there, Pablo just sending one of the men on some errand. The Captain looking stern when he nodded his good morning and Louis knew there was something definitely wrong. "I told Captain Bolt what happened here last night Louis," Pablo said. "The morning watch said they heard a single shot, early this morning Louis, and someone who they had to help aboard because he had an injured arm." "But Pablo told me there were two shots fired," the Captain said. "I was inside when I shot," Louis told him, "my small pistols report would have been muffled some from in there." "That's true," the Captain answered.

Pablo said, "lets go inside," going in Louis following right behind the Captain. They were standing by the boxes when the worker came back with the tools, gave them to Pablo, then left. Pablo pried the lids of the boxes off and they saw what was inside. "I think these are what they were after," he said. "No doubt about it," the Captain told him, "and you'd better get rid of them because there's a good chance they'll be back, they want those arms." "I've got a lot of money tied up in these," Pablo told them. "They told me they were starting a new stage line and said they would pay for the shipment just as soon as it came in." "I don't think they any intention of paying you Pablo," the Captain told him. "These men had to be in some kind of an alliance with the cadet who I'm sure now is a Confederate sympathizer."

CHAPTER IV

"Twelve rifles, twelve carbines and twelve short double barrel shot guns, that's quite a number of arms, isn't it? "the Captain said. "Now think what thirty six men could do armed with those here in California. They could create havoc and probably start something that could end up by the taking over California for the Confederacy. There's sure nothing here to stop them. They'd have control of the gold that coming from here. That would sure put a feather in the Cadets hat, he's ambitious, and knows if they could pull this off he'd more then likely get himself a commission." "What do you think I should do," Captain?" Pablo asked. "Get rid of them, some way," the Captain answered.

"We could take them out of the crates and hide them in the office," Louis said, "then leave the empty crates out on the loading dock, they'd more then likely figure there were gone." "Then you could sell them to others Pablo, there must be stage lines who might need arms." "I'll even buy a rifle," Louis told him. And I can take them apart after if you want to move them out of here in smaller boxes." "It could work," the Captain said. "I don't want you or anyone else hurt Louis," Pablo told him.

"Keep an eye out for any strange faces while I get them moved," Louis said as he picked the first guns. Thirty minutes later they were all moved and covered with an old canvas tarp he found in the warehouse, the empty crates out on the loading dock.

Pablo was out counting hides as they were being taken down to the beach, and the Captain went down on the beach where the lighters were being loaded. Going to the door on the other side of the warehouse Louis found three men waiting to have their hides checked and counted.

Near noon and no one else they're with hides, and he went in to wash his hands and face. He was hungry having missed his breakfast. Pablo came in and told him to wait, that he'd already sent for their midday meal and that the Captain would join them. The ship should be close to being loaded and that the Captain wanted to see how many hides were left in the warehouse.

The Captain had just arrived when the worker came in with their dinner, "I do enjoy Mexican food when I'm out here but I don't get to enjoy it to often," thank you for inviting me Pablo," the Captain said.

They'd barely started eating when the man came with the message for Pablo. Pablo left the table, went out into the warehouse and was gone for a few minutes. Coming back in he look concerned. Sitting down he told them that the man came to tell him that a family out in the country few miles south of there, was forced to give aid to a wounded man early that morning. "The man had hole through his left thigh just a few inches above his knee, and he had trouble ridding, he told me." "Well, "the Captain said, "that gets rid of one of them for a while and should discourage the others." "I hope so," Pablo answered.

They're meal finished, Captain Bolt asked Louis to excuse him and Pablo that they had some things to talk over and check the hides that were left. "I'll take a little siesta," Louis answered. Walking out into the warehouse the Captain told Pablo that he probably should have told him a little more about Louis. "He's a run away Pablo and no older then you or I when we had to go to work and make our own way. I know it's unfortunate that he's had to use a pistol at such a young age, but I'm sure he's mature enough to get through this. I know he wants to stay here, but I will take him back with me if I have to." "He's welcome to stay," Pablo said, "He was doing what I asked him to do, watch over my property." "I'm the one who's responsible for what happened to him." "Do you know how old he is?" Pablo asked." "He's sixteen Pablo," the Captain told him. Madre Dios," Pablo exclaimed, "he's not much older then my youngest." "Don't be hard on yourself Pablo," the Captain told him, "this was an unfortunate happening, but Louis I'm sure will get through it."

They looked at the hides that were there and the Captain said, that he was sure that they could get every one that was there aboard the ship. Walking back by the office they were surprised when they saw Louis at the table. Going in they saw he had one of the rifles taken apart. "See, "he said, "it's only about two thirds of its length when it was together," "The carbines and the shot guns would break down to little more then half their original length." "And don't worry Pablo if I can't put it back together, I'll buy it anyway." But broken down like this you could pack them in shorter boxes that no one would think were long guns."

"What's in the box on the floor?" the Captain asked. "Extra cylinders for the carbines, there really just pistol frames Captain that have been fitted with long barrels and rifle stocks. Empty one cylinder and you can simply exchange it with a loaded one and with that longer barrel I figure you should be able to do some damage out to about hundred yards." "You figure that out on your own Louis?" the Captain asked. "I used to have a rifle Captain and you know I still have a pistol. Picturing them together and it was easy enough to see what some good gunsmith has done."

"You sure you don't want to go back Louis?" the Captain asked. "Like I said before Captain, there's nothing back there for me." "It could be exciting this trip," the Captain told him, "we're going to have get by the Southern States to get home to Massachusetts. The south would like to capture us, though the Cadets uncle I don't think is going to like his ship berthed in Yankee waters." "It sounds like fun Captain but I'll pass," Louis answered, "I've had enough excitement for a while. But talk to me next year when you get back, things might be different then."

With few hides coming in he helped the other workers take the hides that were left down to the beach. They worked that day and all the next morning. The others had left to go some place for siesta and he sat in the shade watching as the Kestrels crew picked up their shorelines and boats. He could easily hear the rattle of the chains as the anchors were brought up. Then as the sails were unfurled, filled and the ship move toward the open sea. In a way he would have liked to still be aboard, but he knew though he would miss it and some of those that were onboard it wasn't where he needed to be. He closed the doors and walked to the cantina, he'd missed eating his midday meal watching the ship as the crew readied it for sea.

There would be little to do now with few hides to check. For the next few days he'd keep busy sweeping the floor and get things ready for the hides when they did come in. Pablo told him that it was getting difficult to obtain hides now. That the cattle were being herded up to the mines, there they'd be slaughtered for their meat and that many of the hides would be lost. But that Pepe would soon be hauling to the stores up in the foothills with the pack animals and would buy what hides he could find.

The warehouse swept clean he wash his dirty clothes then went to the boot makers to see if he'd make him a holster for his small pistol. Figuring that it would be better then carrying it stuffed in the front of his pants. He looked at the boots there and would have liked to buy a pair but told himself that they could wait for another day.

Back to the warehouse and Pablo was there with some boxes that he told him could use to use to pack some the rifles or shot guns in. With three of the guns wrapped in canvas Louis helped him carry them to the Luna's store. They're, Pablo's son Miguel who ran the store would see if he could sell them. He told his father that he thought the rifles would sell all right there. There wouldn't be many people here who would buy one of the short shot guns and probable no one who would want one of the carbines. Have Pepe take some of them up to Angela and her husbands store," he told his father, "the stage stops there." "They'd buy them if anyone would, and if they didn't they'd know someone who would, there's the banks, the mines and the express company's up there too."

Back at the warehouse Louis had little to do but pack some of the short guns and go to the cantina to eat. He listened to the music for a few nights alone, before he decided to go and look at what was happening in the evenings. He tried on his new belt but the holster hanging low on his hip, would be exposed below his blouse. He put it high on his left side, where it would be harder to get to with his right hand but would be hidden by his blouse there. After locking the chain through the door and around the doorpost he walking toward the sound of the music. He came to the edge of the area lit by paper lantern and stopped. From where he stood he could see the platform where the people were dancing.

People walking by him nodded a greeting and he nodded back, but he was a little embarrassed by his dress most of them dressed in nice clothes. He did see a couple of the men he'd been working with and they were dressed just as he was. Pepe surprised him when he walked up and said, "It's good to see you out and about Louis." He stayed a while longer and watched until he saw Pepe dance with a pretty girl. Then walked back to the warehouse and went to bed.

Up early he went to the cantina, that always seemed to be open, having never found it closed when he went there. Back at warehouse he was working on the packing crates when Pablo came in. "Pepe told me he saw you last night, Louis," he said. "I went to watch the dancing for a little while," Louis answered. "That's good, would you come and have supper with us tonight," Pablo asked. He wanted to decline Pablo's offer, because he didn't have the clothes he felt he should have. Seeing he hesitation Pablo figured why, and said, "I was a peon before you were born Louis, and besides that unlike you I could neither read or write. It was my wife who taught me and my children, and she's why I'm able to do what I'm doing today. Now you come to supper this evening and remember that you are not the first peon to sit at that table."

His clothes would be clean and white and he would go and buy himself a pair of boots. The ones he picked were not fancy like many of the boots he saw there. Just plain, but shinny brown and they fit him good. The boot heels higher then his old shoe' s but he knew they weren't for walking in, they were riding boots.

He polished his new boots, bathed and put on his clean white clothes. Walking to Pablo's was a little bit of a problem at first but he was doing a lot better by the time he got there.

Maria was Pablo's sister and took care of his children. Pepe was a few years older then him, Juana about his age and Barbara a little younger he figured. All of Pablo's children had blue eyes, and Louis attributed that to his wife who he knew had passed away. The family talked during the meal but Louis remained silent not used to being in this type of an environment. Determined he get through the meal as best he could. After they'd finished Pablo said he would invite him for a glass of sherry, but knew how he felt about that type of beverage. "You youngsters go and enjoy your selves at the fiesta," Pablo told them.

They had barely started walking toward the music when Pepe said," he'd see them later and trotted ahead. "He's going to go look for dance partners," Juana said, "just like Miguel used to do before he got married."

He walked with the two girls Juana on his left and Barbara on his right. Now he really felt uncomfortable with the girls both dressed in pretty clothes. They were dressed ready to dance and he was dressed in white peons clothes. He saw some of the same people he'd seen before, but now with broader smiles on their faces as they nodded their greetings.

Finding room on a bench they sat down to watch as Pepe danced then came to take each of his sisters to dance. Louis did think that dancing would be fun but didn't know if he'd ever be ready to even try.

After dancing Juana came back and sitting down bumped against his side lightly. Looking down she touched the pistol, then exclaimed, "our you carrying a pistol? Louis." "I am," he answered. "There are some men around that might want to repay me for an injury that one of them has." "You hurt a man?" she asked. "Yes I did, but not because I wanted to. But they were trying to break into your fathers warehouse." "Papa didn't tell us, we heard from others that a man had been wounded but they said nothing about you."

"Do you like working for my father, Mano Noche?" she asked. "What you said in Spanish, I'm sorry but I didn't understand," Louis said. "Night Hand, your friends like to give people names," she told him, "and now I can see why they gave you that one." "It sounds alright, I guess," he answered.

"Do you intend to stay being a peon Louis," she asked, "don't you to want to make something better out of yourself." He had to smile for a minute at the questions, then, answered, "of course some day I want a place of my own, but it takes money to buy land and right now I don't have it. Some day though I will have a farm of my own, you see that's what I was before, and it's what I want to do again. Right now I'll stay working for your father because, I don't want to work at some thing I don't like doing just for the money."

Barbara was giggling and her sister said, "that she doesn't understand, she's just a child." When Juana left to dance, Barbara told him, "my sister wants to grow up and get married," and Louis had to smile again.

When the music stopped he walked the girls home, Pepe having disappeared. He bid them good night and told them to please thank their father. Light enough to walk easily down the middle of the road, yet there were dark places in the night. The little pistol was enough here though, he felt.

The warehouse was quiet, he had no trouble getting in and going to his room in the dark. Laying down he thought about the two girls, so much alike that if they were the same age it would be hard to tell them apart. Yet they were different in other ways Juana was somewhat serious where Barbara bubbly seemed to be laughing at life.

After washing in the morning it went to the cantina for breakfast.

Going back he opened the two big doors to let the sea breeze move through the stuffy warehouse. He was out on the rear loading platform looking at the fog bank that stood off shore, and wondering if it was going to move on to shore. Pepe coming by asked if he wanted to take a walk, "I've got to get things ready for a pack trip," he said. "Sure, there's not much to do here," Louis answered. The doors closed and locked, they walk toward the livery stables. Pepe telling Louis as they walked that he was going to take supplies up to his sister and brother in laws store. "I'm going to go look for hides at a slaughterhouse while we're up there," he told Louis. "With the ranchos selling their cattle for beef now we're going to have a problem getting enough hides for Captain Bolt, let alone any other ships."

It was a fairly large stable where Pepe stopped to talk to a man there. Louis was looking around at the barns, corrals and pastures. What took his interest though was what was going on in and around the arena. Some men out side were tossing loops over what looked like saw horses with horns attached. Other men sitting on the high fence were watching men working with horses inside the arena. One man inside was working with a skittish horse with bloody foam at its mouth and blood on its side. Another horse was snubbed to a heavy post, a man slapping at it with a blanket. Pepe coming up beside him told him that they were breaking mustangs. "There wild horses they go out and round up in the desert," he said. "Their sure pretty rough on them," Louis answered. "Rough, yes but it's a fast and efficient way to break a animal Louis, with their Spanish bits and the large rowled spurs," Pepe told him.

"Come on," Pepe said, "lets go look at the blooded horses Louis, you might like what you see there." They walked along looking at horses each with their own stall. A few of these in the large stalls and some horses coming to the half doors, that they could pet. Horses that Louis knew were well taken care of even pampered, and things of pride for their owners. But he wanted to go back out to the arena and watch what was happening there.

He told Pepe that he would like to go back to the arena and see if one of the men would try to ride the horse they had tied to the post. "I'm sure one of them will," Pepe told him. The men who had been working with their ropes were moving toward the arena. "We made it," Louis said, "I thought we might have missed it." They watched as the chinch on the now blinded horse was tightened. One of the men held the horse as the other man mounted, then released the horse and jerked off the blindfold. The horse tucked his head and bucked almost unseating the vaquero, but he stayed in the saddle. Twisting, turning. bucking and running the horse tried to unseat what was on his back. The vaquero stayed pulling the reins, and raking the animal's flanks with his spurs. Finally the horse quit stood with his legs spread apart, his head lowered, blowing bloody foam and dripping blood from his flanks. The vaquero remaining in the saddle until the horse had gathered some of his wind back, then spurring him into a walk reining him left and right. Finally riding him close to the gate and taking off the saddle and blanket hanging them on the top rail of the fence. He put something on the animal's bloody flanks before opening the gate. Then lead the tired horse up into the pasture removed his bridle and turned him out into the pasture with the other horses.

"He's broke," Pepe said. "I'm afraid in more ways then one" Louis answered. "Broke to ride, but broke in spirit too. He'll work because he has to not because he really wants to, I'm afraid." "You ever have a horse of your own Louis," Pepe asked. "No not really," Louis answered, "we had a work horses that I did ride and used to pack deer on. I would like to have a horse my own some day that I could ride, but that might take me a while. I think I should have a place to keep one on first."

The next day he went to the arena alone to watch, but there were different horsemen there now. Two men riding in the arena with they're horses stepping gracefully under them. He knew they were probable horses from the stables, both with arched necks and combed long manes and tails. Their saddles and bridles adorned with silver, expensive and really only for show. The men dressed in beautifully tailored clothes that fit them perfectly, and he knew they must be comfortable, with those leather lined seats in their britches.

He went almost every day to watch and some days it was only the men on the outside of the arena working with their ropes. Some of these men he knew, having worked with them at the warehouse. They'd greet him with a nod and the word Mano that he knew was Spanish for his last name, and a respectful way to greet some one you knew. He'd answer, with a nod and, Senor.

With no one there in the early afternoon he'd some times walked down along the beach, then into the dunes. There using a dune as a back stop he'd practice with the pistol the Captain had awarded him for the work he done for Cadet Weber. The forty—four was heaver then his thirty one caliber and harder to pull from its holster, but he would get a little better every time he went.

Sunday and he was sitting on the rail fence of the arena with some of the Mexican labors, watching the riders inside. Some one behind him and he turned to find Pepe, Juana and Barbara there. "So this is where you hide out," Juana said. He had to smile when he answered, "I'm not hiding, I'm right here out in the open for anyone to see, if they have their eyes open." Barbara was smiling when Juana said, "sitting just like one of the other roosters." Looking first at the others sitting just a few feet away, then back at Juana he said, "I think I'll flap wings and crow." Don't you dare," she answered, and Barbara laughed out loud. Pepe just shook his head.

"I came to see if you wanted to take a ride Louis?" Pepe said. "Where to?" Louis asked. "Over to the foot hills at the bottom of the sierras to my sister Angela's, she and her husband have a store there with another man and his wife, you know. Were going to take them supplies. We'll get the pack animals and riding stock, you bring your bed roll, pistol and rifle." "If you need any thing else for your self, pick it up tomorrow we'll leave the day after." "I'd better pick up a saddle scabbard for the rifle I bought from your father, I don't think I want to carry it across my back all that way."

He carried his things to the livery after eating breakfast. There were men there already with Pablo and Pepe, working with the pack burros. Pepe told him that his father had to check everything, but it was all right that it would probable saved him from having trouble later on the trail."

Pepe took Louis to the horse he'd be riding. A mustang Louis was sure seeing the scars on its flanks that looked like they'd been healed for some time. He checked the saddle, tied his scabbard on, then tied his saddlebags and bedroll behind the saddle and he was almost ready. Reaching for the bridle the horse shied away, and he talked to it as he reached again, wanting to check the bit. A Spanish bit and he knew he'd have to be careful not wanting to hurt the horse.

Holding on to the horses bridle, he was talking softly to it when Pablo walked up. "You think he understands you Louis?" he asked. "Not the words, but I've haven't seen a horse yet that didn't listen when you talk softly to it." And here was something else that Pablo would wonder about this young man, who always seemed to do things that were a little different. "Are you ready Louis?" Pablo asked. "I am," Louis, answered him, swinging up into the saddle and turning he saw Pablo wave to Pepe." The rider who would lead moved out the line of burros following. "See you when we get back Pablo," Louis said, as he rode out after the last of the column to take up the place where he could best watch and protect the pack train. "Via con Dios," Pablo said as they left.

They would soon leave the coastal breezes moving through a pine and oak forest. Heading east toward the canyon that would take them to the valley on the other side. They'd have to spend their first night in this canyon that would be a hot passage this time of year. But there was water and grass for their animals and wood for their fire. Called to a halt early Louis took care of his horse and brought his gear over to where one of the men was clearing a place for there fire. He helped the others as they unloaded the pack animals then gather fire wood for their night fire, and enough for heating water for coffee in the morning.

Their work done he was sitting by his gear and watching the other men scratching lines on the bare ground where they'd cleared the grass away. Listening, he couldn't understand what they were talking about. But he had been at least learning their names. Finally he could stand it no longer and asked Pepe what they were so interested in talking about? "Their planning to go on a round up after we get back," Pepe told him. "Cattle?" Louis asked, he'd heard there were still some wild cattle in the hills but very few. "No," Pepe answered, "wild horses down in the desert south east of here." Now this was something that interested him and he asked Pepe to ask them if he could go with them? Pepe looking at him for a few seconds, then with slight shrug told him, "I can do that much."

After talking to them for a minute, Pepe came back and sat down. They were talking, looking toward him and smiling for a couple of minutes. Then they grew serious as they continued talking and he thought that, that was it, they'd decided against taking this green horn and he couldn't really blame them. Finally the one called Juan, the one Louis had always thought to be kind of the ringleader of the group, stood up and walked over his saddle. Taking his lazo off the saddle horn he brought it over to Louis, and said only one word, "practica." That was an easy enough Spanish word for Louis to translate into English himself.

Pepe was smiling and told him that he'd show him some of the basics, but that was about all he could do. That he'd never had the time to really learn how to master the rope. The fundamentals gone through, now he'd practice every spare minute he had. Juan would help him if he saw a place where he could, but other wise he was left to rope about anything he cared to. Except of course the men and the working stock.

Stopping at the mission San Juan they'd spend the night to enjoy the evening fiesta. Louis found and purchased a new lazo. He gave it to Juan feeling he abused his when he'd made some really poor throws. Juan didn't want to take the new lazo but Louis told Pepe to tell him the older one fit his hand now. Juan smiled nodded and said, "gracias."

The old rope did show some wear but would last for a long while yet.

Leaving the mission they rode to the trail that lead to the pass called Pacheco, and made their next stop a little way from the spring on the other side. The pass heavily used by the men who had gone to look for gold, and now still used by those hauling in both directions.

Five days and night camps where Louis had time to work with the lazo wanting to become good enough with it so he'd be accepted by Juan and the others.

Reaching the store Louis met Francis Leon, his partner Charley and Charlie's wife Dove. When Angela came out with her daughter he saw a slightly older version of Juana and Barbara. Walking beside her a little one that would fit the same mould, with her dark hair and beautiful blue eyes.

He thought the store was nice but from the loading platform at the rear of the store he could see the large cornfield that had already been harvested. Another area planted in row crops and across a stream a fenced pasture. A nice place where a man could work and raise a family he thought. Someday, he said to himself, I'd like to have a place like this. Why it brought to back to mind the place he had once called home he didn't know, but he wondered then how his father and brothers were doing there. It was Pepe who brought back when he asked, "you seem to like what your looking at Louis?" "That's a nice garden isn't it?" he answered.

They made their camp across the road from the store where they'd spend the night, but were served supper at a table inside by Angela and Dove. Invited to come back in the morning for breakfast, and told not to worry about it. "We're used to serving meals," Angela told them, "we serve meals to the people who come through here on the stage."

Though they wanted to get an early start in the morning the men lingered over coffee after breakfast. Louis standing by the door could see Angela's husband and his partner Charley as he weighted the gold that they gave to Pepe after. Pepe was talking with his sister and her husband as Louis and the others saddled the animals. The pack bags empty now they rolled and tied to the packsaddles. A sure sign that would tell anyone what had been in them had been delivered, and someone in their group would be now be carrying the payment. Pepe was the only one not dressed like a peon and would be easily singled out as that man. From here Louis knew he'd have to stay close to Pepe. He was still there when Juan moved the first string of burros out toward the road, and he waved to him to move on. Louis brought Pepe's horse to him and thanked his sister, and her husband for their hospitality. Pepe put the pouch in to his saddlebag, mounted and they rode after the last of pack train.

Riding side by side, Louis told Pepe about how he felt and how Pepe's dress stood out from the rest of them. "Anyone would know who you were and who was carrying anything valuable, I'd feel better if you'd stayed close," Louis told him. He was looking at Louis, and then glanced quickly toward the pack train before looking down at what he was wearing. It was obvious he knew but smiling, told Louis, "I thought maybe you just wanted company or wanted me to eat a little dust with you back here." "I thought about that to," Louis answered, smiling.

Charley had told them that it was an easy four—hour ride to the Four Corners. That the mine where they'd find the slaughterhouse and the hides, was only a short way, from there and that they'd be able to see it from the road.

A late start and they'd been on the road well past noon and hadn't reached the Four Corners. Coming to a stream Juan lead them down to the water. Pepe riding up told him that they'd camp there for the night that there was water and it was to late to go on. It can't be to far to the Four Corners, we'll get an early start in the morning.

With the extra hours of light Louis had more time to work with the lazo, and the stump near the edge of their camp was targeted time after time. Juan and the others had to smile watching him and Juan continued to help him, pointing out the things he thought he needed to learn.

An hours ride in the morning and they passed between the store and the small building across the street with a man standing in front. The star on his chest told them what he was, and the first and only one they would see while on this trip. He nodded in what Louis felt was an all right in their passing and when their eyes met Louis threw him a small salute.

The road up to the mine only a few hundred yards past the crossroads, where they held the pack animals while Pepe went ahead to check on the hides. He was back within a few minutes with a man from mine, who led them to a building some distance from the mine compound it self. The building wasn't very big and packed to the rafters. They waited while Pepe looked at the hides then came and told them to go ahead, start loading that he'd purchased the hides. It would take them well into the after noon to bundle the hides and secure them to the packsaddles. Then another two hour ride on the road south before they found a place with water and grass where they could camp.

They'd only eat two meals this day but they'd have the rest of the day to rest. Pepe told Louis he'd paid little for the steer hides, that with their storage building so full they were happy to get rid of them.

With the others resting Juan and Pepe watched Louis working with the lazo throwing a loop at every object that looked like a good target.

For two days after they rode south before coming to the road that they'd follow west toward home. There was little for Louis to be concerned about now with people they encountered along the road. The people just seeing them with their loads of hides didn't even seem to warrant them a second look.

They crossed the hot valley where they did find ample water and excellent grazing for their animals. Up into the pass that would take them back to the San Juan Mission. A stop here a must for Pepe and the others, so they could go to the fiesta in the evening. Some of them would dance and they could see some of their old friend and meet new ones.

Louis found another lazo, but thought this time he should ask Juan what he thought about it. Juan looked at lazo as he talked to its owner for a few minutes. Then took a coin out of Louis's hand that he held out to pay with, paid for the lazo and handed it to Louis. It was only half of what Louis had paid for the first one and he was looking at the money left in his hand, when heard Juan say, "trocar Mano." Later he asked Pepe what the word trocar meant. "It means to talk about what you want to buy," Pepe told him, "I think you'd call it to barter in English. But we take it a little farther then that and it's kind of expected, it's a friendly way to make conversation. Learn Spanish Louis, it could save you some silver."

They could have taken the stagecoach road after leaving the mission the shortest route home, if they didn't have the hides. But the steep grade just after leaving the mission would be a tough climb for the loaded animals. The regular road around the base of the hills a longer route, that would mean another day for them on the trail.

Except for the time in his bed roll Louis took little time to relax, determined to master the lazo. Juan and the others watched as he improved and knew he would have something else to learn. Even after he'd mastered the lazo there was something else that was needed to learn, a dar la vuelta or dally in English. Learning the dally a must if he's going to control an animal after he'd put his loop on it

The trail level and the air cooler here moderated some by the ocean air in this valley they were crossing. The last valley then they entered the arroyo seco where they knew they'd have to make camp for the last time.

Listening to Juan and the others talk even after Louis knew as always they were talking about going after the wild horses. He was picking up more words that he understood now, but would still ask Pepe about others.

It was near noon but they were close to home and Pepe led them on. The pack animals voicing there complains as they moved past the livery stable.

Pushing on to the warehouse where they unloaded the hides just inside the door. An insignificant pile in this big building and it would take a lot more to fill the Kestrel, Louis knew. And Louis wondered if Captain Bolt or the ship would come back.

He left everything except his small pistol in his room before he followed the others to the livery.

Rafael built a fire while the others unsaddled the stock and turned them into their home pasture. Louis watched the as the burros ran off not unlike a bunch of children just let out after school, and he had to laugh.

They ate finishing most of what was left from the trip, then they left each going his own way. Louis going to his room at the warehouse, unrolling his bedroll took the canvas cover outside and shook the dust off. Picking up his bar of soap he walked down to the beach and a saltwater bath. Washed his clothes then back up to the warehouse to rinse them and himself off with a couple of buckets of sweet water from the barrel.

He lay down and dozed off thinking about what else he'd need to get before he could make the trip after the wild horses. Waking sometime later he dressed in clean clothes and walked toward the music. Finding Pepe and his father there but Pepe just leaving to go dance.

"Sit down and keep me company for a bit Louis," Pablo told him, "Pepe will be off now and I'll be by my self. Pepe said you wanted to go on a wild horse roundup." "I would like to," Louis answered, "there isn't much to do here right now." "You be careful Louis that's some real harsh country you'll be going into. Are you going to come back to the warehouse or become a rich horse owner?" Pablo asked. "I don't think I'll get rich the first time I go Pablo, I'll be back to work."

Juana and Barbara came and talked for a while, then bid him goodnight with a smile. And he watched after them as they walked toward home with their father.

He stopped at the cantina knowing he could get something to eat there even at this late hour. Then to his room where he'd think again about the wild horse roundup.

Morning and breakfast at the cantina then to the livery wanting to see what plans might have been made. No one there but Anselmo and he went with him to catch the horses he'd need for the day. "Lets see how you can do," Anselmo told him, seeing Louis with his lasso looped around his left shoulder. The horses knew what a man was gong to do as he walked toward them carrying a lasso. Running away bunched together some even dropping their head to keep from being caught by the loop. He missed one but succeeded with his next four loops. "Bueno Mano," Anselmo told him, "you did well for beginner, someday a vaquero, no?" "I'll be happy to be just a farmer,"

Louis answered. "Ah, but no romance, Mano, think about it. You want to be looked up to or looked down at, my friend?" Anselmo said smiling. He had no answer for Anselmo because he knew what he said was true here. He did know one thing though he didn't think a man should have to rope his horses every morning like Anselmo did. His father's horses would always come to him when he went out get them.

Juan and the others still not there yet as they usually were and he figured they had left with out him. Probably figuring he'd be a handicap for them. Though he was younger, he was just as big as any of them and didn't feel he'd be liability but maybe they did. He asked Anselmo if the had left already. "They went to find the Maestro," Anselmo told him, he's the old Peon you see around here once in a while. He knows that desert country about as good as anyone and used to lead the horse hunters. Juan has been with him a time or two and would look to the old man for help." "I want to go with them," Louis, told him, "but I don't know if they'll let me. And if they do I'm going to need a horse."

"I can help you there," Anselmo told him, "I got just the mare you need I took her in trade on buggy. If you'd of got here a day earlier you might have recognized those two. They came in here and gave a story about the one with gimpy leg getting wounded in the war. He was having trouble riding and they needed a buggy. But I saw that wound and it wasn't healed up that well. And you know I'd say if he was shot in battle, he was heading the wrong way. I seen the other one here a time or two picking up supplies. They've been holed up some place in the hills around here, and not to far away."

"You let me bring her out now Mano I think you'll like her, look her over and see what you think." Bringing the mare out Anselmo tied her to the hitching rail in the sun. Walking over Louis reached up toward her head and she pulled back, but once he laid his hand on her neck she was fine. He looked at her closely a reddish brown coat with yellow, gray and white hairs mixed in. "She looks like somebody couldn't figure out what color they wanted, Anselmo. "She's a fresa," Anselmo said. "A what?" Louis asked, "I never seen a horse quite this color before." "She's a strawberry Mano, not to unusual in wild horses and she's a Tex Mex," Anselmo, told him. "Aw come on, how can you tell Anselmo, looking at a horse." Not the horse, Anselmo said, "it's the tack, this and their other horses carried silver on their bridles and the Texas star on their saddle skirts."

"How much?" Louis asked, and winced when Anselmo answered. "I bet you've been taking lessons from Juan," Anselmo told him, "But I'll sweeten the deal with the saddle and the bridle. They've been used some I admit but their still some life left in them." "I don't like the Spanish bit," Louis said. "All right what else are you gonna ask for?" Anselmo asked. "The saddle bags

44

should go with the saddle I think." "Your going to make me lose money" Mano, but that's it," Anselmo told him. Louis knew better, Juan was right but he was happy with the deal. "Bill of sale?" Anselmo asked, Spanish or English." "Both," Louis told him, "you can't tell where, when or who night want to look at it."

While Anselmo was changing the bit on the bridle Louis finding a brush in the livery brushed the mare. She stood calm like every horse he had ever brushed and seemed to like what he was doing.

The saddle blanket stiff with dirt caked into it for who knows how long. "She needs a new blanket," he told Anselmo, "I'll be back in a couple of minutes." At the saddle shop he picked a blanket he liked, a brush, a hoof pick and a rasp the thing's he knew he'd need now.

Coming back he saw Juan, the others and the old man by the arena. Throwing the blanket on the mare, he put the saddle on and brought the chinch up lightly.

Paying Anselmo he took the bill of sale and untying the mare started toward the arena. "Hey," Anselmo said, that halter belongs to me." "It should go with the mare," Louis answered. "Oh no," Anselmo said. Louis flipped him a coin. Catching the coin Anselmo smiling waved and putting the coin in his pocket walked back into the livery.

He led the mare to where Juan and the others stood. "I knew you'd buy her Mano," Juan said, did you squeeze anything out of him?" Saddle, bridle and saddlebags, that are pretty well used but they'll do me for awhile, but I did have to add a little for the halter." "You did all right Mano," Juan said, then introduced him to Tio.

"The Maestro," Louis said. "At one time maybe young man," the old man answered, "but the years have done their work. So you call me Tio now, I think I can still be an uncle. Juan tells me you want to go after wild horses with them and that you can use your lazo. Now there is one more thing you must learn."

With Louis's newly acquired saddle on a hitching rail and his lazo Tio said, he'd show him what else he needed. "You learn a dar la vuetta the [dally] to be successful," he told Louis. He was playing with the rope spinning loops, when Louis saw he was missing the first joint of his index finger. Tio seeing Louis looking at his hand, said, "a lesson the rope taught me when I thought I was good at making my a dar la vuetta. But the rope taught different when I got careless, a bitter lesson my friend."

Chapter V

The Horse Hunt

"You go after horses, but you be careful and when Juan shows you where there is water you remember it well. Where you're going with Juan to find horses is desert and like your dally can be unforgiving and a mistake there could cost you everything even your life. Now let me show you, Tio said, then you work with it, throw your loop and dally until you are sure you can use it on a wild horse."

For the next weeks they worked on heavy rope halters and the reatas, [the ropes], they'd use to keep the wild horses in single file as the led them home. They could each easily lead six or eight horses this way once they were broke to lead.

Louis had to practice the dally now ever chance he got, riding the mare he'd just acquired that he call Fresa. Dropping a loop on a fence post he could practice his dally seated in the saddle. Not quite like it would be when that looped dropped on a wild horse he knew, but it was practice and he'd face the other when it was needed.

Juan and Rafael made a list of the food they'd need, but fell short when it came time to pay the bill. Louis putting up the extra cash told them your not getting out of it with a poor excuse like that.

They had to figure on eight to ten days going and that many or more coming back. Then two weeks to trap and ready the horses for the return trip home.

Louis wanted a telescope like the Captain had let him look through when he was on the Kestrel. At the chandlery he found three different sizes. The smallest one would do him just fine, lighter, less money and it came with a leather case and strap. His rifle in case they needed meat and his small pistol that he'd carry high on his left side out of sight under his blouse.

Everyone there, in the morning saddling their horses, Tio and Juan both checking their gear and the packhorse. Mounting Juan led them out Tio and Anselmo wishing them, bueno suerte [good luck] and via con Dios [go with God]. Louis taking up the last position though no one was assigned a particular place in the line. He was the only one armed and just as when he road with Pepe this was where he should be he knew.

It was cool as they rode off toward the hot canyon trail that would take them to the cooler valley on the other side and the Mission trail. Here they'd turn south and move into the warmer country where the oceans cooling breezes couldn't reach to modify the temperature. Two more days through hot country where there was still ample water then east three days. Now it was Juan they would look to, to show them the way by landmarks he'd recognize.

Most of the low country here so much alike knowing the high ridges and peaks was all important. First for you to find your way into land where you wanted go and after to find the way back out. Plus knowing where to find water that neither you nor you're animals could survive with out in this desert country.

The late after noon of that third day in this dry country Juan was smiling when they came to the first of the three springs that were critical if they were to succeed. This spring back in a narrow rock crevice wasn't excisable to large animals but they were able to bucket out enough water for themselves and their animals. They'd temporarily camp here while they scouted the blind canyon to the south, where there was a small pool fed by a spring. If there were wild horses here, that would be where they'd find what they were looking for. At the third water source would be where they'd make their camp, if there were fresh hoof prints at the pool in the blind canyon. Juan would scout the canyon alone leaving the least amount of the scent of man in the area that might spook the wild horses and they'd leave.

When Juan came back it was easy enough to see by the smile on his face that he had found what he went looking for. At least a dozen he told them but there could be three times that, it was hard to tell. There's a lot of sign but new and old that was mixed with the tracks of other animals.

Picking up they moved near the third spring a half mile to the north past the blind canyon where they'd build their horse trap, make their camp and plan what they had to do next. There was some wild horse sign at this spring too but very little. A small rock spring here where they could only water one of their horses at a time, but the small basin did fill back up fairly quickly.

While the others set up camp Juan told Louis to come with him that there was still enough day for them to do a little scouting. "We need a good place for you to watch the desert for the horses," Juan told him. "I'm the lookout?" Louis asked. "You have the telescope," Juan answered. They found a good place for him to sit but out on the edge of the ridge where he'd be exposed to the sun. Something else they found up along the ridge was deer sign on the trails.

Back in camp they helped the others finish laying out the camp area, after as they ate they talked about what had to be done in the morning. Rafael would take care of camp and the cooking. Louis up on the ridge with his telescope to watch for the horses, while Juan and the others would gather the brush for the barrier at the opening in to the canyon. The deer if Louis could get one they agreed would be a welcomed addition to their meals.

After eating in the morning Louis rolled up his bedroll but kept out his ground cloth to take with him up to the ridge. The night had been cool but as the sun rose in the sky so did the temperature as he climbed up to the ridge. A few broken branches and he had a frame he could lay his ground cloth over and create a bit of shade. From here he had an unobstructed view of a large expanse of desert. Sand, rock and brush for miles and he wondered why anything would want to live here. There was wild life here though, first the birds that flew in to the spring below. Got their drink and flew out to disappear out into the desert brush.

Most of the animals he knew were nocturnal and if man could see like them he would probably do the same, sleeping in the heat of the day in this country. Thinking about these things as he looked out into desert wanting to see something and after a couple of hours would settle for seeing about anything.

By noon he figured he'd looked at about everything that was out there and put his telescope down while he ate, though he wasn't really hungry. It was hot but the slight breeze that came across the ridge kept it bearable in the little bit of shade he had.

He was just finishing his last bit of tortilla when he saw the whitish dot moving north and east through the dessert fairly fast. Behind it a cloud of dust and other objects that caught up to the whitish dot when it slowed but then it streaked away again. Twice more the same thing happened as he watched, then it stopped. With his telescope after the dust cleared some he could see it was different colored animals now moving north. Moving slower now and he knew that they had to be horses, some of them always hidden by the high brush that made them impossible for him to count. The whitish colored one just like the others, only visible part of the time. They must be grazing now he thought and wouldn't be close enough to count for hours.

Time past and the sun was sinking as he continued watching and tried to count them. A least a dozen he thought but maybe many as two dozen, they were still to far away for him to be sure. Juan came up and sat down beside him as he watched. Louis only took his eye away from the glass for a second then went back to looking again. "What is it your so interested in Mano?" Juan asked. Pointing to where he'd been looking, Louis handing the telescope and told him, "there, look for something that's kind of white."

Juan looked for a while before he said, "it's them Mano, at least twenty I'd say. Now I've got to get back down and get the others away from the canyon before they get there. "Their still quite a ways off Juan they shouldn't be here before dark" Louis answered. "Believe me Mano they'll be in, drink and out before dark, there not going to go in that high rocky puma country after dark," Juan told him. Handing Louis the telescope, he said," see you camp, don't stay to long," and hurried down off the ridge. Continuing to watch Louis soon saw that the horses were moving a bit faster toward the canyon. Within minutes they were at a trot moving toward the canyon the white horse in the lead. He still found it impossible to get an accurate count as the animals moved faster, even though they were strung out in a long broken line. Now dodging though the brush the dust now raised by the leaders hiding some of those following.

Wanting to get at least a fairly accurate count of the horses he picked up his things and headed along the ridge toward the canyon. An easy game trail for some distance but then it headed down to the lower desert below before reaching the canyon. Nothing he could do now but work his way through the thick brush and rocks. By the time he was close enough to look into the canyon some of the horses were already drinking at the pond. Even there together it was hard to count them as they moved all trying to get in to drink. Not until the whitish horse started to move back out of the canyon with the others following could he feel he had a fairly accurate count. Twenty—six horses and four colts was what he counted, as the last ones finished drinking and trotted out after the others. Picking he way back out he had to hurry, the night already starting close in.

The others were finishing their meal when he walked in by starlight. "What took you so long Mano?" Juan asked, "You loose your way?" "No not quite," Louis answered, "I went to the canyon to see if I could count the horses in that bunch." "I counted twenty—six and four colts," he told them, as he ladled beans into his tin plate. "That's about what I figured, "Juan said, "I had hoped there'd be more."

"It's going to take another day for us to gather enough brush, Mano," Juan told him. "Then we'll have to halter break them and that will take a few days, go and see if you can get us a little meat, will you?"

He left early in the morning going up the same trail but followed the ridge away from the canyon. The first deer he saw were large full-grown animals and not only to heavy for him to carry but would be more meat then they'd be able to use. The first yearling he saw half the size of a fully—grown animal was what he wanted. The little button buck downed he worked quickly to prepare it for packing.

50

He was headed back when he saw the dust rising out in the flat plain and stopped to see what it was. It was the wild horse herd again running, with the white horse in the lead. Though he wanted to stay and watch he had to get back to camp and start preparing some of the meat for drying.

Rafael and Louis were working when Juan and the others came into camp and now they'd help them with the meat. As they worked Juan told them the brush fence was almost finished and tomorrow by noon they'd be ready.

Louis helped Rafael tending to the fire during the night drying the venison that was left after they'd finished eating. In the morning they continued with what drying that was needed and packed their personal gear. Juan and the others came in at noon, ate and started packing their things. There was an exciting tension in the camp now, every thing they'd planed and been working toward was about to take place.

Juan went with Louis up to the ridge wanting to see where the horses might be. They sat for a few minutes before seeing horses that were moving toward them through a brushy area. Few of them visible at any one time making them impossible to count or know if it was even the same animals they'd seen before. "I'm going back and get ready to ride Mano," Juan told him. Go to the edge of the canyon, when they're all in fire a shot toward us. We'll be ready to ride in and close the opening behind them. We'll leave your horse and the packhorse for you to bring when you get back down." "And I might have to stumble off this ridge in the dark, Huh?" Louis said. "Pray the moon comes up early tonight," Juan laughed as he trotted off toward their camp. Louis starting toward the canyon turned and hollered, "there wasn't any moon last night, so there's sure as hell not going to be one tonight." Juan looking back smiling, waved and hollered back, "see you at the canyon Mano."

Back at the end of the ridge where he could look down into the canyon Louis sat down to wait. The horses still ways out in the brush but were moving slowly toward the canyon. They were coming but it would be a long time before they'd arrive and he might have to walk down off part of the ridge in the dark.

They surprised him when they broke out of the brush running the whitish horse speeding away ahead leaving the others behind for a ways. Then stopping, waited until the others caught up then speed off again. The horse did this three times before starting to graze along peaceably and slowly toward the canyon.

Louis watched them intently as they came closer knowing that they were coming for water, but it was that one horse that he was interested in. With his telescope he studied that horse that he now thought was probably a white horse but discolored some from maybe rolling in a dirty wallow somewhere.

The sun was down before they moved slowly into the blind canyon and the water. The white horse leading steadily the others strung out in little bunches, the mares with their colts the last ones to move in through the gap in the brush fence. He moved quickly now back along the ridge a ways before firing his rifle. On down the ridge in the twilight, then down off the ridge in the dark to the camp. His bedroll already tied behind his saddle and his things hung on the saddle horn. Thank goodness he said to himself, I would have had trouble finding everything in the dark. He adjusted his gear, picked up the packhorses lead, mounted Fresa and headed her toward the canyon.

He saw the light from the fire and rode toward it, finding Juan waiting the opening into the canyon now closed with brush. "About time," Juan said, "we're going to have to eat by fire light." "Eating by firelight is going to be easier then coming off that ridge in the dark," Louis answered. "How'd we do?" "Didn't get a count," Juan answered, "but we got all there was, we'll have to be satisfied with that." "I counted twenty—six again plus four colts," Louis told him as he dismounted.

They ate then slept right on the trail in front of the opening closed with a thick brush barrier. They could hear the horses moving around nervously further up inside the canyon until early morning. With water and grass when the sun came up in the morning, they were calmed down, some grazing placidly.

After breakfast they open the brush barrier and moved everything inside then closed the barrier behind them. The mustangs moved farther up into the canyon and milled around again nervously.

Juan started saddling and told Louis to come on, let's go Mano we're giving you first pick. He saddled Fresa, mounted and uncoiling his lazo moved slowly toward the mustangs. Every one watching, wanting to see the green horn try his skill with rope he'd practiced with so faithfully. He saw that only horse that was that dirty looking white color and worked his way slowly through the other mustangs toward him. Closer now he could see the slight grayish tint, the orange brown spots and the white eyelashes that made the horse look half asleep. When he saw an opening he threw his loop over the horses head. They were all hollering, "no, no Mano, but it was to late he had the horse dallied to his saddle horn and Juan moved in and threw his loop. Their first horse held by the two ropes and Rafael and the others moved in to get a halter and heavy lead line on him.

They were laughing when they told him it was all right but go a try to get a better one this time. He tried to tell them that it was the horse he wanted, but they said they understood and it was all right that he could keep the flea-bit horse.

He dropped his loop on the neck of a hand some buckskin that he liked, and Juan and the others hollered, "bueno Mano," this time.

They worked the rest of the day and all the next day catching the rest of the horses and haltered them as each of them picked out the horses they wanted. The next day they worked getting the horses to lead. Some of them excepting it, but others fought the pull of the rope. The halters and lead ropes were strong though and they would learn that resisting would do them no good and they'd have to except their plight.

Each man had picked the five horses he wanted the extra one Juan said they'd figure out what to do with later. Planning for the ride home they knew they would probable have some trouble with the mustangs the first day or two. While the others led horses Juan would ride free so he could help if any of them had a problem.

Louis thought the flea bit stallion was going to be a problem but he turned out to be one of the easiest ones to work with. He knew too that Juan and the others wondered to why he was paying so much attention to the odd colored horse. They'd find out one day what he already knew that though he didn't look it, that this horse he knew could run.

Ready to ride for home they put each string of horses together the way Tio had told them. Each of the animals tied to a main line by their lead line allowing them little lateral movement. Together this way the main line was always high off the ground and no lead line was ever separated from the halter. This way any horse loose during their changing at camp would be kept from running off by the strong lead line that they'd have to drag. As each horse was taken off the line they were tied to a stout bush. There they could graze some around the bush they were tied too.

Louis knew that if the Flea bit horse was ever to get loose that he would be lost, there wasn't a horse in their camp capable of catching him, he was sure of that.

Their treks across the desert now were governed by the availability of water. At some springs it would take hours to water all the horses. The water coming in to these springs no more then a trickle.

Any fair patch of grass Juan would call a halt to let the horses fed if he felt there was time. Feed many times sparse at their night camps and they were always watching for a place where there was a little grass. But it was water that was always their main concern the horses could get by with little feed, but not without water.

Waking early Louis stirred the fire and tossed a few twigs on it. Between the bright sky and the desert grass he could see the forms of their horses. His flea bit stallion standing out from the others with his whitish coat. A few more twigs on the fire and in the light he picked up the tortillas left over from the previous nights supper and walked out into the desert.

Juan getting up saw the empty blankets and though somewhat concerned he did have an idea where his young compañero might be. He looked out into the desert where their horses tied for the flea bit stallion, where he was fairly sure Louis would be. Walking out he found him breaking pieces of the dry tortillas and feeding them to the stallion. "He could stomp you into the ground Mano," Juan told him, "he was a wild horse a few days ago." "He won't," Louis answered. "You've got a lot more faith in him then I have, Mano," Juan told him, "but come on lets get some breakfast, I'm tired fo this desert country."

By noon they were out of the desert, still in dry grassy hills but now there was ample water in small streams in some of the canyons. Water, grass and wood for their fire at the next camp and they could relax a little now. The desert was behind them and the horses used to trailing were easier to work with.

They'd finished their supper and sat talking when Juan asked, "did you drop your loop on that flea bit stallion on purpose, Mano?" He's the one I wanted," Louis answered, and Juan just shook his head. "It's just like homely women Juan," Rafael said, laughing, "ugly horses need someone to care for them too," All four of his compadres sat smiling at him now. "That's alright," Louis told them, "some times you have look deeper then just what's on the surface, beauty or worth isn't always that visible."

With better feed and water Juan moved them out at a faster pace wanting to make it back to Monterey in five more days. It was in the afternoon when they rode into the livery and Anselmo was right there to meet them and look over the horses. He knew he would probable end up with, or be the one to auction them off after they were broke to ride. "That's all?" he asked Juan. "That's all there was," Juan answered, "we got the last of them there's none left where we were."

They turned the horses into the pasture that Anselmo had cleared for them then they took care of their own gear. Louis leaving Fresa, his saddle and bridle at the livery he shouldered his gear and headed for the warehouse. Leaving he things on the floor of his room he headed down for a quick saltwater bath. With the cloud cover that was moving in it was to cold to linger long in the water.

Back in his room the cover off his bed roll he dusted off his canvas cover in the warehouse and put his blankets on the bunk. Walking to the cantina in a misty rain he ate supper then back to the warehouse and to his bunk.

Early in the morning he washed his dirty clothes and hung then out to let them rinse off in the rain. To the cantina for breakfast then to the livery to see who might be there and what they'd be doing. No one there but Anselmo and he asked him where the others might be. "There probably holed up with a relative or a friend," Anselmo told him. "But that there was nothing to worry about a man with blanket and a piece of canvas could hole up in any dry spot and sleep comfortable in this country. They'll be here when the weather clears, you can be sure of that." "How long will it take for the arena and the ground here to dry so we can work with the horses," Louis asked. "Only a few hours," Anselmo told him, "the ground here is sandy and the rain will sink away quickly."

He walked out to the pasture to look at the horses but didn't stay out in the rain long. Back inside he sat down and watched Anselmo repairing harness. They talked about the horse round up, Anselmo asking questions and Louis answering as best he could. When Anselmo asked, "who got stuck with the flea bit stallion?" Louis looked at him for a minute before he answered, "he's mine Anselmo." Anselmo stopped what he was doing and looking at Louis, asked, "you going to bother breaking him Mano, cause I don't think your going to get much for him." "He'll be the first one I'll work with," Louis answered. "Well he's yours so I guess it's only your time you're using," Anselmo said with a shrug.

Louis stayed until near noon then left for the cantina for his midday meal. At the warehouse he took in his clothes and hung them inside so they'd dry and lay down to rest for a siesta. Waking he looked out side at the rain that was still coming down and went back into work cleaning his rifle, pistol and the other things dusty after the horse hunt. He thought about going to see if there was going to be fiesta and dancing to night. But decided he didn't want to get wet going to find out.

Early morning outside and he looked up into a star bright sky. Leaving early in the dark for the cantina, knowing he was going to need time to break his horses the way he wanted to. He'd seen it done with young horses and realized it was going to take him longer. These horses he'd be working with were older and had tasted freedom. Knowing he could ride was one thing but bucking out a horse the way the vaqueros did it was something else. Their way was not only hard on the rider but did physical damage to the animal he felt. Scars on their flanks, that would be visible for the rest of the horse's life, plus deeper scaring that wouldn't be visible. A horse that worked only because it knew it had to, not because he wanted to.

There was a horse here that he had only seen twice that he would like to emulate. That was the black stallion that belonged to Don Francisco Borba. The Don a proud man who rode a horse with a spirit that was also obvious, with his walk, arched neck and long mane and tail.

Would his horse be like that, no, with that flea bit color and loose sleepy stance he would never be an animal on parade. But he had something else Louis knew, something he could help him with, if the stallion would let him.

In the early morning light he walked into the pasture with the twenty—six wild horses. All moving away as he approached, except one. The flea bit stallion stood his ground and watched Louis as he approached. Picking up the line that was still attached to his halter Louis walked up to the horse, patted him on the neck and gave him his reward. Leading him out of the pasture, through the corrals and out side he tied him to the arena fence.

With the tools he'd purchased when he bought Fresa blanket he went to work, first brushing him, then removing the burrs and tangles from his mane and tail. Washing him after didn't change his color much, the grey and brown hairs mixed with white and the rusty brown freckles were still there. He stood quiet as Louis worked drying him and even when he cleaned and used the rasp on his hooves. All the while Louis listening to the goings on, on the other side of the fence where Juan and the others had started working with their mustangs.

Anselmo came out as he was finishing his work and stood for a moment looking. "Came and check on you Mano I thought maybe he took a kick at you," and he stood again looking. Finally speaking he said, "You just ain't going to make that sows ear into no silk purse, Mano." I know," Louis answered. Picking up the tools Anselmo said, "I'll take them inside if your done Mano?" and he walked away slowly shaking his head.

Hungry he untied the Flea and led him to the cantina where he tied him to the hitching rail, going inside he sat where he could look out and watch. Eating he could see him just standing at the rail, asleep or half asleep he couldn't tell. The owner of the cantina walking over and looking out the window asked, "Your horse senor?" "Yes," Louis answered. He stood a minute longer before saying, "A rare color senor," and as he walked away shaking his head and again Louis heard him say, "a rare color."

Outside Louis fed the Flea the pieces of tortilla and talking to him, told him, "you haven't impressed anyone so far but me, and that was a distance away and some days ago." And he wondered again if he might be wrong and the Flea wasn't the horse he saw that ran so fast in the desert. Walking back he knew once he got the saddle on and rode the Flea he'd know for sure what he still felt in his heart.

Juan and the others out side the arena now having each rode one horse that morning. "That was enough for one day," they told him, "that they'd wait until the next day before riding another."

After they left Louis went to work, first with the horse blanket across Fleas back. Seeing if he'd tolerate something that was strange to him on his back first. Then with the saddle on Fleas back, he lightly tightened the cinch. He knew he was pushing it and Flea might at anytime become unruly, but he just had to know.

That afternoon when he turned Flea loose into the pasture he took off his lead line and rope halter and let him run free.

This evening he'd walk to the fiesta and the dancing if it didn't rain. No one had come to the warehouse to check and he though he might talk with Pablo if he saw him. He saw Pepe first but he was moving away toward the dancing and just waved.

Juana and Barbara meeting told him that they'd heard about the horses but wondered why they hadn't seen him at the fiesta. "First it was the rain," he said, "now it was his horse that was keeping him busy." "I want to get a couple of my horses broke to ride," he told them. "Your going to break your own horses Mano?" Juana asked. "Who else," Louis answered, "I can do it but it takes longer then the way the vaqueros do it." "Could we come and watch," Barbara asked. "I'm by the arena every morning," he said, "come and see."

When Pablo came to take the girls home Louis had a few minutes to tell him about their trip after the horses.

"Things were slow now," Pablo said, "I'll have time to see what kind of a vaquero you are Louis." You might be disappointed Pablo," Louis told him," I'll do things a little different, you'll see nothing fancy I'm afraid."

He left for the warehouse right after saying good night to Pablo and the girls, wanting to get to his bunk early. Wondering if he'd made a mistake when he took the halter off Flea. Would he be able to catch him easily or would he have to work him into a corner and throw a rope on him.

It was still dark when he went to the cantina for breakfast and he watched it getting lighter as he ate and thought about what he do today. First it was to see if he'd made a mistake letting Flea run loose, if he hadn't he'd take another step. This afternoon when every one else went for their siesta he'd make his next move.

The big doors were open when he got to the livery and said, "Buenos dias," to Anselmo and picked up his lazo off his saddle. "Your early again Mano, you like what your doing?" Anselmo asked. "I can't think of anything I'd rather be doing right now," Louis answered, and headed out to the pasture. Climbing up on the fence he sat and waited. It wasn't long before they came and inquisitive like most animals they stood watching. They were just a bit out reach but the closest one easy enough to rope if he wanted to. The flea bit stallion came pushing his way through the others and stood for a minute before walking right up to Louis. He gave him his treat and placed his loop on his neck. Dropping down off the fence he lead Flea out of the pasture gate, out of the livery and tied him to the arena fence.

Tio was there with Anselmo as he picked up his tack and started saddling. "Where've you been," Louis asked, "I thought you were going to help breaking horses." To old for that," Tio answered, "but you look like you're getting ready to ride." "Only saddling him Tio," Louis told him, "I haven't got up on him yet."

He was brushing Flea while Tio watched for a while. Then Tio asked, "What is it about your stallion Mano, he isn't pretty but I feel there might be something I'm not seeing?"

He sat watching for a while longer then went and sat on the fence were he could watch the others inside the arena. Mumbling something about he thought there was more to see there.

Finished with his brushing Louis went over with Tio to watch the others bucking out another one of the mustangs. "How about something to eat Tio," Louis asked, "I'll buy. I can't refuse that," Tio answered but then frowned as Louis led off leading his horse. They sat where they could both look out the window at Flea standing at the hitching rail. Finished eating and Louis was picking up the left over tortillas when the owner came and gave him three pieces of Mexican brown sugar. "For your horse," he said, "panocha he'll like this better then tortilla." Gracias," Louis said. Outside and he gave him one piece and started walking back toward the arena. Flea now with his nose at the pocket, where Louis had put the other two lump's of sugar. "You might just as well give it to him," Tio told him, "he can smell it and he's going to pester you until he gets it." Surrendering the sugar, Louis said, "can't keep any secrets now can I." Not knowing then, that something he would soon realize, would be found out by someone else. Someone who knew nothing about what he would just find out for himself.

The activity in the arena had ended, Juan and the others gone to where ever they went for siesta. Tio disappeared into the open maw of the livery, probably to spend his siesta relaxing and dozing in one of Anselmo's rocking chairs.

Louis assuming that everyone else was enjoying they're siesta led Flea to the warehouse then down the roadway to the beach. This was where he'd planned to mount Flea for the first time. Here he figured if the stallion wanted to buck, the dry sand would make it difficult for him to buck hard. Plus the sand here would be a little softer for him to land on then the packed sand near the arena. He had a little trouble getting him to except Fresa's bit but he had expected it, this was after all the first time. A little adjusting as he talked to him and he had the bridle fit.

It was just between him and his horse now he thought, completely unaware of the pair of eyes that peered down from the grassy dunes above.

Another check of the cinch and wanting to see if he was going to carry him, he swung up into the saddle. A grip on the saddle horn that wasn't needed, he wasn't thrown to the sand as he'd expected and he coaxed him to move ahead. Walking the horse he reined him one way then the other before reining him to a stop then a few minutes of this and he stopped him again and dismounted. Now he took a little time to relax and relieve the tension as he talked to his horse, knowing the worst was over. Back in the saddle he rode along the beach, Flea gradually moving toward the damp firmer sand. He trotted along the wet sand and through the shallow surge of the water from the waves. Leaving the reins slack Louis soon found himself moving faster over the ground then he'd ever moved before. Soon soaked from the spray and he knew now this was a horse that loved to run. He knew too that this was the horse that he'd seen running across the desert, confirming what he needed to know.

Reining him down then slowing to a stop knowing had run a long way and should need time to blow but found him breathing fine. It was almost mile back to where they'd started from but the stallion still wanted to run and Louis let him. He ran just as fast going back and he still wasn't breathing that hard when they reached the bottom of the road.

For the first time he rode his stallion up along the road and right to the livery. Dismounting he led Flea inside and removed the saddle. Juan, Tio and Anselmo sitting together, Anselmo said, "you've finally ridden him, Mano." "I did," Louis answered. "Did he throw you?" Anselmo asked, "you look wet." "No, I stayed aboard," Louis told him, "I got wet playing in the water." "Better work your leather or it's going to dry up like an old tortilla Mano," Anselmo told him, as Louis led Flea toward the pasture.

"He never said a word about how the horse ran," Anselmo said. "You don't say nothing Anselmo, you hear me," Tio said. "I don't want him to think I was spying on him. But you mind my words, that horse can run." "He sure don't look it," Juan told them, "but when he roped that horse first and I found out later it was no mistake, I knew he saw something I didn't. He still looks like a bag of bones to me though." "It's his color," Tio said. "Flea bit ain't a color," Anselmo laughed, "it's an itch."

Back inside Louis worked on the saddle and bridle, they weren't much but they were all he had and would do for now.

"The buckskin next?" Juan asked. "Tomorrow I'll start on him," Louis answered, "after that I don't know. That will be one more horse then I can ride." "You break him and I'll auction him for you Mano, when Juan and the others have their horses ready," Anselmo told him.

Finished working with the saddle and bridle, Louis said, that he'd see them in the morning. At the warehouse he washed the salt out of his clothes, bathed and dressed in fresh clothes. Lying down on the bunk he looked at the ceiling and couldn't remember a day when he was any happier. What someone like him could usually only dream about, he was sure he had. It wasn't an apparition he saw in the desert, what he'd seen was more horse then he could have hoped for, even though the Flea didn't look it.

How long he'd slept he didn't know but he was hungry and walked toward the cantina in the twilight. The proprietor came over as usual, and said, "I saw you ride him today Senor. He's much more horse with you in the saddle." "Gracias Senor," Louis answered, "he became something more to me today too."

Into bed early he'd start with the buckskin in the morning and wondered if things would work out again for him. This would only be the second horse he'd break, if he succeeded. Breakfast at the cantina and he left with a few tortillas. He saddled Flea and would try roping off him, just to see if he could do it. Even though he knew it would take a lot more work to make a roping horse out of him. Riding Flea into the pasture and the horses moved off as he'd expected. All into one corner and as they spilled out it was fairly easy for him to drop his loop on the buckskin. With the flea in close he picked up the buckskins lead line, took off his lazo, coiling it he hung it on his saddle horn. At the gate he got off and lead both horses out side. Walking back to close the gate and Fresa was there, standing and watching him. He wondered what she was thinking, knowing she had to be there for some reason. "I've been neglecting you girl haven't I?" he said, and he took out a tortilla broke it into pieces and fed it to her. "I'll do better just as soon as I finish breaking the buckskin," he said. Walking away he looked back and wondered if she had some of the same feelings people had. She did feel something though he thought, why else would she be sanding there looking after him.

He'd finished working on the buckskins hooves and was brushing him when they walked up. Pepe, Juana and Barbara coming to see the horses they'd caught in their round up.

The tawny young buckskin his black mane, tail and hooves, distinct colors and a proud stance that would warrant a second look by anyone. The flea bit stallion too would draw a persons attention, but for a totally different reason, standing relaxed and of no particular color. But he was the one to draw both girls attention, "he looks so tired," Juana told Louis, caressing his soft nose. With his head held low they could easily scratch his ears. They looked at his long eyelashes as he open and closed his eyes slowly. "He's so sweet," Barbara said softly. "Your horse sure loves attention," Pepe said. "Wouldn't you?" Louis asked, "if someone was treating you that way."

Don Francisco riding up on his black, hesitated, nodded and said, "Senoritas, Señor but his eyes were mainly on the freshly groomed buckskin. Then he and his three vaqueros rode on toward his newly built adobes half a mile father down the road.

No one could help admiring the Dons black stallion or the silver adorned saddle and bridle. Right now though it was his flea bit stallion that was getting the caring attention from two pretty young ladies.

When Pepe and the girls left Louis saw Flea looking after them the same way Fresa had watched him leave the pasture that morning.

He moved the blanket and saddle from Flea on to the buckskin. The first time the buckskin would feel the weight. The tightening of the cinch drew some movement but he quickly seemed to resign himself to it. He walked him around a bit before taking him into the livery, removed the saddle and turned him out into the pasture. Flea he'd left standing outside the arena with only his bridle on. Tio, Juan and Anselmo were inside the livery when he left riding bareback to the cantina. The tidbits for Flea after he'd eaten and he rode to the warehouse then down the road to the beach. An easy gallop for a short way but the stallion wanted to run. Along the wet sand and through the foam and the flea eagerly ran. He stretched out coming back in long smooth gallop and moving fast just as Louis knew he could. As he reined in he didn't know that he had a gallery above in the dunes that hadn't been there before, now watching. Stopping at the warehouse he washed Flea then rubbed him dry, which took him a while.

The gallery from the dunes back at the livery talked about what they'd seen and agreed the flea bit stallion did look fast. But knew too they had nothing to compare him to yet. The distance they were away from beach and the spray of water might have just have made him look like he was moving fast too, they just weren't sure.

Bareback to the arena then as he lead Flea through the livery the three there seemed to be studying the horse as Louis walked by. Flea turned into the pasture, he walked back inside and hung the bridle on his saddle horn. Tio, Juan and Anselmo sitting quietly in the chairs and Louis wondered, but didn't know what to ask. He said, "I'll see you in the morning," and walked to the cantina.

Morning as he walked to the cantina he knew, he was going to try to ride the buckskin today. At the pasture gate Fresa and Flea came when they saw him to receive their reward. The buckskin stood a few yards away and he had to go to him. Picking his lead line he lead back to the gate before giving him his reward with Fresa and Flea.

The buckskin out by the arena Louis brushed him and checked his hooves before he saddled him. The bridle on, he led him down to the beach before stepping up into the saddle. He coaxed and healed him around in the dry sand near the bottom of the road to the warehouse. For close to an hour he did this with out a problem and rode him up to the loading dock. Took the saddle off and leaving it there mounted the buckskin rode back down to the beach. Coaxing the bucking they moved along the beach at a trot until a wave spilled up on the sand. The buckskin shied almost unseating Louis. Twice more Louis tried but the buck didn't want anything to do with the water. On the dry sand it was difficult for a horse to run. And Louis heading him back to the warehouse, he'd have to try him on the road later.

Right now he put the saddle back on and rode to Luna's store. He wanted to buy some of those lumps of sugar the horses like so much. In the store he saw that Pablo hadn't sold all of the arms. Still a few of the six shot carbines and the double barrel shotguns left. He would have liked to buy a carbine and a shotgun but right now he didn't feel he wanted to part with that much money.

Pablo told him there was news about the war and told him about places he'd never heard of before. "There'll be more and better news," he said, "if and when the ships start coming." Knowing little or nothing about the places Pablo mentioned, he would just as well never heard about it, but he said nothing. Leaving most of what he bought at the warehouse but took enough to give the horses a little treat later.

Near enough to noon he stopped at the cantina for lunch. Then rode out north, out on the road passed the Dons adobes, holding the buckskin to a nice easy lope. The buckskin his head held high and with his rocking chair lope was a pleasure to ride. He'd be a nice horse to keep but he knew like Juan and the others he was horse rich and land poor. When Anselmo held the auctioned the buckskin would be put up for sale.

Passing the adobes there was smoke coming out of the chimney of the larger adobe and there were horses in the pasture. The Don must be here he thought but he didn't see his black, but the horse could be out behind the high brush that hadn't been cleared from the pasture yet.

Only a quarter mile out now and he let the buckskin have his head letting him run. Sweating now and Louis pulled him up letting walk the rest of the way back. Then rubbed him down before turning him out into the pasture giving him, Fresa and Flea, each a lump of sugar.

Stopping in side the livery he'd spend a little time with Anselmo, Juan and Tio. "You spend much of your time with two stallions Mano," Anselmo told him. "I guess" Louis answered, "but I think they need it." "Your making puppy dogs out of them," Juan told him, "you want them that way?" "I do, I don't want to chase after them, I want them to come to me," Louis answered.

Approaching the gate in the morning Louis could see there wasn't a problem if Fresa stood between his two stallions. If Flea and Buck stood together there was always a bit of hostility. Flea seem to be the dominant one, the buckskin was still young, but one day he would challenge Flea and they'd surely fight. They needed to be separated but he lacked the facilities and had little chance of acquiring anything soon. He knew that he could only keep one stallion. The buckskin had a lot of potential but he knew that Flea though he didn't look it, was the one that could run. He knew then for sure that even though he liked him, when Juan the others had Anselmo auction their horses that he have to let the buckskin go. What work he did now to improve him, would only benefit who ever owned him later but that was all right he knew it had to be that way. With Flea it was different he himself would be the one to benefit fully by the work, time and effort he put in working with him.

Don Francisco always stopped for a minute or two when he had the buckskin outside and Louis thought he probably liked what he saw. At noon he told Anselmo what he thought. It was Tio that spoke up saying, "you be careful Mano he's going to want a race." "He likes to race that black, he'll be fair but he'll damn sure take every advantage he can." "I don't understand why wouldn't he just buy the buckskin if he wanted him?" Louis said. "He could buy him, Mano if he wanted to," Tio answered, "but he loves the race."

All that afternoon and evening he mulled over what Tio had said, and tried to put it out of his mind. There was that doubt but then that chance to win too and that did intrigue him.

For the next few days the weather was poor and rainy and he used the time to wash his clothes and to clean up around the warehouse. Some thing he'd been putting off for a while but he'd catch up now and still had time to stop in at the livery and check the horses in the pasture.

As soon as the weather cleared he was back riding again. One day riding Flea on the beach where the horse seemed to love running through the water that moved up after the waves broke.

The next day he'd exercised the buckskin running him on the road. The buckskin could run at the start but after a few hundred yards slowed. Then he'd have trouble maintaining any speed over longer distances at a slower pace. He was young Louis realized but with time and some better feed he was sure he'd do better. He'd have to spend some money on grain the pasture grass alone just wasn't enough and Flea could use some better feed too,

Rainy days there wasn't much for him to do but the other winter days in this moderate climate here were fine. He rode the beach for miles with Flea and wouldn't return some times until late in the late in the afternoon. Days on the road he worked with the buckskin then some times he'd ride into the dunes between the road and the sea. Not much to see there and the next time he rode east from the road into a rolling land of brush, grass in small meadows and oak trees. Deer, rabbits and quail and he thought about how hunting here. He wouldn't have the time to do it now but he'd try to remember the trails.

The buckskin was definitely growing stronger now but at the same time so was Flea and able to maintain a ground covering lope for a very long time. His strength and stamina hidden some ware under that flea bit hide.

They'd make another trip across the valley to the gold country at the base of the sierra with the supplies for Pablo's son in law. Pablo hoping they'd be able to bring back a load of hides from the slaughter house at the mine.

CHAPTER VI

Hides becoming more difficult to find, the ranchos were all now selling their cattle for meat, the hides no longer the most valuable part of the animals. Pablo would soon have to send Pepe to look for the hides they needed at other slaughterhouses. The warehouse filling painfully slow and Pablo hoping he could at least gather enough hides for Captain Bolts ship. The hides to help off set the price of his incoming shipments the Captain would be bringing.

Pablo was worried also that the ship might not even be able to come here, the Civil war still in progress.

Shorts stints of work at the warehouse then Louis was back in the saddle every day as the weather warmed toward spring. Don Francisco coming to town more often now and would always stop when Louis had the buckskin out by the arena. Louis still thought he might offer to buy the buckskin, but he never did. It was a little over week before Easter when Louis was riding past the Dons adobes and he saw the Don out in front watching as he passed. Louis waved and the Don waved back, his eyes following and surely watching the buckskin.

Sunday morning and he had both Flea and the buckskin out side the arena. He'd just finished cleaning the buckskins hooves and was ready to use the rasp a little when the Don and his vaqueros rode up. This time he did dismount and walked to where Louis stood. "I like your buckskin Senor," he said, "would you consider putting up in a stake race?" "You mean I put my buckskin as a prize?" Louis asked, "then what would you put up Don Francisco." "My Black of course, it's a race between your stallion and mine. Lets say to just the other side of my adobes, turning around there and the race would finish right here." "I might," Louis said," "but I've never raced before and neither has my stallion, so that's sure not very good odds. I've heard that you've raced your stallion before." "Then I'll sweeten it enough to make it interesting for you, I'll add twenty hectares with the two adobes. Be here next Sunday after Mass, the Don said, and we can race if you likes the odds."

Going inside the livery he told Anselmo, Juan and Tio about the Don wanting to race. "It's my buckskin against the Don's black," he told them, "but he added his two new adobes and twenty hectares of land to his stake,"

"Oh that's a lot Mano, do you think you can beat his black?" Tio asked. "He's probably thirty pounds heavier then I am and that saddle of his with all that silver close to another twenty more then mine. I know that neither the buckskin or I have raced before but with black carrying that extra weight I think can beat him," Louis told them. "It sounds all right," Tio said, "but I think there's something we haven't seen yet. The Don is just not one to race without figuring to win." Now Louis was concerned and naïve as he was about racing he now wondered what he might have let him self in for.

Early Sunday morning and not feeling hunger he walked pasted the cantina in the dim light of early morning without stopping. Out to the pasture and he brought both Flea and the buckskin into the livery. Put his saddle on the buckskin and lead them out to the fence outside the arena. With nothing but time knowing it would be hours before the last mass would be over. He cleaned and checked both horse's hooves and rasped off the rough edges. He'd brushed both horses thoroughly and was combing out their manes and tails when Tio came out.

Glad he'd have someone to talk to maybe now the time would pass a little quicker. "Nervous," Tio asked. "Butterflies," Louis answered, "I've been trying to figure out what I missed." "I don't mean to worry you Mano but from what you've told me the odds are a bit lop sided." "He put out the bait and guess I bit, but I don't want to back out now Tio, what would he think of me? Besides I haven't got much tied up in the buckskin, other then a whole lot of my time," Louis told him. "You keep watching Mano," Tio told him, "you might be able see what the advantage is he's planned yet, and find a way out."

Some people were already gathering near by and Tio said, "there's going to be a crowd here Mano everyone loves a good horse race." He had the bridle and saddle on the buckskin, the left stirrup hung up on the saddle horn. Now all there was to do was tighten the cinch and he was ready to ride. The last mass at noon was out now and more people coming.

He saw Anselmo bring the table and set it up outside of the livery and wondered what he was going to do. Tio seeing his questioning look, told him, "he's getting ready to see what the odds are going to be, after he'll collect the bets and keep tabs on the money." "After the race he'll take care of the pay offs."

When the Don rode up with his vaqueros Louis got his surprise. There it was the something he wasn't expecting. Riding the black was the shortest and lightest vaquero from the Dons rancho. A young man that Louis knew and realized that this vaquero was at least thirty pounds lighter then he was. The saddle on the black was not the saddle that he was used to seeing. The saddle there now was no more then a leather blanket with stirrups.

"I thought I was riding against you, Don Francisco," Louis said. "I said a race between my stallion and yours, I didn't say I would ride senor," the Don answered. "True," Louis said as he turned he saw the look on Tio's face but said nothing. He'd found out now what he'd missed, a supple play words but he hadn't seen it, and now would have to find a way to over come the disadvantage. The difference in his weight and the vaquero's he couldn't change, so it had to be some thing else.

He was looking toward his two stallions standing by the arena fence and walking over took the halter off Flea and put it on the buckskin. The bridle off the buckskin on Flea and he turned around, Tio and Juan now both right there by him. "I'm going to ride Flea," he said. "Wait Mano," "Juan said, "I need to borrow some money I'm about broke, you know I'll pay back." In my room at the warehouse, in my saddles bag there's a leather pouch with my spending money you can take that, "Louis told him, and gave him the key. "Gracias Mano," Juan answered and sprinted off toward the warehouse.

Louis walked out leading Flea and Don Francisco asked him, "your not riding the buckskin?" "No," Louis answered, "I'm riding Flea." "But you said the buckskin," the Don told him. "I said the buckskin was the bet, your prize if you win but as you said before and just said it again, it's was my stallion against yours and this is my stallion." "True," the Don answered, as he walked around flea. "This is the stallion my stallion is going to have to run against, I've never seen him run but I think your making a mistake. I think your buckskin would be a better choice but it is up to you," the Don told him.

He saw Juan come running back and he saw the pouch that he held up, and it wasn't the pouch with his spending money but the one that held his savings. He waved but Juan just waved back, turned around and ran toward the betting table. Louis knew he could never make it there in time to save what he'd worked so long for. Put the money out of your mind he told himself, it's the race you've better concentrate on now.

The Don had a stick in his hand with a bright yellow ribbon tied to it. "It's the turn around marker," he said. "I'll have one of my vaqueros stand in the road with it and you should someone there to represent you also" But none of his peon friends were there they were all at the betting table. Seeing Pepe, Pablo, Barbara and Juana standing across the road he waved and motion for Pepe to come over. They all came, Pablo saying as they walked up," we heard it was you Louis and we had to come and watch." "It's me all right, and I need a favor Pepe, will you represent me at the turn around?" "Take the buckskin you can use his lead line to rig reins, he'll rein all right with just the halter." "I'll be there," Pepe said and a minute later he was riding away down the road.

Unbuckling his pistol from under his blouse he handed it to Pablo to take care of. "That's about all the weight I can take off Pablo, take care for me will you?" he asked. "Maybe I can use it to start the race," Pablo said. "That's fine with me," Louis told him, "but maybe you should ask the Don." Both girls wished him luck and he walk toward where the black stood in the road. Pablo met him coming back from talking to the Don Francisco and told him that it was fine with him to use the pistol. He was looking past Louis at Flea, when he asked why there's no saddle on his horse? "I can't ask flea to carry the extra weight Pablo, Louis told him, "look at the vaquero that's riding for the Don and the saddle on the black." "But don't worry Pablo, I've been riding Flea for a while with out a saddle and he swung up onto Fleas back.

When the pistol fired the black charged out and ran. The Flea tensed at the sound but took off after the black and half way to the flag he'd caught him. At the turn around the black familiar with the race made turn and was ahead again. Halfway back Flea caught the black again and crossed the finish line a length and a half ahead. Louis let him run past the finish then slowly pulled him up as he was passing the cantina. Turning him back Flea was again his wild bands leader and pranced, tossed his head and still wanted to run but Louis held him in check.

Back toward where the people were waving and shouting at them but Louis hardly could see or hear them. His eyes were tearing from the wind and his heart was pounding in his ears. At the arena he dismounted as they came to congratulate him and the Flea. Pepe tied the yellow ribbon from the turn around flag to the Fleas bridle. Tio was there and said, "go Mano and sit down I'll take care of your Pulgas." People were coming to congratulate him but more came to look at the horse that had out run the Dons black. He saw the Don walking toward him and thought he'd be angry but he had a slight smile on his face.

"I got bit by your Pulgas, the Don said, "my congratulations my friend." "I really didn't think your stallion could do it. I've known about sleepers but I didn't think your stallion might be one." "I don't know what you mean by a sleeper Don Francisco," Louis told him. "Your Pulgas is a horse that doesn't look like nothing more then a workhorse until he runs," the Don told him. Louis and the Don were standing by their two stallions as they were cooled down. People were still coming to see the horses and they heard a young boy say, "look Papa it's the sea horse, the one that runs through the water on the beach." The Dons and Louise's eyes met and the Don said, "I guess I should put a second story on my new adobe when I build it, then I can see what's happening on the beach." Louis had to smile.

The people were leaving most of the excitement over when the Don took the blacks reins and held them out to Louis. Looking into the Dons eyes Louis said," no, I don't want your stallion Don Francisco." The Don surprised for a moment frowned, and Louis told him, "he's yours and will always be yours. If I rode him everyone would say, look there goes Louis riding the Dons black stallion. I have my stallion and I only need one." The Don smiling shook his head then asked if he and his men could stay in the adobes tonight?" "Certainly, I'm fine in the room at the warehouse," Louis answered.

Almost every had left except Pablo, Pepe and the girls and now they walked to where Louis was standing. Pablo gave him pistol belt and told him not to forget that one of the chambers in the pistol had been fired.

Pablo had seen the Don leaving with his black stallion and he asked Louis about it. "I thought the black was the prize," he said. "I didn't take the black," Louis told him, "I didn't feel he would ever really be mine, he's the Dons stallion. The twenty hectares and the adobes is more then I could have hoped to win." "I didn't know about that Louis," Pablo said, "but congratulations, you've done well my young friend, you're a man with land." Juana and Barbara both kissed his cheeks and congratulated him before they left.

Tio and Louis lead the buckskin and Flea back into the livery and stripped their gear then turned them out into the pasture. Coming back into the livery Louis said he was tired and hungry and was going to rest for a little while. "Here" Juan told him, "'take this with you," and handed his leather pouch which was a lot heavier then he remembered it, now. "What's this?" Louis questioned. "Your money Mano," Juan answered smiling, "plus half the winnings, I'm afraid all but a few of us bet against you winning." "And you bet I'd win?" Louis questioned. "Sure" Juan answered, "Tio first, then Anselmo and I have watched you ride the Flea on the beach, we knew the flea bit horse could run."

Tio holding up a small sack of pesos," said, "I only had a few pesos to wager, but look."

"Lets go" Juan said, "I'll buy supper and a cervezas or two." "No more then two for me," Louis told him. Juan didn't have to buy their second cervezas the owner of the cantina bought it for them. Then congratulated Louis and telling him, "You see senor I'm not such a poor loser." "Then you bet against me," Louis said. "I did," he answered, "I didn't see how that sleepy horse could possible win, but that's horse racing and I wasn't the only one who was bit by your flea though, was I?"

In his room Louis took off his pistol belt, tossed the money pouch on the bed and taking off his clothes, lay down. Waking he knew he'd slept the whole night, the light of day in the window across the room. His clothes smelling of horse sweat he got up and started a fire. An hour latter he'd taken his bath and washed his soiled clothes.

Hungry again though he'd eaten heartily the afternoon before, it didn't make up for the two meals he'd missed. After he'd left the cantina he was walking toward the livery when he saw the Don and his vaqueros riding toward him. Stopping he waited then bid them good morning.

The Don giving him two keys to the adobes said, that the locks are not strong enough to stop thieves but they would discourage a somewhat honest person. "I'll bring you the papers for the property as soon as I can," he said. "Oh and could my men get water from the well until we get a new well dug." "Your welcome to what ever you need," Louis told him. "Gracias," the Don said, and rode off with his vaqueros riding behind his stallion.

Holding the keys up at the livery he asked, those there, "who would like to take a walk? I want to take a look at the adobes." Tio and Juan were ready to go but Anselmo said that he had better stay at the livery. "You can't tell, it's a nice day and someone might want to rent a buggy," he said.

At the larger adobe they found the front door without a lock evidently barred on the inside. Louis opened the lock on the rear door into a large dining room with a big table, two benches and two chairs enough seating for ten people. A well equipped kitchen to the right with a single bunk off the pantry. At the other end of a large room four double bunks, two on each sidewall, a table with four chairs and curtains on the windows.

"I like that kitchen," Tio said, "I could do some cooking here." "Go head and move in if you want to," Louis told him. "You mean that Mano, I'm tired of sleeping in the hay at the livery." "Move in when you want," Louis answered.

The other adobe with a fairly large room, a corner raised fireplace where you could cook or heat water, a few dishes and utensils. Two small bedrooms and Louis said, "I wonder why the two bed rooms." "One I think would be for the Dons sister," Tio told him. "I didn't know he had a sister," Louis said.

"You've never met her Mano?" Tio asked. "No, I can't remember even seeing her." Louis answered. "You'd remember her, wouldn't he Juan," Tio said. "No man ever forgets seeing the Rose," Juan answered, "see her only one time and you'll never forget her Mano." "That must be where the feminine touches comes from then," Louis said, "with the curtains and tablecloth," "It has to be," Tio answered, "the Dons a widower and that's why he always wears black. Whenever you see her she'll be in black too, she's been a widow for a while now, yet I've never seen her wearing anything else. Have you Juan?" "No never," Juan answered.

"You going to let me move in too, Mano, I don't want Tio to be lonely?" Juan asked. "Go ahead pick your bunk Juan," Louis told him.

They walked the pasture that was already fenced but there was still a lot of brush that needed to be cleared. No fenced area for a garden that Tio said they should have. "We'll have a nice big garden," Louis assured him, "this is my chance to something I really like to do." Walking to the end of the fenced property they found deer and rabbit sign. "What's past here?" Louis asked." "Miles of the same thing," Tio told him. And Louis knew he had a place to hunt now also.

The well their only water source but that would be adequate for the adobes and the horses, but the not for a large garden. They brought up buckets of water from the well and found it sweet and good and poured it into the horse trough.

If they moved the fence back for a garden that will mean the horse trough would have to be moved too and that would mean they'd have to carry the water to it. "Dig another well then," Tio said. "Not me," Juan said, "that's about the only thing I won't do I'll be under ground soon enough."

Louis knew he wouldn't have much leisure time any more but what he had now was always what wanted and the work he'd be doing was what he enjoyed. "Your all set Louis," he told himself.

Moving his horses was his first task then his things from his room at the warehouse. If Pablo needed him to stay he could carry his clothes and bedroll there.

The cash he had now was a problem that he didn't really have before and he needed a place a stash it. A short log he found out in the firewood pile he peeled removing the bark. Four smaller branches for legs and he had a crude wooden horse with no head. He'd use it to keep his saddle on inside the small adobe, dry and out of the weather. A hole chipped into one end and a plug to cover it and he had a place to stash his moneybag. A safe place he figured unless some one was to cut it up for firewood. Wood pegs over the door to hold his long gun and pegs in the wall to hang bridles, belts and what ever else they might be needed for.

Satisfied with his first work project he'd now splurge and buy a couple of things he wanted. Walking to Luna's store he found both Pablo and Miguel behind the counter. In their gun rack there was still a couple of the six shot carbines and the short shotguns too. He told Pablo he was moving to the adobe but would stay at the warehouse when he needed him. "I figured you would, but that would work out just fine." Pablo told him. "You walked here to tell me that," Pablo asked. "No I want to buy a couple of things too," Louis told him. "With your own place Louis your going to be buying a lot of things but what's on your mind today?" Pablo asked him. When Louis told him Pablo smiled and asked if they were necessary? "Tio is going to be doing the cooking so I figured I could do some hunting and bring in a little meat for our table," Louis told him.

"That's good," Pablo told him, "anyone else moving in with you I understand that's a fair size bunkhouse?" "Just Tio and Juan, there now," Louis said, "but maybe the others who were with us on the horse round up." "That's good too, Pablo told him, then I'll know where I can round all of you up at one time when a ship comes in."

A carbine, two extra cylinders, a short shotgun, powder, shot, and primers on the counter and Louis asked how much he owed? "I still owe you Louis," Pablo told him, "you've only drawn cash one time, since you come here we'll just take it off what I owe you." "Alright if I send Tio to pick up things?" Louis asked. "Sure Louis," Pablo answered, "I know Tio."

Walking back he not only had a fairly heavy load but an awkward load with the carbine, shotgun and no slings. At the adobe he put more pegs high on the wall for both guns. And a couple of other pegs, one where he hung the possibles bag. Little by little he'd get things done to his own satisfaction. The next morning he went to the saddle shop and had slings made for two new purchases and a saddle boot that would work with either one of them. His pistols belts he'd hang up close by at the head of his bed when he slept. The next day he and Juan started putting posts in back where they'd put the new fence. Hot work in the sun and they'd quit at noon, eat and Louis went to his adobe. After a cool bath, clean clothes on and he was ready to lie down and rest.

The knock at the door was light and he barely heard it. When he opened the door he just stood staring. She turned and looked back behind her then turned and facing him, asked, "is there something senor?" Gaining his wits he said, "I'm sorry senora Romano you took me by surprise." "You know who I am yet I surprise you senor, have we met?" she asked. "No senora," Louis said, "but I've been told about you and your more then I could have ever imagined." She flushed slightly then said, "You embarrass me senor but I should have been prepared, Francisco said that you were different. Now are you going to invite me in." "Again you'll have to excuse me senora while I'll try to compose myself," Louis told her, "please come in." He pulled out a chair for her and she walked up and stood facing him. Looking into his eyes she was almost as tall as he was in her vaquero riding boots. He felt she was the most beautiful woman he'd ever seen.

Looking toward the door she said, "you can close the door you don't have to be afraid me." "I could never fear you senora," he said, "I'm the one I fear." "I don't have much to offer you but I do have chocolate," he told her. "It's not really necessary," she answered. "Maybe not for you but right now but I need to do something for a minute or two," he said. He kindled the fire and put on the water and walked back looking at her. Dressed in a black vaquero suit, boots, hat even black gloves. More like a Spanish doll then a real person and he found it hard to believe that anyone could look so perfect.

"Do I bother you that much?" she asked. "I'm afraid do," he answered, "some how you just don't seem real to me" "You speak you mind senor, "she told him. "Would you have any other way, should I hold back what I feel even though I realize that it's a complete folly on my part." "No," she answered, "I'm glad you told me and I wish there was some way we could change things. If our ages were reversed it would be accepted but the way it is, it would be frowned upon. I'm expected to except some wrinkled old man long past his time but you my young friend be patient one day you'll find someone."

"My problem will be finding someone who could somehow erase your image Senora." "I'm afraid it is that way though and that is to bad for both of us because I could love you too, my young friend. We can be friends though and enjoy each other's company, can't we?" she questioned. "I'm at your service Senora," Louis told her.

"Gallant too, what more could I ask for? She said. But enough, Francisco will be here anytime he wants to get things started but we'll need water, we're going to camp." "I told Don Francisco he could use what ever he needed here, and your not to camp out senora, you stay in the room that was yours," he said. "That was my room, she said but what might happen with you so close in that other room?" "I know what I'd like to happen," he answered smiling, "but tell Don Francisco to stay here. His men can stay in the bunk house and I'll stay there too if there's room, if not I'll stay at the room at Luna's warehouse."

Putting her arms around his neck and kissed his cheek and he felt the warmth and softness he knew was there. They heard the rattle of the wagon and she stepped back a sad smile and tears when she said, "I wish things were different." Then asked, "do you always wear your pistol?"

"Every since the trouble at Luna's warehouse when I used it and made more enemies that night then I did friends," he told her.

He had his bedroll on his shoulder and his second pistol buckled on when he came out of the bedroom. "The water you put on for chocolate has boiled away," she said smiling. "I guess we didn't need the chocolate but at that moment I needed the distraction," he said.

Louis met Don Francisco as he was walking up to the adobe coming in from where his men were setting up their camp. "You and the senora please stay in the adobe in your rooms, Don Francisco. Your vaquero's can stay with us in the bunk house," Louis told him as he was leaving.

Entering the adobe the Don saw his sister standing looking a bit flushed with a pleasant look on her face, but looking past him a the wall behind him. Turning he saw the long gun hanging above the door, the carbine and shotgun on pegs beside it. "Is he a pistolero Francisco? She asked. "I don't really know," he answered, "but there was a shoot out at the Luna's warehouse when someone tried to break in and that Louis was involved." "I really like the young man Francisco." "I know Rose," her brother said, "I could see it in the brightness of your eyes when I walked in, something that I haven't seen there for a long time. I like him too Rose, I'm sure he's honest also and mature for in his actions but he's pretty young little sister," the Don told her. "I do have a problem then, don't I Francisco? But it's one that makes my spirit soar, I could love Francisco, you know how it's been with me."

"How well I know Rose, we've been walking that same path for a long while now and I realize I've had more to fill time my time then you have. I under stand completely and I am all for you but I'm concerned too, you know how it is with people and you could be hurt again." "I know Francisco", she said, "but I want this, it will only be a close friendship. With the trouble that's been happening here I think I should have a bodyguard. The vaqueros are brave but with only their cattle knives they would be helpless against what I see riding our roads now." "I'll talk to Pablo and when Louis isn't busy working for him and I'll see if he'll do it," he said, "but be careful little sister." "I will my brother," Rose answered.

When the Don told Pablo that he would like Louis to guard senora Rose whenever she rode, he agreed. "It's not safe on our roads I know," he said, "I'll only need him when there's ship in and a few days after, when we'll still have valuables stored in the warehouse."

Later the Don gave Louis the paper on the property and Louis folding it put in his pocket. "Aren't you going to check it?" Don Francisco asked. "Why? If you say it's the paper for property, I believe you." "There's something else Louis, the Don said, senora Rose likes ride sometimes and there's this bad element on our roads now and it bothers her. Would you ride with her as her escort now and then? I've talked with Pablo and we'll make sure not to take you away from your work." "I thank you Don Francisco," Louis answered, "and I'm honored."

When Don Francisco and Senora Romano went back to his rancho a small crew remained to continue the work on the new adobes, plus starting their well. Wagons were sent north to pick up the redwood planks and timbers they'd need for the well shoring and rafters for the adobes.

"There'd be enough for the new well that Tio had mentioned you wanted Mano, by your water trough," one of the men told Louis. "It seems I'm always thanking the Don for something," Louis told him.

The fence and turning the ground for their garden kept Juan and Louis busy. But Louis would stop anytime the senora wanted to ride or go shopping in town. Accepted, but thought of as somewhat of an oddity the beautiful senora always dressed in black, the sign of a widow in morning. The young gringo always dressed in the loose white pants and blouse of a peon and they did know he did work as one when he wasn't escorting the senora. The intimacies between them slight, only when he helped her mount and dismount or escort her into or between stores. She holding his left arm away from the pistol he wore low at his right side. Every one there knew what had happened at the Luna's warehouse some months before.

Only once was there a confrontation between Louis and another man in town. A rather large gringo accosted the senora. Louis gently moved the senora through the doorway of the store they were near. Coming back out he stood in front of the man his hand poised above his pistol. He stood looking straight into the man's eyes, without saying a word. The man evidently seeing something in the next few seconds, held his right hand up, palm out and his fingers spread. "All right young man I understand, I know my place and walked off down the street. Louis watched after for a few moments then turning walked into the store. The people who had witnessed this happening said they knew Louis was determined to stop the man right there. Making sure any idea the man might have about continuing his actions toward the senora, ceased by him confronting the antagonist right then.

He didn't go to the auction at the livery, not really wanting to know who bought the buckskin. When Anselmo gave him the money he didn't ask either, just hoping who did buy him would never use a Spanish bit or large rowel spurs that he knew were not needed to control the buckskin.

As the year progressed and their work diminishing he and Juan had more time to hunt.

Deer, rabbits and quail, that and what they harvested from the garden took care of most of their needs. Water and wood for their cooking fires always a daily chore that they'd have to attend to. Juan liked hunting with Louis's carbine and decided he'd buy the one that he saw that was left in Luna's store. Giving Louis two spare cylinders for his when he got back, that he bought cheap because they were all that was left and the carbines were gone. "I knew we didn't really them but the price was right," he said.

The Dons adobes close to being completed even his added upper room. Now he could see much of the beach and had a sweeping view of the harbor, under cover and out of the weather. They stayed in his new adobe and Louis didn't have to stay in the bunk any longer.

She'd come to the fence sometimes to watch him laboring in the garden. Usually he could take some of the vegetables they'd harvested to her. Only once did she ask why he labored in garden the way he did. It's apart of me he told her, it's what I enjoy doing and look what comes from what I do. And he pointed to the things he'd given her.

They had to carry their firewood some distance now and Louis purchased a jenny and a donkey cart for Tio to use too. Now Tio could use the cart to carry wood up from the beach or haul the extra things they harvested from the garden into town. He'd sell them or trade them for things they needed.

When the Don told Louis he should fence the twenty hectares behind the front twenty, he questioned him why? "You haven't looked at the paper yet have you Louis?" "No I haven't," Louis admitted. The Don smiled, and told him, "because, that other twenty belongs to you also." "But why Don Francisco?" Louis asked, "I don't understand?" "Lets say I didn't want a dog leg in the property line and you'd have to up the fence saving me from having to." "I owe you again Don Francisco," Louis told him. "You owe me nothing more then what you've already done Louis, you're good faith and trust is enough," the Don said.

When he started on the fence she would ride to see him. He often rode with her on the beach, along the roads or into town so she could shop.

Once the fence was built he worked with the three mares he had from the round up that still needed to be broke yet. The weeks and months past and he'd gradually earned their trust. He'd been taking his time breaking them wanting to be like Flea and Fresa.

The Kestrel came in and it was work for peons with the in coming cargo, then with the hides taking them down to the beach. The warehouse was empty of hides and Louis was there with the things that would have to stay until Pablo could get them to the store.

He was sweeping the empty area when the Captain came in. "Your still here Louis," he said, "I thought you might have moved off to some place else." "No," Louis answered, "I like it here." "And you Captain, I thought you might have lost Kestrel with a Southern owner and all." "Like many other men, the Captain said, with the cadets uncle, silver and gold takes precedence over God and Country. He knew he'd receive little compensation from the Confederacy for the Kestrel, other then their script and that isn't worth the ink it took to print it. So the Kestrel remains in my hands and she's a fine ship, Louis. "I'm happy for you Captain, you deserve a good ship, Louis told the Captain, and what happened to cadet Weber?" "He left the ship and headed south, Louis and we heard little about him after that, except something about him receiving some kind a commission. Be hard to tell where he might have ended up.

But now what I've heard from Pablo you've done alright, Louis." "Better then all right sir" Louis answered, "I've got a piece of land and a solid roof over my head." "Then I guess there's no use asking if you want to go back with us, is there? So I guess I'll say good bye and see you next year." "Good sailing Captain, and I'll be here next year."

A few more days at the warehouse then back to the adobe and work there. They hadn't been there for weeks and he went to talk to the two men who were working on the Dons fence. They told him they hadn't heard any thing from the rancho and were also concerned. If they didn't hear soon one of them would ride in and see what might be wrong. Two days passed then in the next after noon, Louis saw the Dons black coach with the Dons black tied behind it. The coach pulled in by the rear of the adobe and Louis saw her as he walked toward the coach.

She was still wearing black but a dress now with a black mantilla on her head. The Don and a woman helped her out of the coach and they went inside. Going to the door he knocked and the Don answered. "I was just coming to get you Louis," he said, "she wants to see you." When he saw her knew she was not feeling well and he didn't know what to say.

"I'm alright Louis," she said, "just a little tired, will you excuse me." He saw the Don shaking he head slowing as she walked away, helped by the women toward her room. Turning to the Don as they walked out side Louis asked what was wrong? "I don't know any more then you do Louis and the doctors here can't tell us anything either. I'm going to take her to Mexico City," the Don said, "maybe the doctors there can help her. I need some help though Louis, we have to go through some dangerous country between here and El Paso, will go as a guard?" "I will," Louis answered. "Could you find another man who could help?" the Don asked. "Juan will go," Don Francisco, "and he's a good hand with his carbine."

'They're getting things ready at the rancho and we'll be here tomorrow, we'll leave the day after," the Don told him. "We'll be ready" Louis answered, "I go and tell Juan now."

Finding Juan he told him what the Don asked and Juan said that he'd ride. They made their plans each deciding that they'd each take an extra mount. Knowing the desert they'd be going through would sap the strength of their horses and that they'd surely be riding as out riders. Assembling their gear they each made sure they had an extra canteen. "Better put some jerky in some place too" Juan said, "you never know when you might get hungry and it doesn't weight much."

He talked with Tio telling him what they were going to do. "You'll be gone for months Mono," he told him," but that's all right I've got every thing I need here." "I might talk to Rafael, Carlos or Julio and see what their doing." "Bring anyone you want Tio," Louis told him and handed him a leather pouch, "just incase you need something."

They were both ready when the wagon and four vaqueros rode up to the Dons adobe. In minutes the Don led the coach out on to the road. The wagon with their provisions followed then four vaqueros. Juan and Louis brought up the rear. This would be the way they'd travel through the arroyo seco. Later turning south on the El Camino Real. Then through valley Juan and Louis had traveled before. Denied the influence the ocean by the coastal mountains it was the first hot area they'd encounter. Not the heat of the desert yet but Louis knew the senora riding in the coach would be uncomfortable.

The Don and Juan road ahead of the coach here while the vaqueros brought up the rear now Louis rode near the coach. Here there was little chance of conflict with any rouge elements but he would still remain close.

They followed the mission trail here, a day's ride between the missions. Settlements along the way where they could buy fresh provisions and here there was ample water. It was hot but not really unpleasant for the men on the coach or the two men on the supply wagon. Neither for those on horse back but he was concerned about the senora and the lady caring for her in the coach, who he knew would be uncomfortable. She'd smile when she looked out of the window of the coach and saw him. A wan smile and so evident to him of how she really felt. He too tried to put on a brave front that he could only hope was working.

He wondered what it really was between them, she was neither lover nor mother to him but he did love her and he knew she cared for him. From the very first second he saw her he knew, but she was so beautiful how could anyone not care for her.

At their midday stops if there wasn't shade near he'd put up a canvas shade for her. She ate little and he'd coax her to take a few more bites. Frustrated because he wanted so to be able to help her and the only thing he knew was that she did need to eat.

At San Diego Don Francisco said they'd take a day to check the coach and other equipment. This would be their last chance to enjoy the moderated temperature near the ocean. "Tomorrow they'd head toward the desert and we can't afford any problems," he told Louis. "The Don seems concerned," Louis told Juan. "He should be," Juan answered. "You've been this way before, Juan?" Louis asked. "Only once Mano and I swore then I never wanted to do it again." "How come you said you go then Juan?" "When you asked me, I knew you'd be going regardless, so I thought you'd need company," Juan said. "I owe you a good turn Juan," Louis answered.

"We've got to do some talking Mano," Juan told him, "the first desert country is just going to be miserable but after we'll move into Apache country. That's when it's going to get dangerous, I'll try to show you what to watch and what to listen for and it's not going to be fun."

They rode side by side as the Don lead them east toward the rising sun. For the first few days they'd move through scrubby trees and brush country, hot country but not desert yet. The trail old, used by the Spanish Friars for some two hundred years and surely a trade route long before that.

Once across the Colorado River and Juan told Louis that it wouldn't be long and they'd be in apache country. "You're not going to see them unless their ready to be seen Mano or your lucky but there are things that are there, that can give them away. An animal doesn't run in the desert unless something disturbs him. The birds and animals are only going to move if there's a reason, they're only use their energies when have to. The silent desert is another warning, when every thing is listing you'd better be listing and looking too. You know what to look for on the trails, are you ready Mano?" Juan asked. "As ready as I can be Juan," Louis answered.

They rode wide now, one to each side of the coach, here they'd be the first ones to come under fire if there was an attack by any hostiles. They came across un-scathed their only trouble was when they had to help the wagons through some deep dry sand.

Reaching El Paso Don Francisco said, "that they would take the road south toward Mexico city from here. We'll be traveling with others and have the protection they needed. That it would be best for you to stay and wait for us here, he told Louis. There seems to be some feelings about people from the states across the border right now. Juan can stay with you, we'll be back in five or six months."

He wasn't happy about it but knew he didn't have any choice. He'd say his God speed to Rose and to get well.

Don Francisco arranged for them to stay at a rancho just out of town. They'd stay in the bunkhouse and take their meals with the vaqueros.

Louis watching the coach leaving and knew he might never see her again, but he had to cope with his feelings and pray. He and Juan went to work helping the ranchos vaqueros on their round up. The cattle they gathered would be added to some of the other cattle from the rancho then driven north. Cattle that would be used to stock the new ranches being established on the thousands of acres up in Colorado and Wyoming, land they heard was free for the taking.

Then two weeks later he and Juan were recruited to help on the drive. Juan knew Louis was having a problem worrying about Rose. He knew he couldn't help him that he would have to leave him to his own thoughts and to find his own way through it. He'd ride beside him knowing that it was about the only thing he could do.

They were riding to join the trail crew when Juan told Louis he heard the war between the states had been over for a few of months. Looking at

Juan Louis smiled a little and told him, "well, I missed the start and now I've missed the end too." "You think you missed a whole lot Mano?" Juan asked. "More then likely a lot of suffering more then anything else Juan," he answered.

They found the chuck wagon and the outfit where they were told it would be. The trail boss was Charlie Porteous who signed them on and gave them the rules they'd have to abide by. Then asked them if they had any questions. Louis told him that he wanted his horses kept out from under any one else's rope that they were his alone to ride. "Their yours," Charlie answered, "so what's your reason?" "I don't like those blood letting spurs or Spanish bits and I know they wouldn't either," Louis told him. "Fair enough," Charlie told him, "I'll pass the word. We'll move out at first light, Fred's got supper on so grab something to eat and get yourself some shut eye."

Awakened before first light by the noise from the chuck wagon that breakfast was ready. They ate their breakfast and were assigned to ride drag at the rear of the herd. "Should have figured that," Juan said, "the first morning out and we get to eat dust." The fourth day and they sat off by themselves, not fully excepted by the other ten drovers who'd started the drive. They were riding the flanks now and riding after the cattle that strayed out away from the herd. Flea seemed to love chasing after these wayward critters then hazing them back on to the trail.

There'd been other herds moved up on the trail before them but there was still enough grass to take care of their herds needs. Breakfast was done and Louis after scrapping his plate off dropped it into the bucket of soapy water. Picked his saddle his bridle hung on his saddle horn, his carbine in its boot. His long rifle he left with his bedroll on the haul wagon. With his gear up on his left shoulder he walked out toward the remuda.

In the morning light he saw Flea with a rope on his neck. The man at his side had just tossed his saddle Fleas back and was reaching under ready to start cinching. "That's far enough," Louis said, "now get your saddle and rope off that horse." When the man turned to face Louis, he knew he was one of the riders and that his name was Will Matlock. Louis heard the others walking behind him and then Charlie the trail boss say, "Will I told all of you I promised the kid that no one else would ride his horses." "I know," Will answered, "I just wanted to see if this pony could really run. I've been watching him and I think he's fast." "I don't care what you think Will," Charlie told him, "its hands off and I don't want to give out orders more then once, all right?" "All right Charlie," Will answered, and turning removed his saddle and rope. Then he stood and watched as Louis walked up, saddled and bridled his horse, the horse standing untethered. After Louis rode off, Will dropped his loop on another horse in the remuda, saddled up and rode out to take his position with the herd.

Louis wasn't in yet at their noon stop when Will came over with his plate and sat down near Juan. "Your partner sure cares about that pony of his," Will said. "Should," Juan answered, "he has his own place out in California because of that horse." "Then you think he would have pulled on me if I would have kept on with his horse?" Will asked. "No doubt what so ever," Juan told him. "But I was standing in front of his horse," Will said. "But your head was well above the Fleas back," Juan told him smiling. "He's that good?" Will asked. "Seen him take the head off a rabbit at twice that distance Will," Juan told him.

When Louis came with his plate, he nodded and said, "Will." "No hard feelings I hope," Will said, "I was out of line but that horse of yours sure doesn't look like a runner until you see him stretch out. I just wanted to see if I was right or just seeing things" "Oh he can run, "Louis told him, that's why I picked him first when we corralled his wild bunch. I'd seen him run across the desert two days before. And he's been broke without breaking his spirit Will, he runs because he likes to run. There's no scars on him from those spurs you fellows like to use, and he's never felt a Spanish bit." "I thought he was a Texas horse, your saddle says Texas," Will said. "I bought the saddle at a livery in California with the stars on it," Louis told him. "Then you're not a Reb are you?" Will said. "No," Louis answered, "I'm afraid I missed the war," "You didn't miss anything," Will told him, "both sides lost to many good men and I don't know of anyone down at our level who got anything more then a hole in his hide for his effort,"

At their evening meal Charlie told them that he didn't want any more problems.

Louis and Juan both could see a difference with the rest crew they were accepted now. "It's odd," Juan said, "what it took for us to become part of the crew and not a couple of outsiders."

The crew both Texas cow boy and Texas vaqueros came to look over the Flea but what ever he had that let him run was still hidden somewhere under his flea bit hide.

Riding Fresa wasn't like riding Flea she was fully capable but she wasn't anxious the way Flea was. Flea took after any animal that started away from the herd doing it without being encouraged.

The days passed one just like the last, day after day only the stream crossings to break the monotony.

Two Indians rode in one day that Charlie rode out and talked to, then came back and had two cows cut from the herd. The Indians drove them away. Louis and Juan learned that they were crossing the Indians land and the two animals were a tribute. "You might call it a toll charge," Charlie told them, "but it's worth it we don't need them stirred up."

More days and weeks and even their meals were becoming routine like everything else, the same thing over and over again. They couldn't blame Fred though he sure didn't have much to choose from with what was left on the chuck wagon.

They saw something moving some distance off and neither one, Juan or Louis were able to tell what it was with their naked eyes. Louis took out his telescope to get a better look and it was a group of riders. "There not Indians, we'd better tell Charlie Juan I don't think he's expecting company," Louis said. Juan rode after Charlie and Louis kept an eye on those moving dots. When Charlie got there Louis handed him the glass and pointed to where he saw them last. It took him a minute to pick them out. "I don't like it," he said, "I don't think their up to any good just following along with us the way they are." "They might try to spook the herd and cut out some for themselves."

"Check your arms, I'll go tell the rest of the crew and keep yourself a horse saddled all the time," Charlie said and rode off. The chuck wagon would always move and they couldn't turn the cattle and bed them down until they reached where Fred had set up for their night camp. They were lucky this day in reaching the bedding ground a little earlier then usual.

Half the crew would remain with the herd at suppertime while the others ate. Juan and Louis were with the first ones to eat, finishing they rode to relieve others so they could come in. The exchange was made and the other half of the crew had left for the chuck wagon. They could see two of their other riders as they slowly circled the herd on the other side. The night was coming on fast now, the sky darkening, the stars starting to wink on as it became more difficult to see.

They were already close when they came in firing, evidently having led their horses in close before mounting and making their charge. They came in a line and both Louis and Juan dropped quickly the ground and on to one knee where they'd be able to fire with the best accuracy. One of the vaqueros ahead was hit just as they started firing and picking off the riders that came. Their carbines firing shot after shot, the line of rider broke and turned back with four less riders then they came in with. A couple more shots to send them on their way as they headed back the way they'd ridden in.

Back in the saddle Louis and Juan rode along the outer perimeter of the spooky cattle to the downed vaquero. His partner with him was already tying a bandana on his arm. "It's a deep wound he told them but it didn't hit the bone. They helped getting the wounded vaquero in the saddle and his partner had just started to take him into their camp when Charlie and the other riders rode up.

Charlie and Will stayed while the rest of the crew split and started around the herd. They went checking on the downed raiders and Juan told them there was no hope for the first one they found. They found the three others and brought them all together then caught their horses. Charlie told Will to take the horses in, strip them of their gear and turn them out with the remuda. "You two stay here on this side of the herd," Charlie told them, "and keep the scavengers away the bodies. I don't think that bunch will be back tonight after the way you shot them up. But keep an eye out for them, I'll send someone out to relieve you when I can but expect a long night," and he rode off. Some of the cattle brought to their feet by the rifle and pistol fire were laying back down now.

They didn't know what time it was when Will and one of the vaquero came out and relieved them and they didn't know how long they'd slept after laying down. It wasn't long they knew when they were awaken by Fred's banging on a pan. Breakfast and Charlie and Will rode out with them to where the downed men lay. They walked around where the men had fallen picking up the arms they'd dropped during the fracas. Then Charlie and Will left them, to take care of burying the men, and rode after herd that was already on the move.

Juan asked, "how come we have to bury them we were the ones who stopped them and now we've got to get punished for it?" "Dig Juan," Louis told him, "Will told me last night that it would up us to bury them that way Charlie could let us have their horses and tack." "That doe's make me feel better about digging," Juan said, "it's not like we did something wrong." They were almost finished when Louis saw the birds circling over something to the east of where they were. The direction the other raiders had taken when they rode away. "I guess we'd better go and take a look," he told Juan, pointing to where the birds were circling.

They found another man downed evidently hit by one of then when they fired their last shots. The man's horse some yards away cropping grass his reins dragging on the ground. While Juan dug Louis emptied the man's pockets tying them in the man's bandana and took off his pistol belt. Brought in his horse and hung the pistol on the saddle horn. The flies had already done their work and Juan complaining said, "I should have started this digging on the up wind side." Their work done and Louis led the horse as they followed after the herd. They were late for the midday meal but Fred had set food aside for them.

"Wondered why you were late," Charlie said, "you find another man down?" Saw the buzzards," Louis said, handing him the bandana. "What's left that of that bunch will think twice about tackling another cattle drive, I bet," Charlie told them. "Put the saddle on the wagon and after you leave that pony with the remuda one of you on the left flank the other on the right."

Will saw Louis turn the horse over to the wrangler and asked if they went after another rustler. "The buzzards led us to him," Louis told him. "One of us must have hit him with one of our last shots." "Old prairie undertakers always there and doing more then one job, aren't they? You two sure shot that bunch to pieces, where'd you learn to shoot like that," Will asked. "Had to bring home the rabbits for stew," Louis told him, as they rode out toward the herd. "You see if there were no rabbits there was no stew." "You help your compadre then?" Will asked. "Some," Louis told, "and he borrowed my carbine a few times then bought his own."

They let the cattle drink at the river then pushed them across to the other side before herding them into a circle and their night beds. Lois and Juan both into their blankets as soon as they finished their supper. Tired they slept until Fred roused them out for breakfast.

While they were eating Louis told Juan he was going to swap his saddle for one of the one's they'd collected. "About time you got rid of that rag you've been sitting on. You've got the best horse Mano but you sit the worst saddle." "It came with Fresa and it's what was available at the time," Louis said.

Another four days and they bedded the herd down out side of Cheyenne and Charlie left to go find a buyer. There'd be no pay until the cattle were sold, so going into town broke the way most of the crew was wouldn't be much fun. The respite and the stream near by gave them a chance to bathe and catch with their laundry. If there was a chance then after for them to go to town they'd now be half way presentable.

When Charlie got back he told them that he did find a buyer but they were going to have to push the herd another sixty or seventy miles to make the delivery and get paid. Coming over to Juan and Louis he told them to go through that gear and take what you want. The rest he told them he'd sell to the new ranches that were starting there, that they needed everything. They decided they'd each keep an extra saddle and saddlebags that the extra horse that they'd brought from California could carry. They'd tie their extra gear and bedroll on the other horse and lighten the load on the horse they were riding. Emptying the saddlebags they got a surprise that they squirreled away. Two bridles without spade bits and rest they'd let go even the arms, both pistols and rifles.

After breakfast the next morning they started the herd moving north. Fred headed into Cheyenne to pick up supplies and would catch up with them when they stopped at noon.

Fresh bread at lunch that the men said it wasn't as good as the biscuits they enjoyed that Fred baked on the trail. What he'd make for supper that evening they knew would be a welcome change though, fresh vegetables. Then the fried potatoes with eggs the next morning that would be a real treat. After that it would probably be back to biscuits, bacon and beans.

Ten days and they were at the agreed meeting place and bedded down the herd early. Charlie rode into town to contact the man that said he'd have everything ready when the cattle arrived.

He didn't get back until after dark, said that he'd eaten in town and that the men said they'd be there by mid morning. They'd take a tally of the cattle and pay just as soon as it was completed.

Midmorning was nine a clock to the men who rode in that morning. Two men in a buckboard and a dozen men on horse back. Charlie had Juan and Louis bring over the saddles, arms and other gear then the five horses they had for sale. He did the negotiations while Juan and Louis helped lining out the cattle so they'd file pass the buck board. The two men and Charlie standing on the buckboard would make the count as the cattle passed. On the other side the ranch crew would take over the responsibility of the cattle. Once all the cattle were past the buckboard, the drive was over and their job was done.

Charlie was given a bank draft that he would take into town in the morning then pay the crew what they were owed when he returned. They'd worked through their usual midday break pushing the cattle past the counters before being able to sit down to a late lunch. Happy their job was over and they could all lay back and take it easy the rest of the day. It would be an easy evening for them, all except Fred who was fixing their supper.

Morning after a good nights rest, breakfast and Charlie left for town. Louis and Juan checked their horses and their gear one more time. Then figured what they'd need for the first leg of their trip back to El Paso. Figuring they wouldn't follow the cattle trail but take the freight road. Then they could stop at the towns along the way where they could pick up their supplies as they needed them, keeping their loads light. They figured at least three weeks if they were lucky and a month on the out side. Graining their horses would keep them in good shape and was a must if they were to make it back the way they planned.

Charlie back from town gave Louis a pouch and told him that's for the horses, tack and arms. You'll have to split it up you're selves any way you see fit. Sitting down he read off the names and paid each man in coin knowing that they didn't like paper money.

They rode into town together every one but Charlie and Fred who stayed in camp. Pulling up at the first saloon they came to all except Juan and Louis out of the saddle. Their horses tied to the hitching rail and they started toward the door. "Aren't you coming in for a drink?" Will asked. "No," Louis answered, "we'll have to say our good byes here." "By the time you fellows get back to camp we'll be long gone," Louis told them. "So long it is then," Will said, "see you on the trail one day then." He shook their hands and walked toward the saloon, turning and waved one more time before entering through the bat wing doors.

They bought the supplies they needed, four canvas bags and a half sack of grain for the horses. I'll pay for it out of out of the horse money," Louis said "and we can split what ever is left after when we get to El Paso, Juan." "Bueno," Juan told him.

Back to the chuck wagon and they saddled their other horses tied on their bedrolls and canvas bags. Gave each horse measure of grain and went to say their good bys to Charlie and Fred the only ones left in camp. "Better have a bite before you pullout" Fred said and handed them each a plate. While they were eating Charlie told them, "I want to thank you two, I knew you were green horns but you both did a good job besides you kept us from losing stock to those rustlers or maybe a man or two. I think I owe you a little something," and he flipped them each a ten dollar gold piece. "Thanks to both of you. They finished the meal, shook hands with their trail boss and the cook, mounted and rode off heading south.

Their horses in good shape they moved at a ground covering fast walk. There were towns where they'd stopped for a meal but were looked at with suspicion. Dressed more like farmers or sheep men then what they'd really been for a while but this was cattle country. The cattlemen here determined that they would keep this way and they didn't look the part.

Riding into a small town the were tying their horses to the hitching rail in front of a café, with a wagon parked in front of the store next door. A rather large man coming out of the restaurant picking this teeth, walked over to the back of the wagon. Taking out his pocketknife he slit the two sacks that were laying on the tailgate. "Your grains spilling out allover the ground lady" he said to the woman sitting up on the wagon seat. "He cut the sacks Momma," the little girl sitting next to her said. "Hush," her mother said. "Mind your momma," the man told her and strode into the store. Louis heard Juan say, "Mano," but he didn't even break stride as he went into the store. "Why'd you cut those sacks mister?" he asked. Turning the man with a look of contempt asked, "what are you talking about Mex?" "You know just as well as I do," Louis answered. Louis didn't see the man with the badge that had walked in behind him. "I saw the sacks Ed," the Star said, "did you cut them?" "No," the man he'd called Ed answered. "He's a liar," Louis said. "You calling a liar Mex?"

"Better be careful Ed," the star said, "the kid ain't no Mexican, but I want no trouble here." "Be alright if we take it out of town?" Louis asked. "If it is, watch my back, and you liar follow me out to the edge of town. When you get there be ready to go for it. Then when I get back, I'll pay for the two sacks of grain." "You hear what he said Boyd, he threatened me," the big man, said. "He's calling you out Ed, I think you'd better pony up for the grain and go back to the ranch. The kids called you out and I don't think you'd come out of this one with a whole skin." Ed put some money on the counter and left. Boyd, the man with the badge said, "I'll go see he heads home but you'd better get your business done here and move on son. His old man pulls a lot of weight around here." "Thanks," Louis answered, "I just couldn't let him do that to a lady and a child."

"Lets get bite to eat Juan then we'd better ride like the man said." Both the storekeeper and man whose wife and child were on the wagon thanked Louis. "That should take some of the hot air out of Ed," the storekeeper said. His father's a tough old man and I don't think he's going to be happy with someone making his kid eat crow. I'm sorry but Boyd's right you'd better put miles between you and this town."

An hour latter later Juan and Louis had eaten picked up the things they needed at the store and moved on. No dust behind them they rode until almost dark before moving off the road to a secluded grassy spot. Unsaddled and grained their horses before bedding down. Up before the sun they rode out on to the road chewing on beef jerky and hardtack.

Up into mountainous country where they did stop long enough to boil oatmeal with dried apples. A day later they met the wagons of some freighters heading north and stopped to talk. Invited to eat and Juan was relieved, when Louis excepted even though there was an hour or two of daylight left. This evening they'd eat a supper better to his liking, beans, bacon and biscuits. Not perfect but a lot better fare then what they'd been living on for days.

They asked about the Indians they might find ahead and were told things seemed to be pretty peaceful but with the Comanche's you just never knew. They stayed the night and early morning right after coffee, they thanked their hosts and were back in the saddle.

With their horses healthy and well feed they were covering a lot of ground. This and with a little luck they hoped to move through any troubled area with out any problems with hostiles. Only once did they see a dust cloud coming up behind that was closing on them. Though who ever it was closing on them fast, they figured they would exhaust their horses before they closed the distance. Riding on until almost dark, then off the road a distance they made camp without a fire.

Hard tack and jerked beef as they rode before sun up in the morning. Checking with his telescope after the sun up Louis saw nothing behind them and hoped that whoever it was had given up.

Coming up on a line of freight wagons, they'd ride on past only slowing long enough to talk to the wagon master riding at the head of the column. From him they learned that if they pushed it they could make it to Santa Fe by nightfall. Good news to them they could enjoy a good meal this evening. They made it early enough to get that meal then out in the half light found a place with good grass and made camp. Breakfast in the morning and purchase grain again for the horses.

Ten more days and they'd be in El Paso. They would have liked to make it to Albuquerque the first day out of Santa Fe but would settle for a mid day meal and broiled beef rubbed with chili and tortillas that they'd taken with them, for supper and the next day. The afternoon out of town they rode until late and made camp by a river that flowed toward Texas. Good grazing for the horses and they took the time in the morning to bathe and wash clothes. Waiting for their clothes to dry and Louis took out the bag they'd found in one of the rustlers saddlebags, one hundred and fifty dollars in gold and silver coins that he divided between them. "We made more off that shoot out then we did wages," Juan said. "I wouldn't say it was a healthy to make money though. It didn't really get to me that first day but I sure didn't feel very good for a few days after."

"Between what I made on the horse race and this trip Mano, I've got more then I could have hoped for. Maybe I can get married now, all I have to do is find a place where I can build a small adobe," Juan said. "Build it on the farm where we live now Juan," Louis told him. "You'd let me do that Mano?" Juan asked. "Why not?" Louis told him, "what would I do without you and who'd watch my back." "I like what you said Mano but I've yet to see when you needed help there," Juan told him.

They made a small fire to make tea, ate the broiled beef and tortillas. Checked the horses and with the fire burned down to embers they retired to their bedrolls. In the morning they finished what was left of the tortillas and beef, took the horses to water, picked up their now dry clothes, saddled up and rode out on the last leg back. Again the days would pass as they rode. Nothing moved faster on the road, no one ever caught up to or passed them. Stage Coaches would most likely be the only ones that could but so far there hadn't been any.

They rode into the rancho they'd ridden away from months before and Don Francisco's coach wasn't there. Louis apprehensive, feeling something might have happened or the Don had left for California without them. Relieved somewhat when they told him that the Don and his party hadn't reach there yet and that they'd heard of no trouble on the road from Mexico City. They were welcomed back, those at the rancho telling him that they had been worried too, because if he and Juan hadn't gotten back, what would the Don have done he was depending on them.

They ate with the vaqueros and in the morning rode out with them on a gather for another cattle drive. Both feeling it would be better that keep busy instead of sitting around waiting. These cattle they were told, would be sent on a drive too but this one was to a railhead that was closer.

It was two weeks before Louis saw the Dons black coach when they rode in after their work. Hearing their horses the Don came out and motioned for him to come. Juan told him to go ahead that he'd take care of his horse. At the door the Don told him that she wanted to see him. He entered and saw her sitting with a blanket around her legs and thinner then when they'd left to go to Mexico but he smiled and asked, "do you feel better senora?""A little better I think," she told him. "Now sit," she said, "I want to hear what you've been doing."

"Juan and I rode up to Wyoming on a cattle drive, he told her. A long ride but an experience that I'll remember for a long time." "You couldn't sit and wait could you, you had to be doing something, didn't you?" She said. "Time would have past to slowly just sitting and waiting," he answered.

She asked Francisco to please tell Rosalie to come there to her. Turning to Louis, she said, "I want you to meet some one." When the girl walked in Louis jumped to his feet and looked from Rose to the girl then back again. "Your daughter Rose?" Louis asked, the girl surely a mirror image of a younger Rose. "No," she answered smiling, "my niece." My brother Guillermo's daughter, but he passed away some time back. Now Francisco has married Margarita her mother and they're going home to Francisco's rancho." "Rosalie this is the young man I told you about, Louis, Rosalie." "Senor," Rosalie said and Louis only answered, "senorita" He was looking at her, she smiled and lowered her eyes. "May I be excused Tia," she asked, "I must help with super." "Surely" Rose answered. "Senor," she said, turned and she left the room.

"Would you have supper with me Louis?" Rose asked. "Be happy to," he answered, "but I need to clean up." "I don't eat with the others I take my meals alone usually Louis but I'd like you with me this evening." "I'll be back in just a little while," he said as he left.

He was all cleaned up with clean clothes on, though still in white pants and blouse his pistol out of sight now high on his left side. He knocked and the woman who opened the door he didn't recognize. She looked him up and down, and then asked, "senor?" "Louis Hand," he answered, and he heard Rose say, "let him in Margarita he's my diner guest." Backing away from the door she let him pass but watched him intently. He was standing by Rose when she introduced him, saying," this is Louis Margarita the young man

I told you about." Margarita had a puzzled smile on her face as she bowed slightly and said, "please will you sit down senor."

When she was gone Rose told him, "one of my care takers now." Filis the woman who had accompanied Rose from California brought her supper and medicine. "The other one of my caretakers" Rose said, "I'm blessed." Francisco brought in a small table for Louis then Rosalie brought his supper. Rose ate very little and he didn't feel very hungry for some reason. He out of habit would clean his plate as usual, the way he'd been taught when he was younger.

Don Francisco came back after super to talk to Louis, asking him if he and Juan could be ready in the morning. "It's getting late in the year," he told Louis, "and though it was mostly desert we do have a couple of high passes to go through." "We'll be ready," Louis answered. He bid Rose and Francisco goodnight saying that he had some things to take of and left.

Though he cherished the time being with her it saddened him the way she looked and he wondered why it had to be this way. At the bunkhouse he told Juan that they'd be leaving in the morning. "That's good," Juan said, "I want to get back I've had enough, it's gotten to the point where it's not fun anymore like it once was. We've still got a long ways to go but we'll be heading in the right direction, home." After checking their things they retired and as usual awake and up in morning before the sun.

The cook had breakfast ready for the early risers and they ate then carried their gear out to the horses. Saddled the horses they'd ride today and took the extra tack they had now and their bedrolls to the Dons supply wagon. The Dons coach in front of the ranchos door and Louis went to help Filis and Margarita with Rose but they shook their heads and waved him away. They'd made a bed in the coach and he could see her propped up with pillows and facing forward. He knew it was going to be a rough trip for her and with the three other women there were four in the coach now.

CHAPTER VII

The Don led with a vaquero followed by the coach and supply wagon. Louis and Juan rode side by side and they could talk, there being little danger along the road here. But that would all change they knew within only a few days. North now but with the coach and wagon they wouldn't make it to Los Cruces the first day. Their noon stop there the next day then they'd turn west toward the coast, California and the setting sun. Three days to the top of the first mountain pass and the continual divide. From here on Louis and Juan would ride on opposite sides of the coach and slightly behind. Don Francisco rode with his vaquero at his side in the lead.

They were in hostile country again and Juan cautioned them again about looking at their campfires after sunset. That their favorite time to attack was morning but that they might try something any time. Now they would also post night sentries.

Any time they came close to a settlement or rancho in the afternoon the Don would have them set up camp. The more people around he knew the less chance of an Indian attack. In the desert and long stretches with no established settlements while the others set up camp Juan and Louis would ride a wide circle around the area, checking for sign. Once back in camp they'd use the telescope and check for anything out of the ordinary. There would always be a spot or two that looked suspicious and they'd have to check them in the changing light as the shadows moved. Any lookout would be sure to move if exposed by the changing sunlight. So far they had been fortunate but knew that it was no excuse for their guard to be lessened.

The weather was a little cooler now but still warm and would be uncomfortable in the coach. Louis would stop by the coach when he could, wanting to see her but would ride away saddened by what he saw. He could see she was not getting better and it was so obvious that she was gradually failing.

They'd camped the night, had breakfast and Don Francisco had taken his position with his vaquero in the lead. Less then a half hour later and the Don with the vaquero had just started riding through a boulder strewn area, when they hit. Two Indians on foot attacked the Don and the vaquero but this was only to draw their attention. The real attack came at the coach and the supply wagon. A half dozen Indians came hollering as they ran. Louis barely had time to drop to the ground and down onto one knee. He broke the charge when he knocked down three of the Indians. The ones that were left were joined by others and charged again. But now Juan was there then and between them they decimated the Indians as they came in. As the Indians, broke and then retreated Juan and Louis quickly changing cylinders in their carbines. Mounted and chased after them and those who turned to fight were then quickly dispatched.

Louis had emptied his carbine and was using his pistol when he rode up on a young Indian who was just standing, having no place to run. Reining Flea to a stop he looked at the young Indian probably no more then fourteen years old. He stood, his muzzleloader most likely already fired and setting with its stock on the ground his right hand on the barrel. Louis had taken a raking shot along the calf of his right leg. The blood that was running down his leg was now showing through his white pants. He watched the Indian as he dismounted and holstered his pistol. He checked the wound, a shallow grove that he tied his bandana over after tearing his bloody pants away. Walking up to the young Indian he took hold of his rifles barrel with his left hand. Holding the rifle he pushed him back with his right hand leaving a bloody handprint on the front of the Indians tunic.

"You speak Spanish," he asked, just as Juan rode up ready to shoot. The Indians expression didn't change and Louis told him, "you go now and tell your people what happened here, you'll need help taking care of them." The young Indian trotted off only stopping once to look back. "You let him go?" Juan questioned. "He couldn't do us anymore more harm," Louis said mounting the spent rifle in his hand.

They rode back though the carnage they'd created, some of the vaqueros picking up the weapons these Indians would never need again. Louis was the only one who suffered a wound and drew the attention of Rosalie, Margarita and Filis. They cut more of his trouser leg, washed and dressed the wound and he'd have to ride with his leg exposed for the rest of the day.

They reorganized loaded their weapons and Don Francisco led off again. Their midday stop late but it was needed this day. His leg was sore and Filis removed the bandage to check the wound. It had already crusted over but she told him that it needed to be bandaged to keep the dust off. With his leg bandaged they were ready to move out again. They had barely started when one of the vaqueros from the rear rode up and told the Don there was a rider to their rear carrying a white flag. The Don riding by asker Louis to ride back with him, "I don't know what this could be about but it might be a ruse," he told him. They rode back toward the rider Louis with his carbine in his hand.

The rider, an Apache who looked somewhat past middle age, unarmed except for the stick with the white cloth attached to it. "Who sent my nephew to come and get us so we can take of our people?" he asked in Spanish. The Don looked at Louis puzzled. "I did," Louis told him. "Why?" the Indian asked, and took the white garment off the stick. Louis saw that it was the white tunic with the blood on it where had place his hand as he took the rifle. "I didn't think that his life would have added much to what had happened already," Louis told him. "True, this is a bitter lesson for our young people, Gracias Mano Sangriento for my nephews life," he said, turned his horse and rode back the way he'd come. Don Francisco sat looking at Louis, "he called you Bloody Hand Louis," the Don said, "How could he have know your name?" "I don't know how he could know, I think he just called me that because I put my hand on his nephews chest when I took his rifle away from him. I guess my hand had blood on it from the wound in my leg." The Don a wry smile on his face said, "a strange happening my friend, I guess I really shouldn't be surprised when something like this occurs. It's happened before to you hasn't it?" He said, turned his stallion and rode back to take up his position at the head of their little column and started them again toward home.

Louis took up his position and thought about what had happened too but figured this had only been a coincidence and something that could have happened to anyone some time in their life.

His leg was doing well except from getting too much exposure to the sun. When they stopped he and Juan went to bathe and he washed his pants working hard to get the blood out. After with clean clothes on he was repairing the tear in his still wet pants when Rosalie seeing him and volunteered to do the job, "men aren't supposed to sew," she told him. "Men without wives have to," he answered smiling. He didn't receive a verbal answer, only a coy smile from over her shoulder as she walked away.

The Streams here were low this time of the year but any day now a storm in the mountains miles away could unleash a torrent of water down any streambed. Many of them here dry and difficult to cross with deep dry sand where a wagon could become stuck for hours at the wrong time.

When the women kept hearing small bits of talk about the battle with the Apaches. They wanted to know exactly what happened and asked Don Francisco to tell them. They wanted to know every thing, even why the Apache who rode in under the white flag called Louis Bloody Hand. Don Francisco explained how Louis told the young Apache how he felt they had lost to many of their young men already. "Louis let that young man go back to his people," Don Francisco told them, "and explained to them what happened so they'd come back and take care of their dead. The name Bloody Hand though it sounds awful it's really a name they gave him and was because of the hand image on that young mans tunic. It will surely be a respected name among them now though. Louis was actually thanked by that boy's uncle, the Apache who'd came in under that white flag and that flag was actually the young Indians tunic, that bloody stain still on it."

The three women were sitting with Rose when she said, "I'd expect something like that from Louis. There really was no reason to continue and taking that young Indians life would have accomplished nothing. I think he might have gained us some respect from the Apache. That's something that we'll all need, before all of the killing by both of our people can come to an end."

They were not out of hostile country yet and they could run into some other band that was seeking vengeance or plunder. Louis talked with Juan about what they'd just been through. "I just don't understand why those young Apaches took the chances they did Juan," Louis said. "They just don't want to change Mano, they want to do just as they've done for hundreds of years," Juan told him. "And they don't realize that in the end that there could be no more of them left." Louis felt that what Juan had just said was true and many more of them would die before it would all end.

After crossing the river then the worst of the deserts that they had to cross was behind them but not the last. There were no hostiles people here but there was the hostile environment and Louis worried about the women in the coach because of the heat. It seemed so much worst now then when they passed through here going the other way. He stayed close by but was helpless there was nothing he do.

The wind now coming from the west, blowing hot and drifting sand across the trail making it even more difficult for their horses. The Dons black didn't look the same now, no longer a proud spirited stallion. The long trail had taken its toll and now his color was even against him. The Don and his Vaqueros now forced to walk to save their horses from complete fatigued and having to be left behind. Even the four vaqueros that were on the coach and supply wagon were off their high seats and on foot. They were struggling too in they're riding boots that were not designed for walking let alone walking through dry sand.

The grain that Juan and Louis had fed their horses was proving it's worth now. Rosalie and Margarita on Flea and Fresa to take some of the load out of the coach. Juan using their other two horses to help the supply wagon and the coach through the particularly difficult places. Louis walked beside the coach making sure Filis had everything she needed to help her take of Rose. Water from their supply the only thing she ever needed though keeping damp cloths on Roses forehead trying to keep her from suffering with the heat some.

The two peons Juan and Louis were better equipped for this desert country with they're white clothes and their flat healed boots, even though they hadn't planed it.

It took them three days longer to cross this desert country this time then it when they crossed going the other way. At the Mission they stayed four days giving the horses a chance to recover some from the ordeal now on good grass and all the water they wanted. Brushed and bathed they recouped enough for them to continue. Everything had been checked the horses and the wagons and they'd pull out in the morning.

He was sitting and listening to the vaqueros talk when he heard what they called that desert wind. Something great, large, important or holy was always given a Saintly name by the Spanish Mexicans. Though he felt that wind was hot enough to have come straight out of Hades and should have been named for what it really was but he didn't say so or tell them what he thought.

The Journey had taken its toll on every one of them but Rose was the one who Louis knew had really suffered the most. He wondered now if it had really been all that necessary. But he felt too that when some one was really ill, the will to regain one's health could be all-important. Then how was he to really know, he wasn't the one who had to try and maybe he would have given up and surrendered to what he felt was inevitable any way.

It was an easier road now and what they needed they could pick up along the way. An easy days ride from one mission to the next but it would take eight days to get to the last Mission. Then almost another two days to the Arroyo Seco and through that canyon to Don Francisco Rancho.

Don Francisco was concerned about his stallion and said that he'd seen how much better Juan and Louis's horses had done in the desert. They told him how they grained their horses on their ride back from the cattle drive. "That had to be it," the Don told them, "I knew the grass was poor on the road to Mexico City but I was to concerned about other things then. In the morning Don Francisco had grain for their horses on the supply wagon and to make sure the stallion was grained, he fed him himself.

All of them weary of travel and even Rose smiled when they left the Mission trail, turning west toward Monterey and home. They'd have to suffer only one more night camp. Louis and Juan rode to the Dons before collecting their gear and heading home, because Louis wanting to see Rose all the way to the rancho. Leaving he told her that he'd return the next day after they'd all had a comfortable nights rest. They stopped only long enough to pick up cervezas Juan wanting to celebrate by having a couple with supper.

Tio greeted them by telling Louis he had two new colts to take care of. He told Tio he'd see them in the morning, right now he just wanted to take care of the horses and get a hot bath. He unpacked some of his gear while the water heated but cleaning everything would have to wait. Bathed he went to the bunk house and found Juan already sitting at the table, he and Tio all ready celebrating with a couple of cervezas. Tio had supper ready and he sat down with them. He had to tell Tio everything about the trip even the round up and cattle drive. And Tio wanted to see where Louis had been wounded. He looked at the already healed wound and Louis asked him how he knew about that? "Juan told me earlier," he told him, "that they attacked you." "And that's all?" Louis asked. "Is there something else?" Tio asked, looking toward Juan. "Not really," Louis told him, finished his supper and told them, he'd see them in the morning.

He laid down in his room the only thing his mind now was Rose's illness. Tired he slept until dawn, dressed he went out side and knew that Tio was up, smoke coming out of the chimney and the aroma of Tio's coffee in the air. Inside he found Juan already sitting at the table eating breakfast. "I thought you'd sleep in this morning Juan," he said. "You forget Mano, "I have something important to do and today's the day." "But you haven't built your adobe yet Juan," Louis said. "If she turns me down I'm not going to need it, am I?" Juan told him. "She told you she'd wait Juan, she'll be there for you." "Wish me luck, Mano," Juan said, his breakfast finished he left.

Tio sat with a cup of coffee while Louis ate. "You going to the Don's Mano, and he asked how Rose was?" She doesn't look all that well Tio and I don't know if the Doctors in Mexico did anything for her." "You go Mano," Tio told him, "I'll have supper ready for you when you get back."

He'd ride Fresa today he'd ridden Flea a lot on the trip and knew he could use the rest and gain back the weight he'd lost.

She was sitting on the veranda in the shade when he rode up and smiled when she saw him. Maybe they did help her he thought, I sure hope so he said to himself. They'd heard him ride in and the Don, Rosalie, her mother and Filis came out all looking much better after a comfortable nights rest.

"You look better Rose a nights sleep must have helped," Louis told her. "I do feel better," she answered, as the Don brought him a chair. "I've got the arms we took from the Apache Louis," the Don told him, "you can take your pick." "I've got all I need," Louis answered, "but I'll ask Juan if he might want something." "They're in house in my study, take a look before you leave and you can let me know later."

When the others had left Rose said that she wanted to talk to him." All right, Rose you know I'll listen, what is it?" he asked. "Do you like Rosalie?" she asked him. And Louis had to smile, "she's a beautiful girl," he answered, "and how could I not, but why do you ask?" "I want to marry her Louis," Rose told him. Louis looking right into her eyes, said, "I think she might have something to say about that, Rose." "Oh I'll take care that," She told him, "and how do you feel Louis?" "How could I refuse but I'm a peon and if I asked a girl like her she'd most likely refuse." "I want you to ask her and she's not going to refuse you, I promise Louis." "Should I wonder why?" Louis questioned. "I'm a Bruja Louis," Rose told him smiling, "and I'll give her a potion." "Bruja," that's a word I haven't heard before," Louis said. "A sorceress Louis, you know what that is. You have to marry her Louis," she said. "I want this for you, she's ever thing you need to make your life complete and it will make me happy too. You talk to Rosalie then ask Francisco."

He couldn't say anything it had all been said and he'd go home wondering how or why this could happen. Rosalie was more then he could have ever hoped for. He was what, a farmer, a peon here and he fully realized it. Telling himself I'd better be prepared if she doesn't say no, the Don or more then likely Margarita will. Rejection would be difficult he knew but he also realized he'd have to suffer through it.

He checked the arms they'd taken from the Apache and they were old and some crudely repaired. Nothing he'd want and was pretty sure nothing Juan would want either.

Out side he told the Don that he didn't think there was anything there that he or Juan could use. Excusing himself he told Rose there were things that needed doing at home and that he had two new colts that he hadn't seen yet. "You tend to your work," she told him, "come when you can, Louis. There's no need for you to come every day, though I would like you to." He kissed her cheek, a cheek no longer smooth and soft as he'd remembered, but dry now and almost parchment like.

Riding home he was saddened, he knew she was still fighting what ever it was and putting on that she was feeling better. When he walked in Juan and Tio were at the table eating. Tio getting up told him that he'd get his supper but Louis told him to stay, that he knew where the pot was. With his plate Louis sat and looking at Juan, asked, "well did she turn you down?" "She didn't," Juan answered, "so where can I build would the corner toward town be alright?" "We'll go and stake it out when I've finished eating. But why so far from my adobe Juan/" Louis asked. "Well there's something else," Juan said, "she wants to bring a couple of pets." "Oh, Oh," Tio exclaimed, "she already has niños." "No, no," Juan answered, "she's has goats." "Can she make cheese?" Tio asked. "I think so," Juan answered, "but I don't know for sure." "What goods a goat Juan if you don't know how to make cheese?" Tio asked. "Alright you two," Louis said with a slight smile, "if she can't make cheese Juan can learn how."

They'd staked the out the adobe in line with the others adobes though they were some distance away.

Tio telling Juan he'd better build three rooms unless he wanted to sleep with cheeses hanging over his head. "That wouldn't be to good, would it?" Juan said. "Only if you get hungry," Tio told him, laughing. Louis had to smile knowing Tio wasn't serious just having a little fun with a younger friend that he was close to.

Going out to see the new colts Louis found he had two grey fillies and no way of knowing their sire. They'd need care and a friendly hand but it would a long time before they'd be ready to break to ride. He looked over the rest of the horses then went to check the yard and garden. Most of the garden work done but he'd turn some soil getting ready for another planting. He worked until he was tired then walked to look at the front yard where he found a row of young trees planted. The work had made him tired but he felt good and knew it was what he needed. Water heated he bathed put on clean clothes and went to relax and talk with Tio.

He asked him about the trees he saw planted in the front yard. "Manzana you know apple trees Mano, a friend gave them to me but I don't think I'll be baking apple pies for a while yet." "It's a start though Tio," Louis told him.

"Are you going to visit the Senora in the morning Mano?" Tio asked, "if you are, I'll have breakfast ready early." "Thanks," Louis told him. "Maybe if you can come back early enough you could go hunting, there's no meat left. Beans and tortillas are all right but meat adds flavor." "Just as soon as I can Tio," he answered.

Coming in Juan told them that Rafael, Carlos and Julio would be there in the morning to help him with building. That they'd bring the first lode of adobe bricks when they came. "You're not going to make your own Juan?" Louis asked. "No," Juan answered, "they've been making bricks and I'm going to buy them from them, and their going to help me build." That way it will get built fast. We're getting married Sunday afternoon Mano, can you and Tio come?" Louis looking at Tio but he was just grinning. "We'll be there Juan," Louis told him.

"We'd like to like to have a little party after but my new family has a very small house and I was wondering if might be able to have it here?" "That's up to Tio," Louis told him. "As long as I don't have to cook," Tio said. "Anna's mother said she would fix everything." "Ah" Tio exclaimed, "and we finally learn the girls name and where you going on your honey moon?" "I've got a tent," Juan told him, "I'll put it up near where were going to build the adobe." "No Juan," Louis told him," "you and Anna can stay in my adobe, use the other room I'll bunk here with the others." "You'll do that for us Mano?" Juan questioned. "Why not, you want me to stay in my room?" "Well no," Juan answered him.

He was up and dressed in the dark then went out to saddle Fresa and this was when he could appreciate his friendly horses. He didn't have to chase around after them and rope one of them out bunch trying to dodge a loop. Saddled he led her to the hitching rail at the rear of his rear door, put on his blanket and saddle but left the cinch loose. He'd tighten it before he'd leave for Don Francisco's. Smelling the coffee made him hungry. Tio's coffee always for some reason smelled and tasted good, but most other people's coffee he would as well leave, it if there was something else to drink.

"Your early," Tio told him, "it's not even light, you'll have to wake up the Don." "I'm not going to leave for a while I'm going to enjoy a nice leisurely breakfast this morning." He ate his breakfast and had then another cup of coffee with Tio and Juan.

He rode out with the rising sun holding Fresa to an easy walk. Alone now gave him time to think and today it would put him in a melancholy mood, he wanting so much for her to get well. But it had been so long now and he had seen no improvement at all. Maybe today it would be different today he prayed. Don Francisco was sitting on the veranda with a cup of something. Louis knew he needed no more coffee this morning three cups at breakfast was one cup to many already, as usual. After tying Fresa he walked up on to the veranda and the Don asked him to sit down and offered him chocolate. They sat for some time in silence, before the Don said, "you look worried Louis." "I am," Louis answered. "She'll be out as soon as it warms up bit," the Don said, and lapsed back into silence.

Filis came out and looked around, nodded to Louis and went back inside. Louis figured she was checking to see if there was a sunny spot where Rose could sit. Two of the Dons vaqueros carried her out chair and all, setting her in the spot where he'd seen sitting before. She smiled at him and said, "your early Louis," I am he answered I have to leave early Tio needs a deer were all out of meat." "And it's up to you?" "Rose asked. "This time yes," "he said, "Juan's busy building his house, he's getting married this Sunday afternoon." "Oh I wish I could be there," She said, I'm sure your going Louis." "He's asked me to I suppose he needs moral support." He told her whom the girl was that Juan was going to marry and she said that she knew the family, that they raised goats and that they made excellent cheese. "Then he's the first of your bachelor group to break the mold and get married," she said. He had to agree but that Tio was a part of the group and he had been married.

"I think Rosalie would like to go to," she told him. "I'll ask her when I see her," he answered. "You'd better and where will they live if their house isn't finished Louis?" "In the room you used to stay in before I acquired the adobe. Before she could ask he said, "I'll stay in the bunkhouse until their house is ready for them to move into." "Your being generous Louis," she said.

"It's not going to be anything but little inconvenience for me and it should only be for a short time. Besides if it was the other way around Juan would do the same for me."

The sun was up higher now and warmer. "If its getting to warm for you," Louis said, "I can move you back into the shade if you like." "It is, would you please, Louis?" she asked. He easily picked he up chair, blanket and all and set her down in the shade. Bundled in the blanket he couldn't really tell but picking her up as easily as he had, he knew that she weighed little.

When Filis came she said that she was tired. "You go do your hunting Louis I need to rest for a while," she told him. Filis went after the two men and Rosalie coming out stood by him. They carried her inside, he stood up and looking at Rosalie, said, "she's not getting better." "I know," she answered, in a low voice.

"Juan's getting married on Sunday would you like to go?" Louis asked. "It will only be a short afternoon affair with a small reception at the bunkhouse." "It sounds nice Louis will you come after me?" "There's nothing but a donkey cart at my place," Louis told her, "can you ride?" "Will that type of dress be alright for a wedding Louis?" she asked. "Don't forget we're all peons at the farm," he told her smiling. She smiled and told him that she'd find something to wear. "Say good bye to your mother, Filis and Don Francisco," and he took her hand. "I think we should pray," she said. "I know," he answered. Turned and mounted, looking down at her he wanted to say something but he couldn't, not now. He tried to smile but couldn't and said, "tomorrow but it will some time latter in the morning." He looked back as he rode away and she was standing looking and he waved then let Fresa pick the pace she wanted, a nice easy canter. It hadn't been a good day for him and wanted to be alone for a while. He rode in and fed Fresa and turned her out into the pasture. Saddled Flea and stopped only long enough to pick up what he needed for hunting and rode away. Without looking back he missed seeing Tio standing in the doorway looking after him.

Something isn't going right with Mano he told the others sitting at the table eating their mid day meal.

Once in the brush and oak it didn't take him long to find a small buck. A well place shot and it was over. He skinned the deer then took the time to bone out most of the meat. Wrapping it in it's own skin he tied it behind his saddle. He realized as he tied it down that the little buck didn't weigh much less then she did when he moved her chair and all. He rode slow going back not in any rush. He stopped at the door of the kitchen and bringing the deer in he set it down on the floor. "Well take care of it from here Mano," he heard Tio say as he headed back out the door.

He took the saddle off at his door and took it inside putting it on its stand. Took Flea out and brushed him as he ate the bit of grain he gave him. Fresa was there and he gave her a few minutes of brushing feeling she was there because he'd neglected her when he brought her in earlier. Now all he wanted to do was lay down and rest for a little while.

Waking to the sound of music he saw that the sun was already down. With cold water he washed the sleep from his eyes. Walking toward the bunkhouse he could smell the fried onions and remembered he hadn't eaten sense breakfast. He didn't feel hungry but knew he should eat something. Tio and Juan were sitting at the table and he knew they'd eaten already. "Hungry" Tio asked, "I've got liver and a piece of steak ready to fry." "I guess I am," he answered, "if you don't mind Tio?" "I saved it for you," Tio said, "you forgot to stop and eat before you left to go hunting."

Seeing the sacks on the floor by the pantry Louis asked, "what's all that?" Three more mouths to feed," Juan said, "so I thought I'd better stock up." Rafael, Carlos and Julio were in the bunkroom and as always were playing their guitars and singing their love ballads. Louis had to smile the three bachelor troubadours and now he'd hear their lonely love songs.

Finished eating Louis sat and watched Tio slice and rub the pieces of meat with ground chili. With the chili on the meat it was ready to hang up to dry. "It's good tender meat," Tio said, "but this little buck isn't going to last long with this bunch to feed." I'll make another hunt in a day or two and maybe find something a little bigger Tio," Louis told him. "Stay with the smaller one's Mano I like them the best, Tio said.

"There's hot water if you want to take a bath Mano," Tio told him. "In a while," Louis answered, "right low I'd just like to listen to the music." "It's nice," Tio answered, "but I'd like it better if a young lady were singing." "You might find one if you go to the fiestas and looked," Louis suggested. "Mano, listen to me," Tio said, "the ones I would want, wouldn't want this old man and the one's who would want me, I probably wouldn't want. Besides, if you catch one that really isn't what it was supposed to be, they may not let you throw it back." "With that Abuelo, (grand father)," Louis said, "I'd better take my hot water and go to my room, Buenos noches Tio." Before he'd finished bathing the music had stopped and like the others he'd retire to his bunk too.

Waking to a bright morning sky he had things that had to be done. Always his first concern were the horses, even though the fences were good and there was little chance of wild predators here. The water trough always demanded some attention and never stayed full for very long. The aroma of coffee told him that Tio was in the kitchen and he could go in and see what there was for breakfast. He could hear the noise from the bunkroom and knew that Juan and the others were up. Tio was in the kitchen and he went in to get his first cup. "Doing better Mano?" Tio asked. "I think so," he answered.

He ate with Juan and the others, and when they left to go work building Juan's adobe he went out to the woodpile. Tio had about all he could do with the cooking and the dining room with the five of them there now. Working with the bucksaw and axe would be good for him right now. Different then working with a shovel but it would tire him and maybe relieve some of the tension he felt but could do nothing about. A break from the saw and axe for a drink of water and he took a half dozen buckets of water to the kitchen Then topped off the trough again before going back to the woodpile.

Whenever he looked up from the work he could see Juan and the others but this time it was different. Past them coming on the road he could see three riders. A black horse in between the other two riders that looked like Rose but he knew that couldn't be. Then he knew that it was Rosalie but the gladness left in the next second when he realized for her to come here now there must be something wrong. Where was Don Francisco?

He walked around the end of the adobe and out to the road to intercept them. Rosalie and two of the ranchos vaqueros that he new from their ride to El Paso. Helping her down, the two vaqueros greeting him with a nod and then led the black mare away towards the Dons adobe. Her face somber when she told him, that they needed to talk. Taking her hand he led the way around to the other of the adobes and into his rooms. Leaving the door open he pulled a chair away from table and invited her to sit down. Then he went to the other side and sat down.

She had an envelope in her hand and with tears she said, "she's gone Louis." Two days ago she gave me this envelope and told me to give it to you but only after it happened." He sat trying to compose himself but it was taking some time. "Would you like me to leave?" she asked. "No," he answered, "Please don't, I need you here." She gave him the letter and told him that she was given one also. He opened the letter and read.

My Dear Louis.

Please forgive me for leaving but I must go and join my beloved husband. What we had was wonderful, we both needed someone to help us fill a void in our lives. I thank you with all my heart. Now you will need someone, let it be Rosalie she needs you and you need her. Think of me now and then.

My love to both of you.

Rose

He folded the letter and put it back in the envelope. Then offered it to Rosalie asking, "would like to read it?" "I know what it says," she answered.

"She'll be buried on the rancho tomorrow Louis and I know she'd want you there." "I'll be there," he answered.

"Rosalie I need to ask you, do you want her wishes to be fulfilled?" Louis asked. "It's easy for me Louis," she answered, "I've watched you from the day I first saw you and I wanted then for you to care for me. In a way though I felt it was Rose who you wanted." "I guess it was some kind of a romance," he answered, "we did care for each other I know but we never held each other romantically, it was something else, a need for both of us." "I understand now Louis but I was jealous in a way. Now I'd better get back they might need me. I'll see you tomorrow," she said and stood up. He was in front of her now and put his arms around her then kissed her forehead. Putting her arms around him she laid her head on his shoulder, and said, "I'm sorry Louis but she's not suffering any longer."

They walked together over to Don Francisco's adobe where the vaqueros were waiting. He helped her to mount and she said, "come early if you can Louis." Walking slowly back he watched as they were riding away then stood and watched until they disappear from his misty eyes. A few minutes to compose himself then inside to tell Tio then there were things that he knew he had to do. Tio when Louis told him said, he knew there wasn't much that he could do to help him right now, other then to take care of things here. "You go and do what you know has to be done," Tio told him, "I'm sorry Mano, I know you thought a lot about the Senora and she was to young to be taken away. We never know when someone will be call though, do we? Then we have to walk that trail until you know you can except it."

He headed into town to the tailors and told him he needed a black suit right away. The tailor told him he only had a couple of black suits and didn't think they would fit him without some work. He took some measurements and said he would get his wife to help him. For Louis to come back in two hours and they should have it done. Leaving, Louis headed next to the boot makers for a pair of black riding boots, and had his belt and the holster for his thirty—one caliber pistol dyed black. It would take a little time and he waited.

Juan and the others wouldn't come in until they were ready to quit for the day they'd taken things to eat at noon. He ate and talked to Tio telling him he had to go and pick up some things later in the day. Finished eating he went to his room, read the letter again, put it back into the envelope and lay down. Waking to the sound of guitars he knew he was late and ran most of the way to the tailors. He told him he was sorry but the tailor said that it was all right it had taken a little longer then he'd expected anyway. "I knew that you would be here, senor," he said. The vest and the pants fit him well, the flair at the bottom of the legs, red. Red as a rose he thought, it was her color and it would do fine. A white shirt two red silk scarves and a black hat, then two sashes one red and one black. If the red one wasn't right he could change to the black one. "That should be all," he told the tailor, paid the bill and picking the packages left for home. Laying out the clothes be bathes before going for something to eat.

Tio had told Juan and the others about Roses passing when they first came in. and that when Louis comes in for them to keep quiet. "Mano doesn't need anyone to remind him, he knows well enough already," he said.

Tio was sitting by himself at the table when he came in, the table all cleared except for his cup. "I figured you might get hungry, Mano I've got some thing for you," he told him as he got up from the table. He set the plate down in front of him and sat down across the table with his cup. There wasn't much they wanted to talk about right then and Tio waited until Louis was finished. Then took his plate and told him to go get some sleep, that he had a busy day ahead of him. "Thanks Tio," Louis said and left.

He thought he'd listen to the music for a while but it seemed different tonight, sadder to him yet he knew he was listening to some of the same songs they'd played before.

Waking early and he thought he'd only dosed off for a while. But he knew better when he saw the morning sun though the window.

Getting up he dressed in his new clothes but left the selection of the sash for later. Not used to the boots he found them a bit difficult for him to walk in as he went out to saddle Flea. Saddled and bridled he tied him outside of the bunkhouse. Now he was ready for that first cup of Tio's coffee. Inside and Tio nodded his head in approval when he saw him. Louis asked about the two sashes he'd bought one red the other black. "Today you wear the black one Mano, Tio told him, "I think if she was here she would have said the red one but it's different now. When Juan gets married you wear the red one." Walking out Juan stopped when saw Louis, "you look good Mano you should have done that a long time ago," he said. "Don Luis Mano, now that sounds good doesn't it?" "I don't think I want to stack hides in these clothes Juan," Louis answered.

Finished with breakfast he was tightening Fleas chinch as Juan stood watching. "My clothes don't go to well with the horse and saddle do they?" he asked. "Next time you buy a suit," Juan told him, "you buy one that matches the Flea." "They don't have a color like that Juan," Louis answered, "you know that but thanks for helping to build up my spirits, Compadre, and don't wait up for me." "You don't have to worry about that Mano and don't worry about the horses. I'll go out and check them and fill the water trough right now," Juan told him, as he was swinging up into the saddle. Juan watching after him as Flea broke into a lope even before they were out of the yard.

After checking the horses and filling the trough Juan going inside sat down at the table across from Tio. "Mano is having a real problem Tio I can see it," he said. "I know," Tio answered, "but think about it for a minute, how old is he Juan, where did he come from and what could he have left behind, besides everything. I think he found something and I'm not talking about compadre's but some one who could fill in who ever they were that he lost. And now after not to long she's gone and you and I are not going to be able help him much. There is someone though and that's Senorita Rosalie and I guess we're going to leave it up to her Juan. All we can do is help with the things here."

He'd settled Flea into his fast walk after he'd had his sprint that he wanted also, just to work off a little of the frustration he felt. Riding into the yard at the rancho he looped Fleas reins around the rail and took his pistol off, hanging it over the saddle horn. The Don came out nodded and said," Louis." Rosalie right behind him said, "I'll stay with Louis." The Don went back after a cordial greeting.

"There'll no viewing Louis," she said, "the casket is closed." He nodded, he didn't want to see her the way she was now, wanting only to remember her the way she was the first time he saw her. "You look nice Louis," she told him, "a new suit?" "Yes he answered, "but I feel awkward I'm so used to loose fitting clothes." "You like nice wouldn't you like to dress this way more often?" "I'll wear them to Juan's wedding, can you go with me? I know it's soon but it was planned before." "I will Louis," she said, "I love weddings, I know that she did too and I'm sure that she would want us to go. Can we take a little walk Louis?" "Yes, but I'm a little clumsy in these boots but should be able to master them with some practice and someone holding my hand." Her hand was soft and warm and made him smile. "It's nice holding your hand," he told her. "Then we should do it more often," she answered. They walked out to the road then walked back to sit on the veranda at the rear of the adobe.

"Stay here," she said, "I'll bring us out something for lunch I don't like eating in the house." They sat quietly eating finished she moved next to him and put her hand on top of his. The time was passing slowly, then she said, "I'd better pick up here it will be time soon."

He saw the Don's coach coming from town. When it stopped the Padre from the Mission got out. Don Francisco coming out to meet him and Louis stood as they were passing. The Padre bowed slightly and said, "Senor Mano," as he passed going inside. When Rosalie came out he told her that the Padre had called him by his name. "Have you met him Louis?" she asked him. "No I haven't," he answered, and wondered. "Then he knows you by word of mouth and by your reputation Louis. He'll know because he watches over everyone in his parish, whether he sees you in church or not you are apart of what he's concerned about."

"I wonder if he knows everything?" Louis asked. "If it happened here I'm afraid most of us do Louis, Rosalie told him. Do you know that Rose even told me about you and why you are so close to Senor Luna." "He was the one who trusted me and gave work and that's why I was able to stay. Other wise I wouldn't be here and I don't know where I'd be today," he told her.

Six of the Don's vaquero's carried the casket, the Padre, Don Francisco, Margarita and Filis following. Rosalie taking Louis by the hand and they followed the others. The service was short, they lowered the casket and Rosalie had her head on his chest crying softly. He couldn't stop the tears from welling up in his eyes and he let them only blinking them away, he was hurting right now. They were walked slowly and could hear behind them the shovels of earth dropping into the grave.

The others going inside but Louis and Rosalie stopped on the veranda and sat down at the little table. Sitting close they remained silent there was nothing they could say right now.

The Padre came out and nodded as he passed, the Don walking with him to the coach. Coming back the Don smiled sadly to them as he passed going inside. They sat for some time then, Louis said, "I'd better go your family will want you inside with them." "We'll be going into town tomorrow, Louis I'll see you then wont I?" she asked. "You will," he said, "but right now I need this and he kissed her for the first time."

She stood watching him as he strapped on his pistol and mounted then blew him a kiss as he started away. He held Flea to a lope, a gait they both would feel good doing for a while then back into Fleas ground covering walk.

CHAPTER VIII

At home he took care of Flea then went inside to change into his comfortable clothes and boots. Going into the dining room he sat down at the table. Tio said he'd put the coffee on, "you look like you could use something stronger Mano. But this is all I have right now." "I probable could," he answered, "but from what I've seen I'd regret in the morning." "Believe me Mano it's true," Tio told him, "I've tried it and have yet to understand how some can do it all the time, but some do." "How well I know," Tio heard him say in a low voice.

Tio brought in the coffee and told him he'd had supper on the stove and as soon as Juan and the others came in he'd put it on the table. He was on his second cup when they came in talking but kind of went quiet when the saw him. Fifteen minutes later and they'd washed up and were back sitting at the table. They hadn't all sat down together for supper in a while.

The talk now was about Juan and his wedding and they told him that he only had a couple days of freedom left. "Your just jealous," Juan told them, "because you are all so ugly, you can't attract any girls." "Go to your room and play your guitars, when you've finished eating," Tio told them. "You sound like a bunch of old gabby hens." After they left for the bunk room Louis said, "its alright Tio, it's kind of nice seeing them have a little fun." "I know Mano," Tio said, "but not today, tomorrows soon enough."

Walking out to check the horses in evening light he pulled up enough buckets to fill the trough. Then stood at the fence with the horses they're for only a bit of affection this night he had no treats for them. Back in his room he listened to the bunkhouse guitars until he fell asleep. Awake early he dressed and in the dark went out into the garden where he could work at turning the soil. Shovel work wasn't the easiest thing to do but he felt good doing it. It was something he was able do with only the light from the star lit sky above him. He turned the soil waiting for the first smell of wood smoke that would come from Tio's morning fire. Then it wouldn't be to long before there'd be the aroma of coffee and he could cease his labor for now and go in for breakfast.

As usual the pot was already on the table and Tio was sitting with his cup. "You all right Buho?" Tio asked. "You call me owl Tio because I work a little in the dark?" Louis asked him smiling. "Maybe part Mano because there are some things about you that make me wonder, but who wouldn't when he sees some thing working in the garden in the dark of night." "I needed to work out some things and I do it better working not laying in bed and staring into the night." Tio shook his head from side to side a couple of times then nodded like he understood, shrugged and smiling said, "I'll get you some breakfast Mano."

He was just finishing with his breakfast when Juan and the others came into the dining room. Juan sat down and talked about a milking shed for the goats, and a small adobe they could age cheese and a place for chickens. "I like goats milk, cheese, chickens and eggs," Tio told Juan, but if your goats chew on the apple trees or your chickens eat up the vegetable garden, it's in to the pot for them." "Just show me where you're going build these things Juan," Louis said. "Then you and Tio figure out how you're going to keep them from doing damage." Then he had to smile and hope for the best.

Out after breakfast with the shovel he worked again at turning the soil. Thinking now that if they were going to expand the garden they'd have to think about getting an animal and a plow. He continued working until he saw the black coach approaching. Three riders in front but he could see the one on the black horse wasn't the Don. To small in stature and he knew it had to be Rosalie. The Don would be riding in the coach with his wife.

Leaving his shovel in the garden he walked out to the road to meet them. Dismounting Rosalie waved to her mother as the coach passed. Leading the black mare she walked over to Louis. Walking together to the rear of the adobe he tied the mare to the rail. Going in he left the door open, "you don't have to do that Louis," she said. "It's better if it's left open," he said and kissed her.

"She left her clothes and the mare to me," she told him. "And she's left you to me," Louis said. "Are you glad Louis?" she asked. "I'm as happy as anyone could be Rosalie, but I wish she was still with us." "Can we go for a ride," she asked "Can you ride bare back, Rosalie?" he asked her. "I started that way but it's been a long time," she told him. Going into his room and he came back out with a pair of white pants and blouse. "Peon clothes?" she asked. "Go into the other room and change," he said, and tossed her the clothes. "Must I," she questioned. "You'll ruin that nice suit if you don't," he told her' "I don't understand," she said "You will, believe me," Louis said smiling.

He took the saddle off the mare while she was changing and bringing it in he set it on the wood horse with his. He had to smile when she walked out but she looked beautiful and he put his arms her. "I need something to hold up these pants," she told him. "I know he said," smiling. A piece of cotton rope did it but she was bare foot. "It's alright," he told her, "we'll be on the beach and the sand will feel fine." She stood on the veranda while he went out to get Flea. He thought that maybe her black would run through the water but if she wouldn't he'd put her up on Flea. He helped her up on the black and mounting rode toward the warehouse away from the Dons adobe. Down the road on to the beach and he let Flea trot along the beach through the first shallow wave surge after the wave broke on the beach. The black like Fresa would have nothing to do with the salty water. Stopping he helped her over on to Flea then told her, "take the reins in your left hand and hang on to his mane with your right." "Do you think I'll need to?" she asked. "You'd better try it that way first," he said smiling. Swinging up on to the mare he coaxed her forward into a gallop then watched as Flea galloped by and not slowing when came to the water. The water flying up and he hoped that she'd be able to hold on for the wet ride. Even with Flea galloping through the water the mare slowed by the dry sand fell way behind.

Don Francisco had gone up to his second story room to look out on the bay and the ocean and from there he could view the beach. Even from this distance he knew the horse that was galloping through the water along the beach was the Flea. But this time the rider wasn't Louis the long hair flying behind that rider belonged to someone else. His telescope told him who it was and he called his wife. Margarita didn't know why he could possibly want her up in his sanctuary but she climbed the stairs. As she sat down he said, "look out on the beach, you see the two rider?" he asked. Then handing her his telescope and told her to look at the rider on the light colored horse. It took her a few seconds to bring what she wanted to look at into her view. "Oh my," she exclaimed, "It's my Rosalie." "Keep watching," the Don told his wife. She watched as Rosalie rode the horse she was on along the beach her hair flying and the spray of water around her when they sped through he shallow water. "Your daughter," the Don said. "She's yours now my husband," she said, as she lowered the glass. "I'm afraid that responsibility will soon fall on someone else's shoulders my dear," Don Francisco answered. "Do you like him Francisco?" Margarita asked. "I do," he answered, "he'll be good for her. He's not a rich man Margarita, by no means, but he'll take care of her and he's one that can protect her. And that's something that's needed here now."

She was flush from the thrill of the ride and wet when Louis rode to her side. "It's so much fun," she told him, "He just seems to fly Louis." They moved on at a walk to the edge of the dunes, dismounted and sat holding each other. "Did Rose ever ride Flea Louis," she asked. "No" he answered, "other then myself you're the only who's ever ridden him." "Thank you Louis," she told him," I know he means a lot to you." "So do you Rosalie," he told her. They sat close together for a while letting the horses rest.

Flea only ground reined stepping closer to Louis lipped his hair first then his arm. "He cares for Louis," Rosalie said. "I think that's a sign of affection, but I'm not sure," Louis answered. "It maybe and I'd like to think it was but he might be just smelling for the sugar that he knows I have some times." "He looks so sleepy and relaxed until runs," she said, "he's a strange horse you have Louis." "I know," he answered, "an odd color but inside that flea bit hide some place there has to be a big heart that lets him run. He seems to love to run and I knew he could, the first I saw him running ahead of his herd of wild ones."

Riding back she let Flea pick his own pace and he ran again along the wet sand and never breaking stride when he sped through the shallow water. She waited at the bottom of the road that led up to the warehouse. The mare was blowing when Louis reached them having had to labor hard running through the dry sand. The Flea and his rider soaking wet but cooled by the water spray still seemed fresh.

"Now what do I do?" Rosalie asked, "I'm soaking wet from the salt spray, I need a bath and I'm wearing your clothes?" I'll heat the water when we get to my place and even wash your back if you like," Louis told her. "Some day," she answered, "but I'd better go home even though it's going to take some explaining how I got this way." Stopping to pick up her clothes, then they rode to the Dons adobe.

The Don and Rosalie mother both standing on the veranda when they rode up. Rosalie mother rather stern faced but the Don with a smile walked out to help Rosalie down. Rosalie smiled back over her shoulder at Louis as she walked into the house. The Don stood by Flea patting his neck and Louis knew the Don admired the horse because he could run.

"Seen you on the beach and Rosalie riding him," the Don said. And Louis knew that the Don's second story room must give him a pretty fair view of the beach. "I let she ride," Louis told him, "I thought she would enjoy the way he runs. Rosalie's important to me Don Francisco and with your permission I like to ask for her hand." "I've been waiting for you to ask Louis and I'm happy for you." "That's a yes then?" Louis asked. "It's a yes, congratulation Louis," the Don told him, "now go take care of the horses like I know you want to. I must tell her mother there's things she'll want to do now."

He took the mare to his place and gave her and Flea a scoop of grain they'd more then earned it this day for him he felt. Both of them by the well he drew water and washed them. Brushed and dried he turned them out into the pasture with the other horses.

Hot water and a bath and he thought about the next day and knew he should go hunting. Tio said that they needed meat and the day after tomorrow was Juan's wedding so tomorrow he knew he'd have to go. Dressed he went out and looked toward where Juan and the others were working. They were still working and he thought Juan sure wants to get it finished but that was fine with him. Into the dining room he sat down at the table and figured he'd wait. He could hear Tio working in the kitchen but he waited. Tio would come out soon enough or Juan and the others would come in, in a while. "Didn't hear you come in Mano." Tio said, "are you ready to eat?" "Anytime," Louis answered, "but I'm not in a hurry I can wait for the others. I figured I'd go hunting in the morning Tio." "Bring it home early Mano were not going to have much time to get it cut up for drying. Juan's new mother in law will take over the whole place Sunday afternoon," Tio told him.

"I guess I'd better go see how Rosalie's mother took my asking to marry her daughter," Louis said to himself. Juan and the others came in and Juan looking at Louis asked, "why so serious Mano?" "I was just wondering how Rosalie's mother is feeling about now, I asked Don Francisco for permission to marry Rosalie?" "You don't have to worry Mano," Tio told him, "her mother will have a wedding to plan so she'll be happy." He stayed at the table talking to Tio, every one else relaxing in the bunkroom. It was past mid afternoon before he decided he'd better go to the Don's and ask Rosalie about going hunting in the morning. He saw the Don and Rosalie's Mother sitting on the veranda as he approached. Well this is it he thought as he drew close. The Don greeted him with a nod and his name. He looked at the senora, and she smiled. He let out the breath he'd been holding as she said, "I'll go tell Rosalie you're here," and went inside. He looked back at the Don and the Don asked, "you feel better now Louis?" "Yes sir," Louis answered, "I wasn't sure it was going to be alright."

She was there now, smiling as she walked toward him. Taking his hand they walked away together, Louis glancing back once, seeing smiles now on both of the faces looking after them from the veranda. He felt better now, the tension gone and he could breath easier.

"Don Francisco saw us riding on the beach Louis, she said, and so did my mother when he called her to come up there with him. Louis, she told me that she at one time loved to ride too but never had the chance to ride like she saw me." "I didn't know for a while," Louis said, "and I was afraid she might say no." "Every thing is fine Louis," she answered.

"Then you can go hunting with me in the morning?" "I don't see why not but what can I wear I don't have any hunting clothes," she said. "The peon clothes will do just fine and we'll be dressed alike that way." he told her. "And what do I wear for shoes," she questioned.

"Wear your riding boots we're not ridding bare back and you'll only have to walk a short distance. I'll take care of most of the walking that's going to be needed but wear a hat we'll be doing some sitting and not always in the shade," he told her.

At the well they stopped, while he pulled up enough buckets of water to fill the trough. And while she sat he said she could tell him what her plans were concerning their wedding. "But there weren't any real plans yet," she told him. "Good," he told her," then lets get married one week from this coming Sunday." "And where will we stay," she asked, "in the bunk house, did you forget you told Juan he could stay in your place until he had his built." "Juan should have his adobe finished in just a few more days," Louis said, but she sensed there was a little bit doubt in his voice. Flea and Fresa there coming to see if there might be a treat for them but a little ear scratching and neck patting is all they'd get this time. Rosalie saying she thought they should go now and see just how close, Juan and the others were to finishing.

They walked slowly through the garden holding hands toward where Juan and the others were working. Juan stopped working to show what they'd accomplished and the little adobe was close to being finished. "Would it be ready by Sunday?" Louis asked. "No," Juan told him, "there's some finishing to be done and some furniture to build but by Wednesday we'll be able to move in."

They talked about their wedding now as they walked back, Louis saying he hoped that their wedding wouldn't be to elaborate. That she was marrying a peon farmer but he was one that loved her. "Do you feel your less then other men Louis because of what you choose to do?" she asked. "No," he answered, "we all came here the same way and when we leave we'll all turn into the same dust. I feel I'm equal to any man Rosalie, maybe not in stature, weight or amount of his riches. I'll respect him for who he is but I'll never bow down to any man.

"Don Francisco Louis what are your feelings concerning him," she asked. "Rosalie, just like Pablo and Pepe Luna, Tio, Juan and Anselmo I owe the Don a lot. He was the one who showed me that I wasn't the only one who cared for horses especially one that could run. More then that he would show me how gallant and generous a man could be even though his horse had lost a race and he lost a bet. I hope that if the time ever comes I'll be able to stand up and be as much a man as he is."

They walked on in silence and Louis wondered if he'd said something wrong but when he looked at Rosalie she was smiling. On the veranda at the Dons adobe she told him that she wanted to wear a white wedding gown. "Isn't it going to take a while to sew a wedding gown for you?" Louis asked. "The gowns already made Louis," she told him, "it was my mothers and it fits me." "Then we'd better see the Padre," Louis said, "maybe after we get back from hunting. I'll have the horses ready by first light you can ride Fresa Rosalie." "Not my black mare?" she asked. "No not this time I doubt that she's ever packed and she might not like the smell of blood." "Lets not take a chance this time, I'll work with her later," he told her. "We'll have breakfast for you here in the morning Louis," she said.

The household was up when he tied the horses at the rear of Don Francisco's adobe. The Don greeted him as he walked across the veranda approaching the rear door. "You're on time as usual Louis." "Always if it's at all possible," Louis answered. "An admirable trait that more men should follow," the Don told him, "but sadly neglected by many to day." Rosalie's mother had breakfast ready and after gave him a flour sack that she told him had a little something for them to eat later. "Now go and have a good time," she told him. "Thank you and don't worry I'll take of Rosalie," he told her.

The Don and Margarita watched as he tied their lunch be hind his saddle then helped Rosalie mount Fresa. He mounted and turning waved as they rode off toward the sun that was already rising. East toward the rear of the fenced properties and into the oak and brush where he knew there was good hunting. They rode side by side until they came to the narrow game trails. Riding quietly with out talking for a half hour before he stopped at a small meadow. Here he put their horses on pickets and told her that they'd have that short walk from here.

He carried his rifle and the other things they'd need and led the way on a narrow game trail through brush. An easy walk to the shoulder of a low hill, here in the shade of a large oak he told her they'd wait. The sacks he brought to carry the meat in he put down for them to sit on. From here they'd watch the little pond below where he told her the deer would come for water during the heat of the day.

They sat close and quiet as the sun moved higher in the sky and it got warmer. It was rather hot now even though they were in the shade but he continued their watch. Near noon they ate and drank water from the canteen he brought, that had become rather tepid during their wait. Finished eating and she was nodding off her head against his shoulder as he watched. It was a while before he put down his telescope and tapped her nose gently with his finger. Then put his finger to his lips meaning for her to be quiet and pointed slowly toward the pond where two doe's were drinking. Finished the two doe's moved off taking a different trail away from the pond. Louis again put his finger to his lips and pointed to the brush where he'd first seen the doe's appear. A few seconds later and a buck stepped slowly and cautiously out moving toward the water.

When the buck lowered his head to drink Louis slowly brought his rifle to bear and a few second later the sound of the rifles report broke the quiet. The sound still resounding in their ears the acrid odor of gun smoke still in the air as he lowered the rifle. The buck down then with just a few kicks of his legs and it was over. "I can't believe it," Rosalie said, "it's all over, it happened so quickly once they came to the water." "It's really only just started" Louis said, "now the work begins."

He kept an eye on the buck as he reloaded his rifle making sure he didn't move then picked up their things and started down toward the buck. "Come on Rosalie," he said, "smiling we've got work to do." At the buck he laid the things down he carried and turning the buck so his head was up hill. The distance he had to shoot wasn't long and he'd elected to shoot it in the head. A cleaner kill that saved more of the meat and an easier animal to work on.

He was skinning the animal out on it's own hide when he looked up the first time. She was grimacing and he smiled saying, "you'll get used to it in time. It's what has to be done if you want to put meat on the table." "I know" she answered, "it's just that I've never seen it done before, except to a few chickens." "It's about the same," he said," only on a larger scale. Just think what it would be like if this were a steer." He continued working and did notice that she turned her head when he was removing the deer's entrails but he didn't let her see the smile on his face. Quickly he cut the animal into pieces for packing removing as many of the large bones as he could. Pieces of meat hung from bushes he told her they'd bleed out better there and that she could help by shooing away the flies and meat eating hornets. Boning out everything but the ribs and the neck took a little time. Done he packed the meat in the bags rolled up the hide and took the head and what was left out into the brush away from the pond. What was left he knew would soon be cleaned up by the bugs and birds.

Washing with water from the pond he was smiling when he came back near her and said, "now that wasn't bad was it?" "Not for me," she answered, "but I have to admit that I was a little shocked at first. Then I realized that it was something that's being done every day to animals and the way we came by the meat we eat. I'll try to help you next time Louis, I promise. I've just never seen anything like this before." "I under stand," he said. "Now we've got to go and get the horses." "But what about the meat?" she asked. "It will be alright until we get back with the horses. We have only a bear or man to worry about and I don't think there's many of them around here right now, the other animals will stay away because of our scent still being here."

Reaching the horses he pulled the pin that held Fresa and help her mount. He stood looking seriously at the beautiful girl that he was going to marry. "Is there something wrong Louis?" she asked, the smile that was on her face had disappeared and was now replaced with a frown. "It's something that just came to me and now it bothering me," he told her. "I don't understand Louis have I done something wrong, what is it that's so important?" "It's you my love," he said, stepping to her, "you've led a sheltered and cultured life and now I've asked you the step into a whole different life. I'm a boy off a farm who sometimes works with peons and you'll be the wife of a farmer." "I know where I'm going Louis and much about you, she talked to me and told me about you and what she couldn't tell me I've leaned from Francisco. I know there are things I don't know but I do know I want to marry you, be patient with me and I'll learn." He pulled her down off Fresa and held her and said, "I've got to learn too," kissing her and told her he loved her. She returned his kiss then pulled back and said, "you'd better help me up we've a lot of work to do." He helped her up and pulled Fleas picket. Swinging up he told her to go ahead and lead the way.

Reaching the deer the horses snorted at the smell of blood. He told her to stay mounted that he'd take care of tying on the meat and hide. "You're not going to bring the horns Louis?" she asked. "I'll pick them up when I'm out here again after the bugs have done their work," he told her smiling. Finished he swung up onto the saddle and said, "Just let her have her head Rosalie, she knows the way home." The way back easy the horses knowing their way had to be held back from breaking into a trot. Passed the Dons they rode to the rear of the bunkhouse where Tio was standing on the veranda. Smiling seeing the bags of meat tied behind Rosalie's saddles and he was they're untying the sacks before Louis could dismount.

The sacks of meat inside Tio asked Louis if he could ride over and tell Juan and the others to come in and clean up. That he'd have an early supper on the table there was meat that had to be cut and hung up for drying. Tomorrows Juan's wedding and his mother in law's going want the kitchen for herself."

Louis was there after taking care of the horses before Juan and the others got there. At the table he saw Rosalie with one of Tio large and very sharp knives slicing the venison. Shaking his head he didn't know what to say. Tio seeing him said, "she's doing fine but I'm cooking and she can't do it by herself, you and the others had better get busy." Unsheathing his knife Louis went to work.

When Tio brought the finely ground chili he told Rosalie, "don't you rub any of the chili on the meat let the men do it their hands are tougher. The chili will make your hands burn."

Juan and the others got there and they went right to work but only got to work a short time when Tio told then that the fried liver, heart and onions were ready. "Eat now he told them while the food is still hot, you can get right back to work after you eat." Finished eating they were back working when the Don came looking for Rosalie. Surprised when he saw her with the knife in her hand slicing the raw meat into strips for drying. Stepping closer to the table he was standing next to Tio. "What do you think Don Francisco, isn't our pretty young lady doing a fine job?" Tio asked. "She surely is," Don Francisco said," our young people do need to know how to do these things that are necessary in this life. Then when the day comes that they inherit this land they'll know what they need to do to take care of it. Now Rosalie it's time for you to go and get cleaned up. There's the wedding tomorrow and you know how mother gets when there's a wedding." Tio brought her a pan of water and a towel and told her, "you'd better wash up a little we don't want your mother to be shocked at the sight of you. There's smudges of blood on your face and even in your hair."

While Rosalie washed Tio packaged some meat and giving it to the Don said, "a hearty breakfast for you senor." Rosalie dried her face and hands. The Don thanked Tio and as they walked toward the door Louis stopping his work and got up to walk Rosalie home.

Walking ahead the Don left the young couple behind knowing he would only be in the way. He was sure that he couldn't add anything to what they were interested in talking about. At his adobe Don Francisco went inside and closed the door behind him leaving the young to say they're good night in private.

When Louis got back there was still some work to be done, Tio wanting everything to be ready for Juan's future mother in law. So she'd be able to do what she needed to do to get ready for her daughters reception.

It was late before Louis was able to bathe and get to bed. He knew there was a lot for him to do in the morning, wanting to leave his adobe clean and orderly for Juan and his bride.

CHAPTER IX

Early in the morning Louis dressed and went out to take care of filling the horse trough. Then took Flea and Rosalie's black mare out and gave them a scoop of grain while he groomed them. He'd have them saddled and ready before noon when he knew they had to at the church. Finished the grooming he thought it would be a nice day for a ride on the beach but instead he headed for his room. The first he'd carry over to the bunkhouse was the wooden saddle rack he'd made. That done he stopped long enough to have breakfast and talk to Tio. Then carry over his other saddle and tack, arms and personal items. Last his bedroll and clothes.

A few minutes with Tio while water was warming then another quick bath before he dressed for the wedding. After buckling on both his pistols he picked the last few things that were left. Looked around and satisfied that things were ready for Juan and his bride he headed for the bunkhouse.

Tio seeing him dressed in his suit smiled until his eyes fell to his waist and the two pistols and his smile turned into a frown. "Do you feel you still need them Mano?" he asked. "I do Tio," he answered, "but I'll put them in my saddle bags before I leave. I'd feel better if I had them on but I know I can't wear them into the church. I'll be all right having them close by. It's been a while I know Tio but the trouble hasn't really ended even though the war is over. There's still the gold and the rumor that the South still has some ambitious ones who would like to start it all over again."

Flea and the mare outside the bunkhouse he saddled them and rolling up both pistol belts put them in his saddlebags. Time now to go to the Dons and see if Rosalie is ready to ride to the church. Leading Flea and the mare he walked over and was tying Flea's reins when the Don walked out on to the veranda. Surprised at first when he saw the Don wasn't dressed in something other then black. Don Francisco now dressed in grey a color that would look still look good when that rode his black stallion. Though maybe not quite as good as his black suits, Louis thought.

He was smiling when the Don asked him what he thought about his new look? He told the Don that yes, he not only felt that he looked good but said he thought it made him look younger too. "I don't know if I want Margarita to know you said that, or not," the Don told him, smiling.

Louis knew the Don had worn his mourners black for a long time after loosing his first wife. It was time for a change plus Don Francisco had remarried. Now he himself was wearing black but not for a wife but someone he thought was of no less importance. When Rosalie came out on the veranda she too was dress in black and in mourning for that same person. It was Rosalie's aunt but what Rose had been to him was everything that he had lost before all over again he felt. But she had known what he needed and that she would never be able to ever fill his life completely. But she cared enough to help bring someone who she felt would be what she couldn't be to him.

He wondered now how long he should wear black, something he or any else had done for his Mother. Rose had worn black and he knew his mother would have had his father passed before her. Knowing Rose and Don Francisco had both been wearing black for years and that it was the custom was one thing. Why and for how long he had no idea and was reluctant to ask knowing it was sure to profess his lack of knowledge about these things.

Rosalie stepping out on to the veranda and saw him with Don Francisco in his new grey suit. "He doe's look nice doesn't he Louis, you can dress that way when the year of mourning has passed." And Louis realized he had his answer to his question without having to make that inquiry. And he smiled, wondering if this might possibly be a part of what the Bruja had told him she would do for him.

He was looking at her as they rode toward the church, when he said to her, "we have to talk to the Padre today." "Oh we will," she answered, "I've been waiting for you to tell me that." They found room near the end of the rail where they tied their horses. Then walked together up to the to the front of the church and stood together watching the people coming. Some of the people had remained after the mass but there was many still coming there. Don Francisco and Donna Margarita came in the coach and Tio brought Juan in the donkey cart.

Juan coming up to Louis handed him a white ribbon with the ring tied to it. "When the Padre asks for the ring you'll be able to find it Mano." "Doe's he need the ribbon too?" Louis asked. "No Mano that's so you won't loose it," Juan told him.

Don Francisco taking Juan off to the side told him that after the ceremony to go to his coach. 'They'll take you home," he told him, "then they'll come back after the Senora and I." Juan really happy by the offer from the Don thanked him and told him that he wouldn't tell anyone until he led his bride to the coach. "It will be a nice surprise for my Anna, Don Francisco, gracias senor." After entering the church Juan and Louis were told where to stand, as the others were being be seated.

When Anna came walking slowly down the aisle on her fathers arm Louis was surprised how small Juan's bride was. He had seen her from a distance but never close. Though small stature she was as beautiful as any Spanish Angle could be. Standing by Juan she came only slightly above his shoulder and he smiled down at her a very happy groom right now.

The ceremony over Juan and his bride led the way out of the church. The Padre followed but stopped on the portico. Don Francisco, senora Margarita, Rosalie and Louis standing by the Padre watching as well wishers saw Juan and his bride to the coach.

The three riders each leading another saddle horse did draw some peoples attention. And Louis moved to get a better look. Then walked back asked if anyone had seen any of Pablo Luna's family. With no affirmative answer from anyone he asked Don Francisco to please see Rosalie home. "What is it Louis?" the Don asked, "you look, worried." "I personally know one of those men, he was on the same ship that brought me to California Don Francisco." "I'm pretty sure he and those other two men were the one's who tried to get the guns from Pablo Luna's warehouse. Those three horses they were trailing Don Francisco were Pablo Luna's." "Are you sure, Louis?" he asked. "Positive," Louis answered. "They might have recognized you," the Don said. "I doubt it," Louis answered, "Cadet Weber would be the only one and he'd look for me in mess mans clothes, much like a peon wears."

"Do you really think they might still seek out Pablo and those guns," Don Francisco asked. Its been so long now and the war it self has been over for a while." "Those were Pablo's horses, Don Francisco and I've heard a few men that said the South will rise again. Right now though my only concern is Pablo and his family." "You go then Louis I'll see that Rosalie gets home safely." He asked the Padre to excuse him that Don Francisco would explain to him. Kissed Rosalie on the cheek whispered I love and ran to the horses. Flea seeming to feel the urgency broke into a gallop as soon as he was in the saddle. The distance to the store was short he pulled Flea up and simply dropped reins knowing he'd stay ground reined for as long as he be. Buckling on his thirty-six—caliber pistol, before approaching the door and knocking. With no answer he quickly remounted and rode around to the rear of store and the back door where he knocked again but had no better luck there. Across the to Miguel's adobe and knocked several times and called out, "It's Louis Hand, Miguel and I'm alone you can open the door." Finely he heard someone on the other side. Miguel opened the door and Louis saw the bloody bandage around Miguel's head.

Asking what happened he was told that it was the same two men who had ordered the guns years before but that there was another man who he'd never seen before. 'They wanted the guns Louis," Miguel told him, "I told it had been to long and the guns were gone. Angry the one with the limp struck me with his pistol and said they'd take what they needed as part payment for the loss of the arms but that they wanted to talk to my father."

"They took what they wanted even the money my father didn't take home with him. Then took me to the house and told me to stay there, that if they saw me outside they'd come back and kill me, my wife and the children."

"I'd better go and check on your father and the rest of your family Miguel," Louis told him. "Would you Louis?" Miguel questioned, "I've been worried but it could be dangerous for you." "I think there're already on the road leaving here," Louis said, ran to Flea, mounted and wave as Flea galloped out of the yard toward Pablo's adobe. At Pablo's he had to rap hard on the door and announce who he was a few times, before he heard some one lift the bar inside and open the door. Pablo opening the heavy door said, "thank the good Lord that it's you Louis for a while I thought I was going to have to use the shot gun to protect us in this house." "Then every one's alright?" Louis asked. "Safe and sound," Pablo answered, but they took the horses." "That's why they using stock saddles instead of pack saddles," Louis said. "Then you saw them Louis?" Pablo asked. "Yes, I saw them Pablo," Louis told him, "they rode past when were standing on the Portico of the Church, after Juan's wedding." "Maria and the girls wanted so much to go to Juan's wedding," Pablo said, "but when I saw those men coming Louis, I made them go back inside and I bared the windows and the doors. Just seeing them after what they tried to do at the warehouse I knew it could mean trouble for me and my family."

"You did right Pablo," Louis told him, "Miguel felt some of their anger." "Did they hurt Miguel Louis?" Pablo asked. "He'll be just fine, just a headache for a day or two," Louis answered. "I'll try to get your horses back Pablo but I can't promise anything." "Let them go Louis, it not worth it," Pablo told him, "All of those things can be replaced." "If they get away with it this time Pablo, what's to stop from coming back again when ever they want something?" "Then I'll go with you Louis." "No Pablo," "your family needs you here, I need someone like Juan but I can't ask him right now."

As he headed toward Flea Maria, Juana, Barbara and Pepe came out on to the veranda. "I'd like to stay a bit longer but the longer I linger the longer I'll have to ride to catch them," he said. "I need a horse," he heard Pepe holler, as he was mounting. Turning in the saddle he hollered back, "pack your gear

Pepe I'll send someone with a horse for you." He held Flea to an easy lope wanting to keep him as fresh and strong as possible, just incase he'd need Flea's speed and endurance later. Riding right to where he kept the grain he gave him a full scoop, then went to bring in Fresa.

Chapter X

Rosalie, Don Francisco, and Tio were there when he went in to get his things. The Don asked why he was readying the mare to ride? "Pepe Luna needs a horse the three those men were leading were all the horses that the Luna's had." "Then your riding after them Louis?" the Don asked. "They took what they wanted from the store including what cash was there. One of them also slapped Miguel along side the head with his pistol. Then they threatened to kill him, his wife and his children if he didn't do what they told him to do. I can't let them get away with this Don Francisco, if I do they'll be free to come back and do what ever they want anytime."

"There's some thing else, I'm sure they know who it was at the warehouse that night that I hit Cadet Webbers arm with the axe handle and the put the pistol ball in his cohorts leg. The Cadet can identify me and I'm sure they'd both like to exact some kind of payment for what I did. So you see I have a stake in this, I want to able to feel safe and not have to look back over shoulder all the time." "Then it's just you and Pepe?" the Don asked. "I'd like Juan to go," Louis said, "but there's no way that he could leave now but I have to." He was looking at Rosalie when they heard Tio say, "I'll ride with you Mano, but I'll need a horse."

"I'll saddle one of the mares for you Tio," Louis told him but when Tio started to go inside to get his things Juan told him, "I can't go I know but my horse can Tio." Out to saddle his horse before Louis had a chance to even start saddling a mare when Juan told him that he'd saddle his horse for Tio. "You are going to take him, Mano aren't you? "Juan asked. "There's no way I could deny him Juan," Louis answered, "as difficult as he might fine it I know he'll carry his end."

They walked together leading the horses, the reception going on even though Juan had left for that few minutes. Tio had his things packed and said he was ready. Louis told him to take Fresa to Pepe while he got his things ready.

The gaiety of the reception diminished somewhat when Louis walked through the party area carrying his things, a rifle slung across his back and his carbine bringing particular interest from those there. Juan told him to go ahead, that he'd explain to those were there what had happened and why you, Tio and Pepe had to leave.

Anna and her mother with Rosalie and Margarita prepared food for them that they could take. Other then that they would only take some hard biscuits, jerked venison and coffee. Rosalie had a plate of food that he could eat after he'd packed his things on Flea. She sat with him as he took these few minutes to eat waiting for Tio to return with Pepe. He took her hand as they walked out on to the veranda. Tio and Pepe already in sight coming by Juan's nearly finished adobe. He kissed her for a long minute before mounting and she stood by his left stirrup her hand on his leg. "I'm sorry," he told her, "but this is something that has to be taken care of."

Juan coming out with his carbine, pistol belt and possibles bag. The carbine into the boot on the saddle, the pistol belt and possibles bag he hung over the saddle horn. "The pistols handier then your shot gun old man if you keep it on your hip," he told Tio. "I can't shoot good with a pistol Juan, you know that," Tio said. "Just point it and keep pulling the trigger," Juan told him, "if nothing else you can scare the devil out of them." "But with the shot gun I don't miss," Tio told him.

Rosalie now almost in tears knowing what they were leaving to go and do but she did keep from crying. Tio seeing her, said, "Don't worry senorita I'll stay close to him, we will be fine you will see."

Via Con Dios and they were on they're way, Louis setting the pace at a fast walk. Moving at this speed he knew they'd close the distance between them quickly. They'd be covering ground twice as fast as those men trailing other horses. This was the way he planed to over take them, not this day but maybe late tomorrow. For sure on the third day if they didn't loose the trail they'd have them in sight.

Tio would stop the few travelers they met asking about the men they were following. Most had seen the three gringos that stood out from other travelers. All of them standing out, wearing some remnants of military clothing and one having a sword strapped to his rifle scabbard. They'd spend they're first night on a grassy slope where the horses could graze on the ample grass there after being fed the grain Louis brought. They ate the food from the reception that had been packed for them and slept with out a campfire that first night.

Rising early they saddled their horses and would have to ride for over an hour before coming to a cantina that Tio knew about. At the cantina Tio asked about the men and was told that the men had stopped there. That they had camped just down the road and out of the village a little ways, and had ridden out only about an hour earlier. They ate quickly and Tio ordered some other things that they packed for him, and they were back on the trail. They followed a wagon trail that paralleled a small river called the Pajaro and continued at that fast pace. Reaching the Junction with the El Camino Real they found that any sign there left by those men already obliterated by other travelers. They followed the most obvious route toward the mission San Juan Bautista and the pass that led to the Sierras and the mines in gold country. With in an hour they knew that they had gone in the wrong direction. Learned when Tio questioned some men with a pack train coming on the road toward them. Reversing their direction Louis led them at a lope hoping they could some how make up the miles they'd lost.

Back on the El Camino Tio questioned everyone the met but with no luck until he talked to an old man leading a single burro. As Tio was talking Louis heard the old man say the words aqua caliente and he knew it meant hot water and now thought that they were on the wrong trail again. Remembering a place called Los Banos when they were on the way with the pack animals to Pepe's sister and brother in law's store at the foothills of the sierras. Half sick now figuring they would now have a real hard time trying to catch them. It could mean days of trying to straighten things out and get back trail again. Pepe rode up closer to Louis and seeing the look on his face, asked, "what is it Louis, what's wrong?" "From what I've heard so far," Louis answered, "we might have lost the trail again." "I sure hope not." Pepe said. "I heard the old man say something about hot water Pepe, what do you think that might mean?" Louis asked. "I've heard about some hot springs around here, but I don't know where they could be," Pepe told him. And they sat in silence waiting for Tio to finish his conversation with the old man.

Their conversion continued for some time and finally the old man stood up from where he was sitting. Tio handed him some thing and the old man waved toward Louis and Pepe. Then walked off leading his burro. Tio coming back toward them a smile on his face and that was encouraging.

"Was he the first one you gave something to Tio?" Pepe asked. Tio's smile broadened as he said, "It was, but what he told me was well worth it. It did take a while but it was what he wanted to know about you two." "Us?" Pepe asked. "Not so much you Pepe," Tio said, "but he wondered about the gringo dressed like a peon, who carries so many more guns then he has hands to use them. But it's done and we are close behind those men. He saw them he told me this morning that they were on the trail to the hot springs about a mile or so North of here." Tio mounted and they traveled at a trot passing the old man, they waved and kept going. They found the trail easily and checking found the telltale prints of the six horses that had moved up that trail not to long before. At a side trail a mile or so ahead Tio checked and found only the tracks of a single burro. "He told me about this trail to his camp," Tio said, "and his burro tracks are here, the hot springs are still a ways ahead on the trail were on." On up along the dry wash trail for thirty minutes then the smell of smoke. Louis dismounting told Tio to lag behind him a ways while he scouted ahead.

Only a few hundred yards and he could see a small encampment. No sign of the three men or the horses only a few Mexicans. He stopped and motioned for Tio and Pepe to come up to where he was. Then let Tio go ahead and talk to the people and see what he could find out while he and Pepe waited with the horses. Returning Tio pointed to a trail that lead out of the camp area toward the higher country to the northeast. Walking to the trail they checked the sets of tracks that led away from the springs now the tracks were so obvious that almost anyone would be able to follow them.

Again Louis led them out at a fairly fast walk until the came to a stream. Here he stopped so the horses could drink and rest for a few minutes. The trail from here started up a fairly steep rise up toward the next ridge. A more difficult trail for their horses that already had a hard day. They knew nothing about this country only what the old man had told Tio. After refreshing themselves in the stream they ate their meal cold and without the benefit of a fire for coffee. Talking about what they'd do next, they decided that they'd climb the ridge before dark. Then stay where they could look over the country ahead and get an idea of what they were in for. The route they took was away from the trail they were following. Now they followed a trail that was no more then well used game trail that Pepe brushed off after they'd passed.

Below the top they stopped on a grassy slope where they'd picket the horses. A dry camp and without a fire again knowing that any smoke or the light could alert some one about they're presents. Their horses and camp set for the night and Louis said he was going to take his telescope and take a walk up to the top of the ridge. "Maybe I can spot some thing, if nothing else I'll get a look at what's ahead." "Three of us looking will be able to see more," Tio said, and they walked together going to the ridge. Finding a good spot to view from, they sat down and could relax as they looked, talked and contemplated what they would do next.

From here they were looking at a country of rolling broken hills with side canyons, dry washes, oaks, pines and brush patches. "It looks like a place an army of men could hide," Pepe said. "If they moved or did the other things a man has to do survive only at night like some animals, yes," Louis said, "but they can't see well at night. And some thing else, they don't like to eat all their food raw so they'll build a fire to cook by. They've got to be there some place, they just couldn't have ridden all the way through here."

Tio said he thought he saw a wisp of smoke come up out of the trees. Like someone had added more wood to their fire and it smoked a little you know the way, like it always doe's. He pointed out the spot that was some distance off the main trail and up a side canyon. Using his telescope Louis studied the canyon then handing it to Tio said, "you try maybe you can see something I've missed." After some minutes of looking Tio said, that he could see nothing either.

They sat and continued to look and studying the terrain as the sun disappeared into the west and the shadows lengthened. The grassy areas paled to a yellow glow as the brush and trees darkened, affording a different way of looking for what could be out there. They continued their watch as the landscape they were looking into darkened into ghostly parks, dark gray hills and black canyons.

Louis heard Tio say," Mano, look at the trees in that canyon, I think there's something you can see there now." It took him only a few seconds to locate the trees and see the flicker of light the shown through their canopy. "There's a camp fire down there're Tio," he said, "and I'd be willing to bet that it's Webber and his two friends." "The old man told me they could have a camp some where's back here," Tio said, "he said that he saw those men a lot when he hunted in the hills above here."

"Now what?" Pepe asked, "I guess we've found them, now it's what to do next." "I'll go and look around tonight," Louis told them. "In those white clothes you wear Mano and in a place strange to you, you'd better think about it," Tio told him. "Better we sleep on it tonight and talk in the morning, then plan what we have to do."

Before the sun came up over the crest of the hills to the east Louis studied the lay of the land in the first light. Looking for the best way to approach the area where he'd seen that flicker of light. They also needed a place where they could leave the horses, an out of way spot where there was feed and water for them. Then he could scout the country, find a place where he could look over the camp and see if he could find where they were the weakest and the most vulnerable.

Pepe and Tio came and told him that they had the horses saddled and were ready to move. He barely had time to point out the place he figured they would camp when the suns rays seemed to burst over the ridge to the east. Now directly in to their eyes and making it almost impossible to look into that country any longer. "Let's ride," Louis said, "we'll keep to the edges and find our camp site." They worked their way along just below the shoulder of the ridge using the animal trails, the least obvious route. After they'd left the trail Pepe dropped back and with a branch brushed out their horses hoof prints. They moved into a small rocky bottom canyon with pools of water, though not connected they were clear and cool evidently flowing through the gravel between pools. There was the water they needed now all they'd need was grass. That took them another fifteen minutes to find a trail up that rocky side canyon and there a small flat with grass The water near by and dry wood for a smokeless fire to heat water for coffee, the only thing they had that needed heating. It would be dried meat and hard biscuits for a few meals now.

The horses on pickets and their simply camp set, Louis said, "I'm going to take a walk. I want to look around and see what we're up against." "Remember your clothes Mano your still wearing white," Tio told him. "I'll smear a little mud on them from the clay bank I saw there in the creek bed," Louis said. He went down to the pool near the clay bank, took off his clothes and bathed then smeared mud on his clothes front and rear. Back to pick up his things up and Tio told him, "you smell clean Mano but you look dirty." "I am clean but dirty," he said as he picked up one of his pistol belts, his rifle, possibles bag and telescope. "Don't look for me until after dark," he told them, and walked across the creek bed and up toward higher ground.

When he figured he was high enough he picked a game trail to follow that he thought would take him above that grove trees. That flicker of light that he knew had to be from some ones camp fire. It had to be them but there was still that chance that it wasn't though. The sun was almost straight overhead now, it was hot walking and his clothes had dried on him. The warm rising air that he knew would carry his scent up and away from their horses. He slowed his walk not wanted to scare any wild animals or birds into flight that would be sure to alert anyone else in the area of his presents.

He was thinking how nice it was here with the sign of game, the grass to graze animals and ample water but he was on a mission. Moving off the trail so he wouldn't leave any sign on it but he'd follow, paralleling it walking in the forest litter where he'd leave little sign. The smell of smoke, something on the cooking fire and the odor of horses all brought up to him by the warm air currents. All these and he knew he was close. Now he needed to find a place where he could view what he knew was close by. Moving cautiously he slipped through the trees and brush looking for that place. It took a while to find that over look with a clear view of the camp below. A place in the shade, where the glass of his telescope couldn't reflect even the smallest flick of sunlight that could give warning to someone below.

First a quick look over the encampment then to individual things. There was a man at the cooking fire that he knew wasn't Cadet Webber and he thought that Webber and the other man might be inside the cabin. The cabin small but well built of logs, not for a temporary camp but a place set up to be used for a long time. A corral close by where there were three horses saddled and where that smell of manure came from. The corral was small and the manure deep, more then likely not having been cleaned in quite a while, yet more then likely never. Continuing his watch he again looked at the man at the fire and saw that he had a limp. Bolstering his belief that they had found what they had come looking for and this was Webbers camp. A few minutes and Webber himself appeared coming out of the cabin to the campfire, the man tending it and the kettle. Though he knew they were talking he couldn't tell what they were saying. Now he wondered where the third man of the trio was and the question was soon answered. When out of the corner of his eye he caught the movement of that third man. He was there walking on the same trail that he had walked parallel to when he came here.

He lay back slowly and slipped the loop off the hammer of his pistol. Though the brush and grass did offer good cover he realized that if the man continued along that trail he'd pass with in thirty foot of him. Apprehensive now and he slowly pulled his pistol from its holster holding it ready at the front for hip. It seemed a long while before he heard his footsteps then a glimpse of him through the brush as he came closer. He was so close when stopped that Louis felt he suspected something and was afraid he'd be able to hear his heart beating. He seemed then to stand for an eternity before moving farther along the trail. Then walked down the slope toward the men at the campfire below. Louis letting his breath out wondered how the man had missed hearing the way his heart had pounded.

For a minute he had contemplated taking him out but not shooting from ambush. Standing up he would have challenging him knowing the outcome was still assured. That though he knew would have put the other two either on their guard or on the run. Now he could only hope that he'd made the right decision.

Staying longer and watching though he wanted to leave, paid off. The man with the limp was riding off toward the stream. Only two of the horses saddled now in the corral and Louis wondered where the other three horses were. Somewhere out on grass and if he was right this man was going out to bring those horses in now. The three corralled horses would be put out grass and the horses that had grazed all night and day brought in watered, saddled and corralled. Horses always at the ready for a fight if attacked by a small force or a quick get away if they needed it. Now he would have to watch where that man went, he needed to know where they were grazing their horses. Watching with his telescope and time was passing but he couldn't leave he had to know. Across to the other side of the stream then up only a few hundred yards and the man and disappeared behind a screen of trees. There seemed to be a bench along that other slope but the trees on this side hid it well and Louis knew he would have to check it out which meant a longer route going back.

When he finely saw the rider reappear bringing in the horses he had wondered about. He readied his things and would first check the trail behind where he'd been, the one that he'd followed and the one their man walked on. He found more then one set of boot prints evidently this was that mans daily patrol route. He knew now he should have checked the trail before and that he had better be more watchful. These were men with probably some military training, evident by that mans using the same patrol pattern every day, just the way a garrisoned soldiers would.

Leaving he had to walk a ways up above the area before crossing to the other slope. Across through pines, oaks and grassy little meadows that he saw would be a good grazing for cattle or horses. Across the bottom where he filled his canteen in the small stream that flowed down toward that secreted cabin. Then up the other slope high enough that he'd be well above were the horses should be. The best trail with good cover for him was just off shoulder at the top of the ridge and the main game trail. Walking along the side of it he checked for boot or hoof prints but saw none. Deer sign though and a lot of it and he would have liked to linger and watch but that would have to be some other time. The sun already low in the west and out of his sight but the warm air was still moving up as he moved down watching for where they leaving the horses. Finding it, a long slightly sloping bench only a short distance above the stream and just few minutes from that cabin. Somebody had selected well when they picked this place he thought, there was plenty of feed and he watched as that man came back with the exchanged horses and put them out on pickets.

Now it was time to move out of here, he was still a ways above the easiest route but didn't want to chance using it. He wouldn't move down and along the steam where he knew where best trail would be, because it was also their escape route and he'd check it but a little farther down. It was in and out of the side washes for a ways now, rough and slow traveling for him. Finely feeling satisfied that it was safe he move down across the stream and along that trail. Checking it until there was to little light and he moved faster now only interested in making his way back to where they had camped.

Finding the rocky canyon in the dark then walking up wasn't easy but he finally saw the flicker of firelight around a bend and whistled to let them know that he was coming in. Tired, dirty and hungry he ate and told Tio and Pepe what he found. Then said he'd tell them more in the morning and laying down with his head on his bedroll he slept.

Waking to the aroma of Tio's coffee and it made him think of the adobes, and the place he now thought of as home. It was the same thing for breakfast that they had for supper but it could be worse I guess, he thought. They talked again and Louis drew on the bare ground by the fire where things were, the cabin the corral and where they were grazing the horses that weren't kept saddled.

Now it was how they would after go after them. The trail that they followed coming there was their most obvious escape route. It would require the least amount of walking and effort to get there and that would be where Tio could wait. Louis told him where he thought the best place for him was. Where boulders had slid down and narrowed the trail and that they would be good protection for him too. Pepe would go after their horses that were out on pickets and cover the route up through that pasture that they could use. That was the only other trail he told Pepe that he'd found they ridden horses out of the canyon on. "Keep to low side of that grass bench Pepe and you can use the trees there for cover all the way," Louis said. He told them about the man he saw patrolling the trail above the cabin and that would be the man that he'd go after first and try to lessen the odds. From there he told them he would go after the man who tended their cooking fire and the cabin. "When you hear the first shot from above the cabin where I'll be, that should be the start of it, and all I can say, is be ready," Louis told them.

They were quiet for only a few seconds then started to pick up what they would each take with them. Louis picked one pistol and his carbine wanting it's multiple shots. Tio of course his shotgun and Juan's pistol. Pepe his father's shotgun and a pistol and they were ready. Their fire out their horses had already been taken to water and their gear hung up in trees. They nodded to each other, Pepe and Tio moving down toward the trail below, Louis heading up to the higher ridge and the trail that would take him above the cabin again.

He'd go up a little higher today staying well above the trail the man walked along on his patrol. Not really knowing exactly when he'd take that walk. At his spot again he sat down and took out his telescope to check things again today. Everything seemed the same the man with the limp was by the fire and he figured that Webber would be in the cabin. Now all he would have to do was wait for the man on patrol to show. But things changed quickly when saw the man with the limp take one of the saddled horses out of the corral.

Tense now he sat watching and wished he had brought his long rifle then he could have taken that man now. There was no way he'd try the shot with the carbine it was just to long a shot for it. He could only sit and watch now and see what was going to happen. Leading the horse to the stream he let it drink then mounted and rode toward where Louis knew Pepe would be. He was helpless there no way he could help Pepe from here. Tense minutes went by before he heard the two reports the first a pistol then that boom he knew had to be Pepe's shot gun the rider was only carrying a pistol when Louis saw him leaving.

There were running footsteps on the trail behind him and he stood quickly bringing up his carbine. Their eyes met and he saw the man pulling his pistol as he dove for the closest tree. The pistol had hardly cleared it holster when it fired at the same time Louis's carbine did the same. The pistol ball plowed into the dirt as the carbine ball struck the man high to the right center of his chest and it was over.

Swinging around and back toward where he could look down at the cabin and Louis saw Webber as he mounted a horse by the corral and rode toward the trail down along the stream and Tio. Again Louis wished he had his long rifle that he'd left in camp. Now the seconds would tick off slowly as he hurried down toward the corral and the one horse that was left there. There were two distinct pistol shots that he heard from the direction of the trail were Tio was waiting, then booming sound of a shotgun. Now it was Tio that he was really concerned about as he hurried toward the corral.

Then he saw the rider that was coming in from across the creek and he thought that it might be all coming apart and brought up his carbine. But then quickly saw that it was Pepe and waved. Pepe waved back and Louis swinging up into the saddle rode quickly down the trail toward where Tio would be. He found him standing on the trail and Cadet Webber laying on his back beside it, his horse standing only a few yards away it's reins on the ground. And he breathed a sigh of relief realizing that for the most part it was over and Tio was all right. "I heard two pistol shots Tio," Louis said. "I know," Tio answered, "he threw a couple of shots at me Mano but from a running horse there wasn't much of a chance of him hitting anything." "Well I'm glad it's all over," Louis told him. "All of them Mano?" Tio asked. "Yes all of them Tio, this one was the last one and the only one that would have had the chance to make it but he took the wrong trail, "Louis answered.

Stepping down off the horse he stepped over to where he could look at Webber and their eyes met. "I should have known it would be you mess boy," Webber said, "and that was probable you guarding the guns that night too." "Yes, it was me Cadet," Louis answered. "It's not Cadet Webber any longer mess boy, it's Captain Webber now," he answered. He wanted to tell Webber what he thought about what he'd just told him but he knew it would have made little difference. He could see the three black holes in Webbers grey shirt—front. A crooked triangle with one hole below his rib cage, two above and with very little blood. There wasn't much they could do though it was heavy shot but they didn't go all the way through.

"Think you can ride?" Louis asked him. "Help me up on my horse and I'll show you I can," Webber answered him. His horse still had a rifle in the saddle scabbard and a saber strapped to it. "Tio can ride your horse and we'll put you up on the horse I rode out on," Louis told him. "Think I might try some thing mess boy?" Webber asked. "I could let you and put another hole in your hide but we've wasted enough lead and powder today already,"

Louis answered. With him up in the saddle Tio led off leading the horse that Webber was on and Louis walked behind them.

At the cabin they put Webber on the porch in the front of the cabin were he wanted to be, telling them that it was to hot to be inside. Tio rekindling the cooking fire and said he'd put together something from the stores he saw in the cabin. There's plenty there he told Pepe and mostly I'd say from it's your father store.

Pepe and Louis went after the other horses and the body of the man that was to heavy for Pepe to load on a horse by himself. Pepe telling Louis as they rode that he didn't want to fire at the man but that he refused to surrender and fired first. "I heard the report of both his pistol and your father's shotgun Pepe," Louis told him, "you gave him more of a chance then he would have given you. You don't have to feel guilty at all by what you were force to do." Bringing the in horses to water, they then picketed them around close to the cabin for the night on some small patches grass. Then up to where Louis had dispatched the third man and brought him down, then Pepe said that he would start digging.

Louis taking one of the horses from there and rode off after own their horses and gear. That would take him the better of two hours and Tio had their supper cooked when got back. He finished putting their things there where they would spend the night. Tio helped him put the four horses out on pickets so they could sit down together and eat.

Louis talked with Webber that evening and gave him small sips of water. Opening his shirt Louis checked his wounds and saw there was little blood but he knew there was sure to be some bleeding going on in the inside. "They'd build a litter the next day and take him out to a doctor," Louis told him. "If I don't make it," Webber said, "would you do something for me?" "I guess if I can," Louis answered. "Bury my sword with me please." "I think I could do that," Louis told him, "but I can't say I understand unless you're figuring on fighting on from some other place." The look on Webbers face told Louis that yes, he believed in what he and the others believed in and what they had tried to do. Now sure he had no more chance of being a part of it, but he still believed that the south would be one day be what it was before. That they wanted what the south ounce had and regardless what they had to do to return to the way of life they'd do it. In a way he had to feel sorry for Webber and his kind but they had cause him strife. He wasn't the only one who felt they were wrong in the way they were trying to do it. To cause pain and suffering to others the way they did, would help to defeat them in the end he was sure.

They finished what they had to do by firelight then went to their blankets. In the morning they found that Webber had passed away some time during the night. There would be more work to do for Pepe and Louis, making the grave Pepe had started digging a little wider.

Tio busy with the cooking and packing, there were the arms he found stashed in the cabin and the other things from the store. By noon the grave work was finished, Webbers sword buried with him. Louis with the poker from the stove in the cabin burned the Roman numeral III and REB in aboard and put it up at the head of the grave sight. A sprinkling of manure from the corral over the grave sight that should help to keep the varmint's at bay.

Now Louis had another concern he didn't have but a few days to get back home.

They had six horses to carry what they would haul back and no packsaddles, all stock saddles that would make it a little difficult. Tio had rolled the long arms that they'd found hidden under the bunks in blankets and canvas, long bundles that they could tie one on each of a saddle. There were some canvas bags and boxes that they utilized and soon had everything they'd take packed, including the stores metal cash box.

Louis led them out on a fast walk that Flea could do easily keep up for hours and the other horses all carrying fairly light loads should have no problem for these next couple days. Louis had three horses in tow, Tio had three behind him and Pepe kept and eye on the loads from the rear.

Early evening and they came on to the old man with the burro who insisted they stop and take supper with him. They told him about the cabin and how to find it. "Be a good place for you to hole up during the winter months," Tio told him, "and that there was a stove there too that would keep the place warm." They saw the old mans patched up stock on the flintlock he had and Tio got one the rifles that they'd found in the cabin. They gave it to him along with enough powder balls and caps to take care of his needs for a while just before they left. I didn't do anything to earn something like this he told them. "You did a lot more then you realized old man," Tio said. "I ain't that much older then you," he told Tio, "just had me a few more hard winters maybe. You come back again though when you can and at some better time and see me. Few use this trail past the hot springs and I do long for good company now and then." They thanked their new friend for the meal and again for all the help he'd been. Louis now determined to spend every hour they possibly could on the trail led them out and toward home.

Out of the valley trail that led to the hot springs and Louis didn't stop until they came to the junction with the wagon trail that led to the Sierras and they'd rest there. After unloading and putting the horses out on pickets in the dark they slept. In the morning nothing to eat for them Louis telling Tio and Pepe they'd stop when they reached the Pajaro river. There they'd only stop long enough to water the horses. They'd chew on a piece of dried meat and hard biscuits until they finally came to a cantina on the river. Tio went in and ordered for them while Louis and Pepe gave the horses what little grain they had left. Inside and Louis sitting down looked at Tio and Pepe wondering if they might want to say something about the way he was pushing to get home. But they knew that Sunday was going to be important day for him.

They had nine horses all with riding saddles and every saddle boot with a rifle in it. Only three riders but all of them well armed yet all dress like Peons, the gringo one even with a second rifle strapped across his back. The rifle there even as he cared for the horses and still there, when he walked into the cantina and sat down by a window. They looked tired and unkempt, the gringo's clothes even looked dirty. They knew how they looked and that they were unsmiling but that was because they were bone tired and only wanted to eat and ride on. No one questioned them though not even the girl that brought them their food. It was better this way though, there was no way that they could explain in a few words where and what they'd been doing the last couple of days.

They could easily hear the murmur of people talking and would be able to pick out the word vigilante more then once. Louis thought about the word and yes he figured that was what they really were. They ate quietly and that was all they wanted to do, paid their bill and walked out. It front of the cantina they were checking the packs on the horses as people gathered. Serious questioning looks from them but no one asked for an answer. They mounted ridding away with the group of people in front of the cantina watching after them.

If they rode straight through now they wouldn't get home until well after dark and that would mean unloading and caring for the horses in the dark. "We just as well stop when we get to the river," Tio said, "then we'll ride in the morning and be there before noon." Louis was a little disappointed but he realized that Tio was right. He'd already taken the horses to water and had started unsaddling when Tio started building a fire for coffee. Hard biscuits and coffee but this would be their last trail meal.

Tie the loads on in early morning light and they were in the saddle before the sun came up to warm their backs. Their own horses knew they were getting close to home and would need no urging from here on.

It was midmorning when Louis led them into the rear yard of the adobes. Seeing Tio as he got down off Juan's horse he saw how his shoulders sagged. The trip had taken its toll on the older man. Stepping down he went to him and asked if he was all right? "I'm fine," Tio told him, "just tired, a hot bath and a couple of hours rest in my own bed and I'll be as good as new again Mano."

Everyone converging on them now and Rosalie reaching him held on to Louis and cried on his shoulder. "I'm all right," he said, "why are you crying?" "I've been so scared," she said. Even as Juan and the other horse hunters ran up she didn't let go of him.

"Would you take Tio's things in and can we borrow your horse, Juan. I think Rosalie's going to want to ride with Pepe and I taking the horses to the store." He's yours to take any time Mano you don't have to ask," Juan answered. She rode by his side to the store then helped them unload and carry the things inside. The horses unloaded and Pepe said that he'd take their horses to his fathers but there wasn't pasture enough for the others. And he asked if Louis if he could take care of the other horses. "I can do that," Louis answered. "Then I'll leave it up to my father Louis and he can sort this all out," Pepe told him.

Leading Fresa and the other three horses he rode back toward home, Rosalie riding at his side. Juan, Rafael, Carlos and Julio were waiting for them to return and said that take they'd take care of the horses. "There's water on in your adobe Louis," Juan told him, "thought you might want to take a bath." "Thanks Juan, I guess I could use a bath," Louis answered. "I'd say that you sure could Louis, it's hard to tell how you got that dirty, Juan said. And Anna's fixing something in Tio's kitchen if you're hungry after."

Going inside he found the water nice and hot and turning he hugged her and told her," I promise I won't be long." She lingered for a minute reluctant to leave then she lowered her eyes and told him that she'd wait outside the door. He walked out in clean clothes and she smiled again. "Will you always be a peon Louis?" she asked, "you know we have to go talk to the Padre tomorrow is Sunday." "Do you think he might not want to talk to me dressed like I am?" Louis asked. "No not him ever," she answered, "he would be the last one to ever do that."

They found Tio, Juan and the others at the dining table. Rosalie said she'd go to the kitchen and help Anna as Louis sat down. "You're looking better Uncle," he told Tio. "A warm bath and little rest was all I needed Mano. I'll be fine now and you Mano, how are you?" Tio asked. "I had my bath and to night I'll sleep it my own bunk, that's after I see the Padre."

Their food was on the table when Juan told him, "when you go to saddle your horses you might like to take a quick look at your new filly." "Which mare?" Louis asked. "The grey mustang," Juan answered, and he knew why Louis asked. "What color is she Juan?" he asked. "I'm afraid that's one for you to answer Mano," Juan told him, "but it is a filly." "I'd like to go with you Louis," Rosalie said. "Can I go too Anna?" asked. "Why don't you all go," Tio said, "then while you're all out of my way I clean up in here."

They were all lined up along the fence when the horses moved toward them, all but the three horses from their recent expedition. Even the new filly but she stayed behind the mare. Louis could see the filly had dark hooves and a light mane and tail, but he wanted a much closer look at her. Long legged and with fine neck and head, a some what lighter coat then her dam but he wanted to know more. Going over the fence he walked along side the mare and did get a closer look at her before she saw him and moved away. Now he was pretty sure he knew the fillies sire, the rust colored little spots were there she was a flea bit.

Surprised by Rosalie who was close behind him and even more surprised when she asked, "Can I have her Louis?" "They go together Rosalie," he said, "you want the filly the mare has to go with her but they're yours." "They can be my wedding present?" she asked throwing her arms around him. "Stay with the mare," he told her, "and I'll go get a halter we'll take her to the small corral close to the adobe the filly will follow. When their there though they'll have to be feed and watered." "I'll do it I promise," she told him.

"All right then," Louis said, "and what do I get?" "You get me, isn't that enough?" she questioned. "More then enough," he answered, "now I'll saddle Flea and your mare and we had better go see the Padre." Their ride to the church was short and they walked together holding hands going inside. They found the Padre waiting for them. "I knew you'd be here Mano, he said, I heard that you were back. There's been some concern but I see your all right, and the others?" "We're all fine Padre," Louis answered. "Then I'm not going to ask about the other men or what happened. It's a shame that these things have to happen but I'm afraid it could again here, but I'll pray that it doesn't."

"Now I see you still wear the clothes of a peon though Mano, the clothes of a humble laborer." "I wore them for the time working as a mess boy on a steam boat coming down the Mississippi to New Orleans, Louis said. "I learned to like them plus their comfortable and they do fit my needs. I know some may judge me only by what they see and if that's all they feel is necessary it's all right." "One never knows what might be hidden under some things with a different colored outer covering, does one Mano?" the Padre said. "You know, like some one might do with an odd colored horse that he's never seen run." Louis had to smile but wondered if this man knew as much about every one else here. "Now before you leave today," the Padre said, I'd like to get a close look at this Sea Horse of yours."

He talked to them for a few minutes giving them their instructions. Blessed them then said, that he'd like to see this horse he'd heard so much about. They walked together out across the portico to the rail where Flea and the black mare were tied. Flea standing as usual, his head slightly lowered and his eyes looking half closed. Raising his head he'd turn as far as his tied reins would let him, looking at who was coming. So far in his captured life he'd never been mistreated and didn't flinch when the Padre reached up to touch his cheek. The horse only turning to smell and gather the scent of someone who was treating kindly and who he'd now remember. "He is an unusual color," the Padre said, "but not for a mustang I'd say, and I've heard there are some other things." "No spurs scars and no Spanish bit Padre," Louis told him, "and that doe's make a difference."

"Now I see there is something else," the Padre said, "though I've really only seen your horse from a distance before Mano. It is the first time I can remember seeing him without a rifle in the saddle boot." "You'll only see a rifle there when it's needed Padre and I'll try to keep that down to when I go hunting for something for the table," Louis said. The Padre smiled and told them, "I'll see you then tomorrow." Louis helped Rosalie mount and they rode toward home with a wave to the Padre standing on the portico smiling after them.

"There's still time for me to brush Flea" he told Rosalie, "he's been a bit neglected for awhile and if you let me I'll brush your mare too she needs to be spoiled a little." "And what about me?" she asked. "You'll have to wait until tomorrow night I'm afraid, unless you ask your mother for permission," he told her. "Oh that's not funny," Rosalie answered, "but I'll make you a bargain, if you ask her and she says yes, I'll be there." "I'm nether that foolish or that brave," he answered, "but it is tempting." She kissed him and said that she'd go in and see if Anna or Tio needed help. "I'll be in, in a few minute," he said.

Rosalie, Anna, Juan, and Tio were sitting at the table when he walked in and she told him that supper was all ready before she came in. "I'd better go now," she said, "mother will have some loose ends that will need to be take care of I'm sure." They walked to the Don's and found the Don and her mother both on the veranda. Her mother nervous now, said, "I hope you've talked to the Padre." "We have mother and everything is fine," Rosalie told her. Turning to Louis, she said, "I'd better go I'll see you tomorrow," kissed him lightly and said, "until tomorrow."

Don Francisco stepping toward Louis said, "I wanted to talk to you before Louis but when you rode in it looked like had your hands full already. Then with all the empty saddles I saw I knew that it was most likely all over, that what you went to do had been done. Yet I do wonder about a couple of things." "I've got nothing hide," Louis answered. "Those men were your country men and yet you went after them Louis because of what they did to someone who really isn't. Yet I know that Pablo Luna is your friend, I'm just wondering some Louis," the Don told him. "I can understand," Louis answered. "It was some years ago that I left home and that was before the war between the states, had started. There were those in my family who argued in defense of both sides but I was to young and to busy to take either side or argue about it. I came here on a ship and Pablo Luna gave me a chance by giving me work. On that same ship there was someone else who had tried to exercise some authority over me, which he didn't have the right to do. So we were at odds with each other. He was Southern sympathizer and was also one of the men who were after the arms in Pablo's Luna's warehouse. When they tried to break in that night I was the one who there. That war is over and been over for a while but these are the same three who exacted their vengeance on Pablo's son Miguel, because of those arms. They stole from Pablo's store then went to his house after him but at his house they were only able to take his horses, because Pablo had bared his doors and windows. I talked to that same man, who was on the ship with me only a few hours before he died and that was the day before yesterday, Don Francisco. He was Cadet Webber on board that ship but now he told he was Captain Webber a Confederate officer. He recognized me and told me that he knew it was I who was at the warehouse but he still asked if I'd bury his sword with him. I don't know if that explains where my alliances are today but I think we both know what flag will fly over all of us this country and California, don't we Don Francisco?"

The Don nodded his head then said, "I'd like to see that new filly of yours Louis, maybe in the morning before we leave for church, all right?" "Good night then Don Francisco," "Louis said, "I'll see you in the morning." "Good night Louis," the Don answered.

Tio and the others were already eating supper when he walked in. "Why so serious Mano or is it your still tired?" Tio asked. "A little bit of both I guess," "he answered, "but things have been happening pretty fast too, I think after a good nights sleep I'll be fine." He wasn't really hungry and ate little and then lingered until Tio told him, "go to bed Mano, tomorrow is going to be an important day for you." Juan and Anna walked with him to his adobe then continued on to their new home, after bidding him buenas noches.

He slept, and awoke to a grey misty morning, dressing in the dark, which was nothing new for him. Dressed he stepped out onto veranda into a cool morning mist and the smell of the ocean. The pale yellow glow that came through the mist from kitchen window told him that Tio was up as usual. But the aroma of Tio's coffee either unable to penetrate the mist or not ready yet.

Ready to step off the veranda and he saw the figure moving through the mist. Quickly going back in he took down his pistol belt and strapped it on, then moved out toward where he'd seen the figure. He then quickly realized halfway there just who it then most likely was. Not surprised then when he saw her at the fence hand feeding the grey mare. The filly was still reluctant to venture close to anyone and stayed behind the mare. "You're starting early," he said, "as he was approaching. "I'll be finished early and have time to dress for my wedding then," she answered. After giving the mare an arm full of hay and couple of buckets of water Louis said, "come on lets go see what Tio has for break fast." "I can't stay but a minute, mother will miss me and she's nervous enough already," Rosalie told him. "She's so afraid she's going to forget something or something will go wrong with the wedding." "Be patient with her Rosalie, she only has one daughter," Louis reminded her. He walked her back and after a quick kiss she slipped in through the door of the Don's still dark adobe.

"Coffee or chocolate, cornbread and molasses if you want it," Tio said as Louis walked in, then his eyes dropping to the pistol, and he asked, "what is it Mano?" "Nothing Tio, really, I just thought I saw someone out in the fog this morning and went out to check. It turned out to be Rosalie looking after the grey mare and the new filly." "It's good she cares," Tio said, "but in the dark?" "Today it had to before her mother was up Tio," Louis told him. "I can understand," Tio told Louis smiling.

Louis ate then lingered at the table waiting until it was light, then he'd go out and take care of the water trough. He stood to leave and Tio said there was hot water for him when he was ready. "Mi Carro Romano will be ready too Mano," Tio told him smiling. "You can call it your Roman Chariot if you like Tio but it's still a donkey cart to everyone else, but I'll ride in it today, Louis answered. Only because I don't know if I could walk that far in these riding boots."

The water trough full and he'd checked the horses, bathed and was dressing when it was there again. The only thing that he ever really feared and it was back, why he asked himself. Lonesome now when he wasn't alone and yet he could be alone and not lonesome but it should end now she would bring it to an end, she would keep it at bay for him. The other Rose had told him she knew, yet how she knew he had no idea but he had to believe it now.

Over to the kitchen for Tio's inspection the red sash he'd wear now for the second time but this time it was for his own wedding. "You look fine Mano," Tio told him, "maybe a little uncomfortable but that I can understand. Maybe if you'd wear clothes like that more often you could relax and feel comfortable in them." "It might me take to long Tio, how long doe's it take to change from what you are to something your not?" Louis asked. "What is it Mano, is there something wrong?" "Tio asked. "I don't know Tio but I thought every thing was fine until a few minutes ago, now I see me again as lone farm boy. Someone who might be trying to a step to high Tio, you know when he's still got one foot on a shovel." "I'm an old man Mano who can hardly read or write, I've only had the years of time here to teach me but I will say this. It's time Mano for you to stop looking down, look at what you have done already when you saw what you could do. Look at what you have, she saw something in you too, I know and she must have told you what she wanted for you. But if you don't feel for this girl, there's that too," Tio told him. "Oh you know I care for Rosalie Tio, it's that I don't want to be a disappointment to her either," Louis replied. "You go after wild horses, you faced a challenge in a horse race and went after a man who was yours and a friends enemy, now this step should be an easy and happy one for you, Tio said. Now believe this old man Mano, this more then any of the other things, it's what you need. Now let me see how you look, have you got the ring?"

Outside they found Don Francisco who told them he had a few minutes while the ladies were dressing and came over to take a minute to look at the new colt. He and Louis stood at the corral while Tio went to harness the jenny. "She's a fine looking filly Louis," the Don told him, could I look at the other one's you have?" Tio was coming with the cart and Louis told the Don, to go ahead but his carriage was coming to take him to the church. The Don smiling said, "then I'll see you there in a little while Louis."

The ride to the church in the little cart was bumpy but a lot easier then having had to walk that distance in his riding boots. The Padre standing on the portico was seeing his parishioners off as they left after the mass and nodded to Louis as he passed going in to the church.

He found Anna and Juan sitting in one of the front pews waiting." Did you bring the ring Mano?" Juan asked. He took a folded white silk neckerchief from his pocket and handed it to Juan, the ring knotted on to one corner. "I didn't a have ribbon," he told Juan. "A white silk neckerchief Mano, I can't remember ever seeing one before," Juan said. "It was the only one that Pablo had one time when we were in the store Juan, Louis said. Rose bought it that day, then few days later she gave it to me and told me that, one day I would have a use for it. I guess this must be the day, you know it is the first and only time I've ever really had a use for it."

They sat waiting for the Padre, Louis fidgeting and Juan asked him what was wrong, "you nervous Mano? "he asked. "I guess that's it Juan," he answered. The Padre came and motioned for Juan and Louis to follow him. They were standing right where they'd stood the Sunday before and the Padre asked if they had the ring. Juan had the folded neckerchief and held it up in the palm of his hand. The Padre seeing the silk neckerchief like Juan recognizing what it was and said that he'd never seen a vaquero wear that color but that it was an appropriate color for this day.

Louis stood looking out over the sea of faces of the people who had come to the church and sat down. He wasn't focused on anyone or seeming to see a familiar face only that there were people there. It was Don Francisco he saw first then a girl dressed in a white gown whose face he couldn't see hidden behind her veil. He heard the music and the Padre ask if he was all right? "I'm fine," he heard himself say without turning or taking his eyes off her.

He could finally see her through the veil when they stopped and the smile that was there. Then it was the, I do's and little else until he was told he could kiss his bride. He was walking out of the church on weak and shaking legs plus the healed boots he wasn't quite used to yet. Then out side they walked through the crowd of well /wishers that waited and he felt something raining down on them. He did remember to help her up into the Don's coach that was waiting for them. In the coach he lay back against the seat with his eyes closed, until she asked if he was all right? "How else could I feel," he said, as he took her into his arms," when I've just married a beautiful Angel." They sat in each other's arms until the coach stopped at the door of the Don's adobe.

People were already coming into the yard when they got out of the coach and the coach left to go back to bring the Don and Rosalie's mother home. They were waiting for the coach when Tio, Juan and Anna came in. Juan had the white silk neckerchief and started to hand it to Louis but instead gave it to Rosalie. She looked at it and he told her that it was used so they wouldn't loose track of her ring. She looked at it for a moment then folded it one more time and tucked it away.

They danced and Louis had almost as much trouble on the dance floor as he did walking in his boots. Rosalie and the Don danced and it surprised Louis at just how well the Don did on the dance floor. Though he only danced to the slow pieces leaving the fast dances to the younger dancers. The cake was cut and there was the food but the dancing never stopped.

Rosalie and her mother left to change their clothes, Rosalie returning in the black vaquero suit that Rose had given her. She had a small valise that she left out on the veranda because there was no way they'd be able to sneak away until after dark. They ate and danced a little more and it was finally dark. Don Francisco came over and whispered to Louis to be ready, that he would distract the guests by proposing a toast. Taking Rosalie's hand Louis moved toward the door. When Don Francisco on the other side of the room raised his glass to propose the toast, the guests moved toward him and they slipped out the door. Only slowing long enough to pick her valise they melted into the dark. Both dressed in black they were like shadows as they moved toward the adobe and their first night together. They undressed in the dark and went to their bed without risking a light.

Waking early he kissed her gently awake and they lingered a little longer before he got up. It was still dark when he went out to water the horses. No light and no aroma of coffee coming from Tio's pot yet and Louis had to smile. Realizing then that maybe Tio and the others might have tasted in a little too much of the Don's wine.

He saddled Flea and the grey mare knowing they were only going to take her on an easy ride. Both horses at their adobe and he went inside to the aroma of chocolate. Chocolate and a sweet roll for their breakfast and they were ready to ride. Both dressed now in the simple clothes of a peon they rode side by side the little filly following behind the mare. They rode toward Don Francisco's rancho, an easy level ride that wouldn't stress the mare or the young filly that followed her. Drawing little attention to themselves except from those that knew Flea and the race he'd won.

Reaching the rancho they were greeted by the Don's oldest and most trusted vaquero, Mateo. "I'm so happy to see you," he told them, "I missed your wedding but someone must stay with the rancho." "Most times it's good to be the capataz [foreman] but not so good this time." "But I knew you'd come to visit her and I'd get to see you and tell you how happy I am for you, now you go see her, I'll tend to your horses."

Hand in hand they walked to the little graveyard and sat down in the grass next to her grave. Sitting for a while in silence in that small graveyard that was always so well taken by someone from the rancho. Walking back they found Mateo and his wife waiting for them with four small glasses of wine. "It's not good to drink so early," Mateo said, "but we would like to drink a toast to you." Taking his glass and smiling he held high and said, "Salute Manos Dos," and drank his glass down.

They rode away but he didn't head for home but rode around to the rear of Luna's warehouse. He stripped the saddles off the horses and set them up on the loading platform. Boosting Rosalie up on Flea he told her, "go down to the beach and have some fun he needs a little exercise." They rode together down to the beach and he watched as she sped off on Flea. He let the mare walk her foal scampering around behind her and experiencing her first taste of water that wasn't in the water trough or bucket. She got nose full of foam once, that she shook her head at what was evidently to her not liking, that salty flavor. But she did continue prancing in the shallow water that ran up on the beach after a wave would break. Not running yet she was reluctant to get more then a few yards from the mare but maybe one day. Rosalie sat on Flea and was smiling as they were approaching and Louis knew that she liked what she saw the filly doing. "She might take after her sire," she said as Louis drew up close. "We'll no in a year or so," Louis answered.

Resting there a few more minutes and Louis said, "I wonder if Don Francisco is watching?" Riding back Rosalie kept Flea in check only letting him prance a little in the shallow water. The little filly too seemed to be enjoying the foamy shallows but was satisfied now without putting her nose even near it.

Back at their adobe Louis going to take care of the horses while Rosalie put water on for their bath. Their clothes in a bucket of water to soak they stood together pouring warm water over each other. Without drying off they went to their bed to enjoy their first siesta together. He said he would stay longer but there were things he had to do. "I'll go help with supper," Rosalie told him. Water for the horse trough always his first priority then check the other horses for any problems. Then a little while that he'd spend with the new filly. First he'd make a rope halter for her then it would be coaxing her to except him. He worked until near dark before he quit but was satisfied with what he'd been able to do so far.

He found Juan and Tio sitting at the table both Anna and Rosalie working in the kitchen. "I've got two pretty helpers," Tio told Louis as he sat down. It was different now two women in the household and just the way Tio had greeted them, Louis saw that it was now like a small rancho. With everyone finished eating, Tio said it was time for him to clean the kitchen and that he would have coffee for them when they got there in the morning. The three troubadour horse wranglers to the bunkroom, Anna and Juan, Rosalie and Louis walked together. Rosalie and Louis to stop at their adobe while Anna and Juan continued on to their new adobe home.

Morning and that never ending chore of drawing water up for the horses then to the small corral with the mare and her filly. She would come now though still a little reluctant but with the coaxing noise and the outstretched hand with the brown sugar and she'd come to him.

Two buckets water for their adobe and he took them in after the aroma of Tio's coffee stirred his appetite. "Tio's coffees on," he said. "I'll be right there," Rosalie answered, and a few seconds later walked out dressed like a peon. He was smiling but shaking he head at the same too, and she said, "I've got work to do remember, I don't have all my clothes here yet, besides these are comfortable, you know that."

Stepping out side they saw Anna and Juan coming and waited, Juan carrying a small bucket plus a smaller one. In side the dining room he gave them to Tio, "milk he told him for chocolate and cheese for lunch." "Ah," Tio exclaimed, "gracias, "rich chocolate today made with milk that's good." Their breakfast finished, Anna and Rosalie were picking things up when Tio shooed them out.

Rosalie said she had to go feed the mare and the filly. She and Anna were almost to the corral when she saw the halter on the filly. Turning to him, she asked," how did you ever do it Louis?" "It was easy," he told her, then he made a noise with his tongue and teeth twice and both the mare and the filly came to the fence. Taking out two brown sugar lumps he said, "here go make friends with your filly she needs to know you." She went into the corral the coaxed the filly over to where Anna stood and they were both petting her. Then she asked Louis, "if he had anymore sugar?" "That's enough for her now," he said, "she's there with you, don't spoil her."

Don Francisco was there now and said, "good morning Louis," as he stopped and stood looking at the filly. Then he went into the corral walking around her checking. "She's a fine looking filly," he said as he came up to Louis. "Don't even ask Papa," Rosalie said, "she belongs to me she's my wedding present from Louis." "Like with the Indians the horses for the bride go to the father," the Don said. "It's not going to work Papa," Rosalie told him, "the filly and the mare are mine." "I guess I'll just have to be satisfied that there're owned by some one in the family," Don Francisco said but he was smiling. Then he told Louis that he did see them on the beach yesterday.

"Can we take a look at the other colts," the Don asked Louis. "Come on Louis told him. They walked into the pasture and the horses came there surrounding them, except for the three horses from Webbers camp. "You've spoiled them Louis," the Don said. "But I don't have to run down or rope a horse I want, do I?" Louis said, of course if I had a barn and stalls for each of them it would be about the same. But then I'd have to cut hay to feed them all the time, no I like it this way." "I'll have to admit it, it doe's have it's advantages," the Don said, but we've just never done it that way except for one or two horses. You've got some good colts Louis but I think the filly you gave to Rosalie is the best."

Back at the small corral Don Francisco was looking at the little filly again when Pablo and Pepe rode in. Even before he dismounted Pablo said he was sorry that it had taken them so long checking everything. "You brought back everything except for a few staples, Mano. Even the cash box and its contents were all there." Off his horse he went to Louis and held his shoulders and said, "I owe again my young friend." "You don't owe me Pablo it was the same men both times. They just couldn't let go and they would do it again or maybe even something worse, here or any place they thought they could get by with it."

"We'll sell the arms if you want Mano," Pablo said, "they're worth something." "Tio might want a rifle," Louis said, "he only has a shotgun now and I'll ask him." There's the horses too," Pepe said, "I wouldn't mind keeping one but we barely have enough pasture for the three my father has now but of course I would like to have a horse of my own." "You can leave them here Pepe," Louis told him, "there's enough pasture so consider one yours." Tio has the jenny but he might like a horse of his own too." "There's the third horse Mano and one's a mare, you could add her to your breeding stock," Pepe told him. "Then its done Pablo said, "except for the arms and we'll sell them except for any you want to keep." "I'll tell Tio," Louis said, "he can stop by your store and see if there's something he likes."

"How's Miguel?" Louis asked, "I haven't seen him to talk to since we got back." "He's fine physically," Pablo answered, "but that day is still haunting him."

Pablo had seen Don Francisco looking at the new foal in the corral and went to talk to his long time friend. Louis went to where Pepe was now holding their horses. "You had a nice wedding," Pepe told him. ""Thank you Pepe I was a bit nervous through it but I'm happy now," Louis told him.

When Pablo and Pepe left Don Francisco and Louis went in to see if Tio had coffee. Louis told Tio about the rifles and the horses. "I never kept a horse we always sold the wild horses we caught. None of us had a place of own or the money to keep one," Tio said. "There's pasture enough here Tio," and I want to fence more this winter," Louis said." I would like one of those rifles, then maybe I could do some hunting," Tio told him smiling.

Their cups empty Don Francisco said he had things to attend to and Louis told Tio he needed to build a couple more of wooden horse saddle racks. "For now you hang your saddles out under the veranda, then think about building a place to keep them Mano, Tio told him. Saddles in the house are all right for men but with most women it's different. They might not mind if you smell a little horsy some times but saddles and horse blankets can be a little to much for them in the house."

Rosalie and her mother were in side unpacking Rosalie's things as Louis was pealing the four-inch poles he'd hang under the veranda. He was cleaning up the wood shavings when Rafael, Carlos and Julio walked by heading for the bunkhouse. They said that they'd finished early and Louis told them that he'd be there after he finished picking up.

They were all sitting at the table including Tio when he got there. Their conversation stopped abruptly as he walked in and before he had chance to hear what they were talking about. "Why so quiet all of a sudden?" Louis asked. "They were talking about leaving," Tio told him. "We've finished the work at Juan's Mano," Rafael said. "The ships do in and there's not enough hides in Luna's warehouse to fill a row boat let alone a ship. We think the hide business is over, it's time for us to look for some other kind of work."

"How about building me a pole barn with a loft that I can use for a drying shed and an adobe that I can use as for a tack room. They're to many saddles and bridles here now to store in the bunkhouse or in my room," Louis told them. And I don't think it's good for leather to be hung out in the damp on the veranda. Then there's brush to clear and fence to build too. At lease stay until spring then maybe you can go on a horse hunt." "You know we'll stay Mano for as long as you want us to," Rafael said.

"I'll go on horse hunt," Tio said, "I've got my own horse now but the hard riding and roping will up to you young fellows." "You just lead us Maestro you know where to find the wild ones. We'll take care of the trap and the roping," Rafael told Tio.

Louis knew it wasn't likely that he or Juan would be able to go now as much as they would have liked to and it wasn't just being married this place the land and the animals were a responsibility that they couldn't ignore and didn't have before.

When Pablo rode in as he was working in the garden he didn't know why he was there. With out getting down off his horse Pablo told him that the Kestrel was anchored in the bay and he needed him and the others for a day or two. "They're not many hides but I do have things coming in," he told Louis. Can you and the others be there in the morning?" "I don't see why not but maybe not Juan, he has some things to take care of every day now," Louis said, "but I'll check." "Be better with all five of you but if we have to, we'll just have to get by with four," Pablo answered, "see you in the morning then Louis."

He walked the short distance to Juan's to ask him about working in the morning. Juan assuring that he'd be there glad for a chance to make a little money the way they always did. Anna could take of things there but said he would ask Tio to check once in a while. "I'll talk to him when I get back," Louis told him. He stopped first to tell Rosalie what they were going to do the next morning and that it should only take them a day or two. That there were few hides in the warehouse for them to take down to the beach. They walked together toward the other adobe and she asked if this meant that he would be away at night. He stopped for a second and then said, "I didn't even think about it but Pablo will want some one to stay at the warehouse if they have to leave some things there." "I'll stay at the warehouse with you Louis," Rosalie told him. "I'd like that," Louis said, "but I'm afraid others would frown at it and there is a chance that you could be in danger. A slim chance maybe the way things are here now but I don't think that we should take that chance." "Can I show you something when we get back?" she asked. Now he had to wonder what it was that she would surprise him with this time.

Close to noon and Tio and the others were at the table when Rosalie and Louis walked in. Louis told them about what they were needed for in the morning. Rafael, Julio and Carlos said that they'd be there.

Tio brought their mid day meal and they talked about what they thought about the work they'd do the next day. Agreeing that there was less then a half days work with the hides and with what Pablo usually had shipped in another half day. A bit disheartening for them being their working at the warehouse had been where they earned a fair part of their yearly income. "Pablo is going to need someone to stay at the warehouse for a few days," Louis told them, "because I can't do it now." He was looking at her and saw the frown on her face that turned into a weak smile, when she realized that he was right. "Not one us Mano," Rafael said, "you know who we are we don't have anything that we could use to protect us or what's going to be in Pablo's warehouse, except a lazo or a skinning knife." It was quiet for moment then they heard Tio say, "I'll do it Mano if it's alright with Pablo, I've got my shot gun and a rifle now too." "I can't guarantee it Tio but I think Pablo will say it's all right for a man with a shotgun and I'll talk to him in the morning."

They had just started walking from the dining room when she said, "I'm sorry that you can't take that work guarding Pablo's warehouse Louis." "Tio can use the work more then I can, don't you think?" he answered. "But that's not the real reason and you know it," she told him, "you did it for me." He had to smile but he asked, "and what else can I do for you my love."

"There is something," she said, "let's go get your mothers pistol I'd like to show you some thing." Inside he went into their bedroom and took the pistol off the bedpost and turned toward her. "Come on," she told him, and he took the possibles bag down off its peg as they went out the door. Around the adobe, across the road then out into the dunes toward the ocean she led him. Between two dunes that were about twenty yards apart she stopped for only a few seconds. Then said for him to wait right there and walking the short distance to the other dune and drew about a twelve-inch circle on its slope. Walking back she asked if she could see his mothers pistol. He figured what she was going to do but she surprise when she fired three shots and they were all inside that circle. Not real close together but they were close enough that if it were a person they would have been hit all three times. "And where did you learn how to do that?" he asked. "My father," she answered, "he taught when I was only twelve years old," "He told me that it was something everyone should know how to do even a girl, he taught my mother too." "What else am I going to learn about you?" Louis asked. "Nothing bad I hope," she said smiling. She handed the pistol back to him and they walked back and went inside their adobe.

Going to his where he kept the tools he used to repair his leather things first, then came back to where she stood. Taking his pistol belt off he fit it around her waist, marked a spot on it and put a hole there. Putting it around her waist he buckled it on and said," there now it's yours, can you reload it your self?" "I can," she answered, "but it was your mothers, Louis." "It was, but I think she'd like it for you to have it,"

They walked together out to take care of the horses, she to her mare and Louis to the well to draw up the water. The trough filled he took two buckets to the mare and the filly where she was. He had to smile when he heard her talking to the filly and he heard her call the colt Tasa and he wondered. "Did I hear you call her Tasa?" he asked, when he was there by her. She smiled and answered, "yes, I thought it would be a good name for her you know like the standard price for a wife." He just shook his head knowing to make a comment about what she'd just told him might get him in trouble. All he knew he could do right then, was to tell her that he loved her and they walked together to see what Tio had for supper.

Morning in the dark he'd pull water up to fill the water trough and buckets for the mare and the filly. This was the never—ending chore that would even take more of his time when he had the garden planted. Back inside to get Rosalie then to Tio's table for breakfast. Juan and Anna there too so that the five workers could leave together going to the warehouse. The sky was barely turning grey when they said their goods byes and left Tio to watch over the two young ladies and the place.

Pablo already had the rear doors open when they got there and they started carrying the hides down to the beach. The first lighter from the ship hadn't reached the shore yet so they had time to get some of the hides there ready to load before the lighter off loaded the in coming cargo.

The Captain and the Purser reached the shore in the long boat and Pablo asked Louis to come with him. Telling him that he thought he could better explain what happened with those three men. It was friends meeting friends again a once a year occurrence now. "And what brings you to meet us this time Louis," the Captain asked, "you're usually working when we first come into the beach." "Some thing happened here Captain that Pablo feels I might be better able to explain to you about." He told the Captain about the robbery and how Pablo son Miguel was hurt how the family was threatened and the horses stolen. "That's not a good thing," the Captain said, "but how doe's that concern me." "It was the same three men that were at the Pablo's warehouse after the arms that night when I was guarding it," Captain," Louis told him. "Webber? That was some years ago Louis, are you sure?" the Captain asked. "Positive Captain and this is why you need to know. I talked t him before he died and I helped bury him. He told me he held the rank of Captain in the Confederate Army and his last request was that the sword he carried be buried with him. If its any comfort for his family Captain you can tell them that it was," Louis told him." "I really don't have the right to ask, but was it you, Louis?" the Captain asked. "No Sir, it was not my bullet that brought him down," Louis answered. "Thank you Louis, and I will let his uncle know and he'll have to pass it on to the rest of his family." "Maybe we can get together and talk about more pleasant things before I leave," the Captain said. "I'd like that Sir," Louis answered and left to go back to his work.

The Captain talked with Pablo about what happened but Pablo told him he knew little about what happened except what he learned from his son and that he was a prisoner in his own house when those men were here in Monterey. That his son Pepe who was with Louis when they went after those men doesn't want to talk about what happened.

It was the third day of work for them and Louis told Tio that he didn't think that they'd work all this day but he wasn't sure before they left. Tio had pack a mid day meal for Louis and the others and was going to take it to them in case they did have to work later. But Rosalie asked Tio if she could, that she would like to do it. "I'll take Flea and my mare so if Louis wants to we can take a ride on the beach," she told Tio. "Hear you go," Tio said as he handed her the flour sack, "there's enough in there for you too." She saddled Flea and her mare and was going to ride the mare but Flea didn't like following with the little filly and she had to change horses. The mare though was perfectly content to follow with her filly.

She sat aboard Flea near the rear of the warehouse and watched them as they were unloading the cargo from the lighter. Everything off loaded on to the beach and they starting carrying the crates and boxes up the sloping road to the loading platform. She continued to wait even though Flea fidgeted not really content just standing. When everything had been brought up and then taken into warehouse she rode closer. Louis and the four others in their peon togs, Pablo and two men in uniform that she knew would be men from the ship.

She waved when she saw Louis looking toward her and she saw the questioning look on his face when he saw who was there. He turned to Pablo and the men in uniform said something then turned and walked along the wooden platform toward her. He was smiling now as he walked and she knew he was happy to see her. "I brought us and the others something to eat." she said when he drew close.

Louis knew when he saw her riding Flea, that she either wanted ride on the beach or Flea had acted up when she tried to lead him with the mare. But he'd find out later and he asked her to ride to where Pablo and the other were standing on the loading platform. "I want you to meet some one," he told her. "But I'm not dressed to meet people Louis," she said. They're not going to mind and if you don't meet them today they'll be gone and you're not going to be able to meet them until next year." When they reached those standing on the platform he didn't have the chance to introduce Rosalie. The Captain speaking up first, asked? "Well now Louis, who's this pretty young lady you brought to us?" "This is my wife Rosalie Captain," Louis answered." Senora Hand, the Captain said, "I'm Captain Bolt," and bowed slightly, "and this is my Purser Mister Neil and I'm happy to meet you." Turning toward Louis he said, "I guess there's no use asking if you wanted to go back with us this time is there Louis?" he asked. "No Sir," Louis told him, "this is where I live and it's my home now." "I've heard some other things about you too Louis, so I know your doing all right in more ways then only in your marriage. Is this the Sea horse your wife's riding that I've heard about?" the Captain asked him. "It is sir," Louis answered. "I'm happy for you Louis and we'll see you next year now it's time we get back onboard," he said. Then he and the Purser biding Rosalie their good byes, saluted and headed down toward the beach and the waiting skiff.

Pablo locked the warehouse and giving Louis a key told him not to for get to tell Tio unless he wanted to watch the ware house tonight himself.

Rosalie and Louis ate sitting on the steps of the loading platform while Juan and the others said they'd eat as the walked toward home.

Louis and Rosalie after they were finished eating removed the saddles from Flea and the mare leaving them on the platform. Mounted bareback and rode down the slope and on to the beach. Rosalie riding Flea let him run along the wet sand and through the shallow wave surge that moved up the beach. Louis following on the grey watching now the two prides of his life ride as they moved through the spray of water that flew up. Serious for a few moments then he smiled as he saw the filly play though the spent wave surge and foam. His life was full now and he thought about what had brought this all about.

But the two who were the most responsible were no longer here for him to thank. Their time on this earth had been cut short and this day he could only thank them again as he did every day.

They were there now, the melancholy spell was broken and he smiled. "We'd better go now" he said, they're things I have to attend to. Back to the warehouse and dry Flea as best they could, saddle up and ride home.

Louis to ride with Tio back to the warehouse where Tio would spend the evening and night with his shotgun watching over Pablo things stored there. Rosalie and Anna would take over Tio's work preparing the meals for everyone.

Tio's job at the warehouse would only last more two days and he was back to his kitchen and sleeping in his own bed. Asked how he liked having a job? "He asked, "what job? ""There was nothing to do but sweep a little and try to sleep in that creaky wood building that makes odd noises all night long. It's worse then sleeping in Anselmo's livery with the horses stomping all night. I sure can't see why they build with wood when there's all this adobe to build with."

Back to a routine Louis in the morning was out bringing water up from the well, something he knew was a must every day and usually more then one time. Rosalie to the kitchen to help Tio and when she was done there she would go out to take of the grey mare and her filly.

In the morning Rafael, Carlos and Julio at the table when he walked in planning their day work on the pole barn and tack room.

Tio sat down at the table and said that he needed to go Luna's and get some things.

"Can we go to?" Rosalie asked Louis. "Sure," there's some thing's I'd like to look at," she answered. He saddled Fresa and Rosalie's black this morning knowing they hadn't been ridden in a while as Tio hooked the jenny to the cart.

She was walking from the dining room to their rooms when she saw him bringing her black mare out. When she came back out she had changed from the white Peon's clothes and was now dressed in her black vaquero suit. "I'd bet if I was saddling Flea," Louis told Tio, "she wouldn't have changed clothes." "It's better this way," Tio said, "Young ladies should dress nice when they go shopping."

They rode by Juan and Anna's who were busy, Juan building fence and Anna tending their goats. They hadn't been able to come to have breakfast lately with all the work they had. Even after Juan had the fence's built he'd still have water to haul they had no well there were they lived. Louis and Rosalie reaching Pablo's store before Tio and tied their horses, then went in to look around and shop. Louis to go and look at the arms they'd brought back from the cabin near the hot springs. Pablo's daughter's Juana and Barbara there, and Rosalie stopped to talk to them.

He was looking at the pistols and Pablo asked him if he was interested in one of them and then asked him why? Saying he knew that he already had two that he'd seen him wearing many times. "I gave the pistol that had belonged to my Mother to Rosalie," Louis told him, and she knows how us it." "Well that is unusual," Pablo said, "but today that might a wise thing." "There're yours Louis you can take one of them or all," Pablo said. "Just one Pablo and lets hope I don't ever have a need for it," Louis answered. He selected one that he liked and buckled it on, high on his left side, high where it was out sight.

"I've got something to show you Louis, "Pablo told him, "the good Captain brought them and told me that they would sell here." "And you think I might need what ever they are Pablo?" Louis asked. "More then anyone else around here," Pablo answered. There was one setting on a packing crate and

Louis looking at it and had seen something similar aboard the steamboat when he came down the river but not exactly like it. He looked at Pablo and Pablo handed him a paper that explained it, how to use it and how to put it and other things that went with it together. "I want one Pablo," Louis told him, "if I works it's going to save me hours of labor." They carried it and the parts that worked with it out on to the loading dock at the rear of the store. Pablo telling Louis to bring back the extra pieces that he didn't need.

Tio was there bringing out the things he needed for the pantry and looked at what Louis told him needed to be hauled home too. Tio stood looking for a minute but didn't ask about what he was looking at, then just shrugged and went back into the store to get more of the things he wanted. Tio's cart loaded he headed home and Louis went in to see where Rosalie was and found her still talking to Juana and Barbara.

Now wondering what had been so interesting that they were still talking about. They were smiling, though not broadly and he felt but wasn't sure that he wasn't what or whom they were talking about. He said, "hello to Juana and Barbara. Then told Rosalie that Tio had left and that he was through shopping. They hugged each other like they were all sisters together and said their good byes. He said, his good bye to the girls and they left with out Rosalie purchasing anything.

She asked if he had bought what he came for and he told he had but that he'd also bought something else. Something that he hadn't even thought he would because he'd never seen one before. She looked at him questioningly but he told her that she'd have to wait until they were all together at the table. "Can't you tell me now?" she asked. "No," he told her it would be too hard to tell you about it, but you'll see the paper that will tell you everything.

Most of what Tio wanted already taken inside by Rafael and the others when the got to the adobe and Louis told them to leave the other things on the cart by the well. The horses his first concern then to their adobe where he found Rosalie waiting. She had a questioning look on her face and he asked her if there was a problem.

"No," she answered, I had just been wondering about something and they told me what had happened." "What are you talking about?" he asked. "I've wondered about you and Pablo's daughter's, and why when they were there and so attractive that you never became involved with one of them?" she told him. "You jealous of them?" Louis asked, "because if you are there's really no reason to be." "I know," she answered, "they explained how at one time they thought there was a chance." "That was when you were you were working with the horses by the livery and they would go there. Then the race and how you won it and this place but you didn't take the black stallion that was part of what you'd won.

Then she came into your life and they saw little of you after that. But, that when they did see you, it was only when she came in to shop or she was riding her black mare and you were there by her side. Even how you confronted a man who accosted her rudely right there by the stores." He stood looking at her for a few seconds, then said, "I thought you knew all about those things that happened then." "No, not everything," she said "I'm still learning and still wondering but I know now that you were there to keep her safe. At the same time though she was in a way saving you also and I'd like to feel that it was for me."

"It was after we returned from the trip and you were here then Rosalie. She told me that she that she was a Bruja," Louis said, "and that she would give you a potion so you would care for me. Do you remember taking that potion?" "No," she answered, "but I must have." He stepped to her and before he drew her close she saw the tears in his eyes. "What is it Louis?" she asked. "I miss her," he said, "and I owe her so much, of course there are others I owe too but not like I owe her."

"Now we'd better go," he said, "I have to show you and the others what I bought from Pablo. Just let me wash my face in cold water first." "You sure you shouldn't lay down for a little while first?" she asked. "If we went to bed now," he told her smiling, "they wouldn't find out what it was until after breakfast in the morning." He washed his face and was drying his hands and face when she stepped close and he pulled her to him, and kissed her forehead. She reacted by pulling his head down, kissing him on the lips and holding him there for a little while. When she released him, he said, "we'd better go, I'm not going to be able to hold out much longer."

They were late the others having already finished and Anna was helping Tio clean off the table. "It's time for siesta," Tio said, "and we have to wait to see what thing is you purchased." "It will be worth it you'll see," Louis told him, and the others sat squirming in anticipation as they watched them eat."

Finished eating and the table cleaned off he laid the papers that Pablo had given him out on the table. Every one looked at the drawings but no one could figure it out and he let them all work at it for a few minutes. Then told them that it was to bring the water up out of the well. "We'll be able to have a lot bigger garden once we get it to work," he told them. Tio was smiling now and asked how long was it going to take? "A few days if we can get the boards we'll need," Louis said.

"But I'll still have to carry the water for us," Juan said. "You, Rafael, Carlos and Julio get a well dug down by your adobe and I'll buy another one." "It will cost you a lot though Mano," Juan said. "That's all right, it's for the place and I'll pay for it and the lumber you'll need to," Louis told him. "That, with the other work should keep them busy until spring and time for them and Tio to go after the wild horses. Now it's time for siesta I think."

Juan and Anna leaving with Rosalie and Louis but left them at the door, saying their buenas tardes and continued on to their adobe. Louis went to check the horses and pulled up a few buckets of water then two buckets that he gave to the mare and the flea bit filly.

Coming back he in he saw Rosalie standing with a white neckerchief in her hand, the one that he was pretty sure Juan had given her after the wedding ceremony. "Is that the neckerchief I had with your wedding ring in the church?" he asked. "It is," she answered, "but it did once belong to Tia Rose." "I know," Louis told her, "she bought it at Luna's store one time when we went there. He told her that it was a color that just didn't sell well here, so he said that she could have for half price. Rose bought it, then some weeks later she gave it to me and told me that she knew I'd probably never wear it, even though it did match the clothes I wore. But that I should keep it because one day she said that I would have a need for it. I didn't know then how I would ever use it, until our wedding and I didn't have a white ribbon like Juan did. But how did you know that it once belonged to Rose?" he asked. She held it out by one corner for Louis to look at. Something small and red on that corner and looking closer he saw that there was a small red rose embroidered on it. "I don't understand," Louis told her. Rosalie taking his hand, said, "come with me, I want to show you something."

In the room some of the clothes that Rose had given to Rosalie were there still laid out on the bed. "If you would look at every piece of her clothing Louis, you'd find that someplace on every item there's a red rose embroidered. Sometimes times on a collar, sometimes on a pocket but always that red rose somewhere." "And now you have all the rose's," Louis told her. "No Louis," Rosalie answered him, you sill have one, me."

"You know when I went to school I was called Rose and at home I was also call Rose. The only time they called me Rosalie was when Tia was there with us. Both of us were Rosalie's you see I was named after her because they said I looked so much like her when I was born. And that did prove to be true even as I grew up. We were close so you see there were really two Rose's Louis." "How well I know," he answered, "and now I have that one Rose."